In turbulent times, what we need is possibility, and in this rich gathering of diverse voices, Watts and Smith give us just that. A girl molds clay against her deaf brother's ears to heal him. A gay man finds his Appalachian clan in a dark world. These are stories and essays about the blues, about poverty, about families lost and made. *Unbroken Circle* is about broken and unbroken lives, and ultimately, hope.

—Karen Salyer McElmurray, author of *Surrendered Child*

BOTTOM DOG PRESS

UNBROKEN CIRCLE:
STORIES OF
CULTURAL DIVERSITY IN THE SOUTH

EDITED BY
JULIA WATTS AND LARRY SMITH

APPALACHIAN SERIES
BOTTOM DOG PRESS
HURON, OHIO

© 2017
Bottom Dog Press
ISBN: 978-0-933087-73-6
Bottom Dog Press, Inc.
PO Box 425, Huron, OH 44839
Lsmithdog@aol.com
http://smithdocs.net

CREDITS:
General Editors: Julia Watts & Larry Smith
Cover and Layout Design: Susanna Sharp-Schwacke
Cover Image: "Patch of Blue", photograph by Bob Orsillo

We thank all of those who supported the publication of this book.

Table of Contents

INTRODUCTION

The tiny Catholic high school which I attended was in Corbin, Kentucky, a town best known as the birthplace of Kentucky Fried Chicken. In rural Appalachia, Catholics are often regarded with confusion or suspicion, so Saint Camillus Academy became a haven not just for Catholic kids but for others who were too different to find acceptance in the football-obsessed public school. This included East Asian and Indian kids, whose parents worked at the hospital, gifted nerdy kids whose parents wanted them to benefit from the rigors of a Catholic education, arty weird kids like me who started out in the public schools but were bullied or shunned there. Added to this mix were the boarding students from all over the U.S. and from Mexico and Honduras. As a student body, we were small but diverse.

The spring of my junior year, my family agreed to host one of the Mexican boarding students, Silvia, over the long Easter weekend. As my mom drove Silvia and me to the house, our conversation turned to cultural stereotypes. Silvia said Americans always pictured Mexicans as the lazy guy with the sombrero pulled down over his face, taking a siesta leaned against a cactus. Mom said the equivalent stereotype of our Appalachia people was the scraggly-bearded hillbilly, barefoot and in overalls, with a jug of moonshine and a hound dog close to hand.

We turned down the road to our house, and our first sight was one of our neighbors, scraggly-bearded and barefoot, dressed in overalls with a hound dog trailing behind him. We laughed, but with the shared understanding that our scraggly neighbor wasn't representative of all Southerners any more than the snoozing sombrero guy represented all Mexicans.

That was thirty years ago, but the stereotypes persist. People who would never publicly disrespect another group are happy to dismiss Southerners as slow, illiterate, and inbred. Recently, an East Tennessee teacher friend told me about a colleague who had relocated to Connecticut. When the woman enrolled her children in school, the principal, seeing the family's state of origin, said in all seriousness, "Now I do need to let you know that we require all of our students to wear shoes *every day*."

One of the goals of *Unbroken Circle* is to subvert stereotypes—to show that Southern people are not simple, shoeless, rural white people. We are a people as varied as the Southern landscape, from the mountains of Appalachia to the deltas of Mississippi to the skyscrapers of Atlanta. We are black, white, Latino, Native American, Middle Eastern, Asian, and multiracial. We are Christian, Jewish, Muslim, Buddhist, Hindu, Wiccan, atheist and agnostic. We are lesbian, gay, bisexual, transgender, queer, straight, and questioning. We are urban and rural, old and young, poor and rich, and all points in between. We are all these things, plus more that don't fit into neat categories. The voices in this collection represent some of the diverse voices of our region, just a few spoonfuls from the giant pot of gumbo that makes up our region.

When Larry Smith of Bottom Dog Press agreed to co-edit this anthology, we struggled with the title, but once he suggested *The Unbroken Circle*, the vision for this anthology materialized. "Will the Circle Be Unbroken" is a classic in the Southern songbook, sung at pickins and funerals alike and recorded by artists from the Carter Family to the Nitty Gritty Dirt Band to Mavis Staples. In the song, the speaker grieves the loss of his/her mother but takes comfort in the fact that the circle of love created by family will be "unbroken by and by." In a country where politicians and pundits draw lines and build walls to separate people, it is especially fitting to embrace the circle, a shape symbolizing openness, wholeness, connectedness.

One of the things that unites the pieces in this collection, both fiction and nonfiction, is the Southern love of stories. Each author, whether established or emerging, has created a distinct Southern voice which is nobody's stereotype. In a time when many people have lost the ability to listen and empathize, we the authors and editors of this collection, invite you to pull up a chair, join our circle, and listen to our stories.
　　—Julia Watts

　　The writing gathered here is the result of some deep questioning and brave sharing. Whether in personal nonfiction or projected story-telling, the writing witnesses life as it's lived today. Character and voice are paramount, as are theme and style. These are real people caught in authentic situations and struggles for acceptance and caring. In a country where division and judgment are so prominent, they open the circle of acceptance. As Ram Dass declares, the circle is a wonderful image and concept, only keep it ever expanding, including more. We thank these writers and welcome you reading it as part of our unbroken circle.
　　—Larry Smith

The great Circle of Life is a Circle of Unity with all things in the Universe, including our Creator about which all life evolves. We are all equal in the circle.

No one is in front of you, no one is behind you. No one is above you, and no one is below you. We are all equal in the Circle of Life.

— From the Tewa Indians

TO THE CONFEDERATE DEAD
James E. Cherry

Robert McBride circled the block for the third time. No one had to tell him he had to be careful. He'd made a habit of circling the block three times just before midnight for the past weeks. If you've circled one courthouse square in one small southern town anywhere in America, you've circled them all. Actually, he could've circled *this* block with his eyes closed. Each morning Monday through Friday, he reported to work on the third floor of the courthouse as a clerk in the Registrar of Deeds Office. At noon of each weekday, he usually ate lunch at the Derby Diner across the street. But this was Saturday night. He circled for a final time, parked his car yards away from the courthouse lawn, killed the lights and the engine.

He squinted, narrowed his field of vision for movement deliberate or impulsive, strained hearing to distant voices, approaching footfalls, passing automobiles. After five minutes of surveying the landscape, there was only the sound of his breathing. Robert adjusted the rearview mirror, reached under the front seat and grabbed a .38 caliber revolver, slid it down the small of his back. He exited the vehicle, the closing of the door sounding like a cannon blast. Again, he waited to be confronted by anyone who may have spotted his coming, heard his goings. And apparently someone did. Without turning around, he could feel the presence of someone behind him, moving in his direction. No one had to tell him he had to be careful. He'd factored Murphy's Law into the plan. Car trouble. Damn thing just died on his way home and he had to park it here. And if that excuse didn't work, he would do what he had to do.

Robert reopened the door, began to whistle a tune with no melody and pulled the latch to the hood of the car. At any moment, he expected a voice to confront him out of the darkness, and when there was none, he looked over his right shoulder to find a cardboard box scraping the sidewalk at the behest of the wind. He wanted to laugh, but he had to be careful. There would be plenty of time for laughing afterwards.

He walked to the back of the car, checked over his shoulder once again and opened the trunk. When the lid slowly lifted and squeaked to a stop, it revealed an athletic bag, baseball cap and black leather gloves inside. Robert pushed his hands into the gloves, pulled the cap low over his eyes, grabbed the bag and moved towards the courthouse lawn before quietly closing the trunk.

He reminded himself to breathe and walk at a normal pace. Not slow enough to be accused of loitering and not fast enough to draw suspicion. Even though he was dressed in black from head to toe, there were flood lights surrounding the base of the courthouse, and he had to make sure if he was picked up on surveillance cameras or spotted from a passing auto that they would only see the movement of shadows. The last thing he needed to do was to knock something over, trip and fall, or drop the bag.

Robert felt himself relax in the sticky warmth of an August evening, walking towards the courthouse lawn. There was nothing he could do about being the only African American employee in the Register of Deeds Office at the Burroughs County Courthouse. He endured the racist jokes bantered around the office, emails his co-workers forwarded that weren't supposed to appear in his in-box, conversations cloaked in code words of inner city, welfare and gangs. Nor was there anything he could do about being passed over for a promotion for the third time to lesser qualified coworkers, coworkers whom he had trained. But, for now, he was about to do the one thing he could do. For the past five years, it was the first thing that greeted him in the morning and the last thing he saw at the end of the day and outside of his third floor office. In a few moments, looking upward from its base towards the sky, it would trouble him no more.

Blowing something up nowadays wasn't such a hard thing to do. The instructions were right there on the internet and the parts to do it with at the local hardware and electronics store: duct tape, a timer, battery, detonator and a spark. Securing the explosives was the hardest part, until he ran into a high school classmate, Junior Yarborough. Junior had graduated to a junkie now, had been so for the past five years. Junior's daddy still had a farm, just like when they were in high school and on that farm old man Yarborough had cows, pigs, ducks, ammonium nitrate. E-I-E-I-O. A couple of weeks later, Junior had cash and Robert had what he needed to do…what he had to do.

Robert checked over his shoulder, dropped to one knee, and removed the device from his bag. From where he knelt, he read the inscriptions on the monument: "History is an impartial witness to its philosophic judgment we commit the motives and deed of our immortal dead." *Bullshit,* Robert wanted to yell. Confederate soldiers were nothing but traitors to the Union and like traitors, should've been given a blindfold, a cigarette, and a bullet through the brain, instead of a monument outside his office window. "Burroughs County furnished the South more soldiers than she had voters." *That's because,* Robert mused, *the illiterate bastards were too stupid to do anything else; couldn't spell vote if you gave them v-o-t…*"Federal records show they had from first to last 2,6000,000 men in service while the Confederates all told had but little over 600,000." *Proves my point right there,* Robert smiled. If you've got only a quarter of the men that the enemy has, using the same tactics the enemy uses, with your strategy predicated upon the fallacy that white skin has more value than black skin, you're doomed before the first volley is fired. "Erected in 1888: To the Confederate dead." Robert's mind flashed back to the history lessons he was never taught in school how the war could've went either way until Lincoln signed the Proclamation and before it was over ten percent of the Union forces were Black playing decisive roles in major battles, 40,000 sacrificing all in hot pursuit of something called freedom. Yes. The statute was erected in 1888 and rightfully so. It was simply dedicated to the wrong Goddam dead. But it didn't matter now. Robert placed the bomb at the feet of Colonel Reb, set the timer, and walked back to his car, bag in hand, one measured step at a time.

Behind the steering wheel, he slid the pistol back under the seat, cranked the Honda, and it turned over on the first try. He didn't bother to check over his shoulders when he tossed the bag back into the trunk or worry about every little sound that bumped against the night. He simply backed out of the parking spot, shifted into drive. He had scripted everything for months and all went according to plan.

Robert pulled to a stop light at the intersection of Main and Cooper, rolled down the window. He reached for a pack of smokes above the visor and, upon discovering an empty package, crumpled and tossed it onto the pavement. He tilted his head, framed the Confederate statue in the side view mirror and could only imagine Monday morning without it being there, only brick and mortar scattered across the manicured lawn. *Maybe I should've left a note? Something to throw them off the scent. The Sons of Nat Turner. Ministers for Malcolm. The Marcus Garvey Association.* Robert chuckled. He was a tie-wearing, button-down collar, nine to five bureaucrat with no political leanings left or right, whose every word and action was carefully measured with neutrality or restraint. The gist of his conversations consisted of weather, sports, hunting and fishing, classic cars. That was the best way to get along with white folks in the office. Just talk about stuff that doesn't matter. He wanted to express his political ideas with his coworkers, but knowing their political leanings like he did, this would only serve to deepen the isolation he felt every day. For example, on the morning of November 5th, he wanted to climb atop his desk and scream from the bottom of his lungs that it was a new day, that the country had progressed and having a Black president was a definitive step in that direction and had to be a good thing and there was no need any more for Klansmen, Confederate flags or statues. After all, it was the white vote that put the man into office.

Robert wanted to say that and a lot more, but, instead, like he'd done for the past five years, he merely sat at his desk recording transactions and maps, marriage licenses, birth and death certificates. Meanwhile his coworkers barely acknowledged his existence anymore, blared conservative talk radio in the afternoon, spoke of tea parties, town hall meetings and taking the country back. He couldn't wait to see the look on the faces, hear what they had to say when he got back to work. Naturally, he would feign shock, horror and disbelief and exchange speculations regarding the nature of events, if asked his opinion. But emotionally, he would be standing in a nearby corner, cup of coffee in hand, laughing his ass off. And when he got tired of engaging in guffaws, he would savor the sweetness of having had the final word without ever opening his mouth. There was no need to worry about throwing off any scents. Who would believe he, Robert McBride, capable of doing such a thing?

A car horn startled Robert from his reverie, and seeing the light had changed from red to green, he mashed the accelerator and pounded the steering wheel. He had to be careful. A quick stop at a gas station down the road for cigarettes and he'd be the hell away from there.

He pulled into the Safeway Service Center, dropped five bucks on the counter and was surprised to see that the clerk was not an Arab, but a young Black girl, who dog-eared a copy of *Blessing the Boats* by Lucille Clifton; after handing him his smokes, a beer, and change, she wished him a good day and picked up the book, resuming where she left off.

Robert checked his watch before sliding into his car, strapped on the seat belt, set the bottle beside him and merged back onto Main Street. In ten minutes the Fourth of July would come in August to the Confederate dead. The traffic light winked from green to yellow and he accelerated through it, finding nothing on the street except a few teenagers out way past curfew. A solitary car coming in the opposite direction moved a little faster than a crawl, and the nearer it came towards Robert, the lights atop of the car and a City of Perry police emblem on its side became more distinct. The police car made a u-turn, sped up behind him and lodged flashing blue lights into his rearview mirror.

Robert swallowed hard and eased onto the well-lighted parking lot of a used car dealership, shifted into park, left the engine running. He knew the drill, had learned it years ago in the classroom of Black man in America: keep both hands on the wheel, don't make any sudden movements, address the officer in a respectable manner.

Again, out of his side view mirror he watched a white officer approach circumspectly with a light in hand flashing its beam upon the backseat, then briefly into Robert's face.

"Good evening."

Robert squinted, matched the voice with the tall muscular figure before him, Officer Gary Hill. He'd seen him several times at the Derby

Diner and read about him in the daily papers receiving civic awards or making a major bust.

"Good evening, officer. Is something wrong?"

"Well," Sergeant Hill recited, "you almost made that light, but almost ain't never made nothing." He hesitated, peered deeper into the car as if hoping to detect something he'd missed upon approach. "May I see your driver's license, registration, and proof of insurance please?"

"My license and insurance are in my wallet and the registration in the glove box," Robert said and waited for Sergeant Hill to acknowledge his statement.

"Okay," nodded the officer. "Get it out. Take your time doing it, now," he added for emphasis.

Almost my ass, Robert seethed. He watched out of his rear view mirror as Sergeant Hill checked for warrants, violations, expired licenses from the confines of his squad car. That light was yellow and they both knew it. Robert shook his head, resigned himself to the fact that it was always something: an illegal lane change, busted tail light, a suspect that fits the description. Or just plain old DWB: driving while black. He glanced at his watch and it was ten past midnight. Sunday morning.

He could smell onions on Sergeant Hill's breath as he leaned his elbows on the doorframe and dangled Robert's ID in his hand, his face inches from Roberts. "Where you coming from this late?"

Robert tapped his breast pocket. "Cigarettes."

"Got you a cold one too, huh?" The bottle of beer was wrapped in a paper bag.

Robert glanced sideways to the bottle of brew beside him. "Yeah. A cold one would go good on a hot night like this. It hasn't been opened."

"Alright. Take it easy, man," pleaded Sergeant Hill. "I can see it hasn't been opened." He cleared his throat. "Where do I know you from?"

"I don't know, officer."

Robert heard Sergeant Hill grunt, followed his eyes as they traveled the length of the hood and followed its lines back to Robert. "Any reason why your hood is up?"

Goddammit. Robert's mind flashed back to daydreaming at a red light, not being cautious at another and forgetting to close the hood while at the courthouse square. He was supposed to be careful, but now had put himself and all his plans in jeopardy. Beads of sweat materialized upon his brow and formed circles under his arms. He gripped the steering wheel tighter to prevent it from slipping through his hands and prayed that Sergeant Hill couldn't hear the jackhammer inside of his chest. He had to remind himself to breathe and that, no matter what happened next, he was in control.

"Oh," Robert flashed a smile, "she was running a little hot earlier. Guess I forgot to close it tight."

Sergeant Hill slowly nodded his head and meticulously measured him. Robert knew he didn't even have an outstanding parking ticket, let alone warrants or a rap sheet. He was clean. Maybe too clean for Sergeant Hill, who looked at the hood a second time before making a sucking sound through his teeth and handing Robert his identification. "Okay, Mr. McBride. Don't get in too big of a hurry, now. I'll let you off with a warning this time. You're free to go."

He watched Sergeant Hill take a step toward the squad car, immediately took it back. "Oh, by the way. You don't have any drugs or weapons on you, do you?"

"No sir," Robert said stuffing his driver's license and insurance card back into his wallet, "I sure don't."

"You mind if I search your car?" Without looking up, Robert knew Sergeant Hill was smiling as though he were a cat and Robert the canary.

"Uh…yeah I do mind." Robert understood what was about to happen next. He would be ordered spread eagle on the ground, handcuffed, tossed into the back of the squad car until Sergeant Hill's supervisor arrived with a search warrant in one hand and a canine at the end of the other. "I thought I was free to go, officer."

Sergeant Hill stepped away from the driver's door, unfastened the strap of the semi-automatic on his hip. "Mr. McBride. I'm going to ask you to step out of the vehicle please."

Robert studied the young, blue-eyed, blonde hair, muscular, six foot officer whose lips were set in a thin line of determination. Robert breathed freely, felt a sense of peace like a man who had been revealed his destiny and accepted it. He calmly stated, "Yes sir. I'll get out of the car."

He opened the glove box to deposit his registration and thought about the gym bag with its residue in the trunk and how when he closed the glove box he would open the door to exit the vehicle and in one deft motion reach under the seat and grab the .38 revolver and come up aiming for Sergeant Hill right between the eyes.

Robert closed the glove compartment, had one hand on the door handle and was reaching the other towards the floorboard when the night exploded in the background. There was a brilliant flash, thunder dying in the distance and a cloud of dust billowing towards the sky. Sergeant Hill jumped three feet, hit the ground in search of cover, then resurfaced. "What the hell!" He sprinted towards his squad car, got on the radio and with tires screeching and siren wailing, sped towards downtown Perry.

Robert reached over and grabbed the beer, unscrewed the top and took a long hard swallow, securing the bottle between his legs.

He pulled the cigarettes from his pocket, drew one from the pack, lit it. He released smoke into his reflection in the rear view mirror before easing back onto Main Street and then onto Grayson Avenue that would eventually lead him safely home.

BIG QUEER CONVOCATIONS
Jeff Mann

I.

In April 1978, the spring semester of my freshman year at West Virginia University, my lesbian friend Laura drove me home to attend my paternal grandmother's 75th birthday celebration. I was penniless and without a vehicle, but Laura and I rode in style in "Prince," her 1963 Plymouth Valiant convertible, down I-81 and Route 19 and on along the wood-lined back roads that led to my hometown of Hinton, West Virginia. The redbuds, I remember, were in full bloom: explosions of pink champagne amid spring's green-gold hills.

We descended Sandstone Mountain—a tortuous kiss-your-own-rear-bumper road that must be nerve-wracking to flatlanders—then the road leveled off, following the railroad tracks. Soon Hinton came into view, sprawled along the New River. We were only three or four blocks into town when Laura looked over at me, grinned, and said, "So…where are the gay bars?"

We both howled at the absurdity of the question. That plural noun, "bars," was the funniest part. As if a small, isolated, conservative town like Hinton (population: around 3,000) would have one gay bar, much less more than one. For decades now, I've been telling this little story to folks curious about where I come from. It's a way to emphasize how very much *not* queer-friendly Hinton is, how very far it's situated from any public places where gays and lesbians might safely congregate.

In this respect, Hinton is like innumerable rural towns all over the nation: because of religious fundamentalism and the homophobia that inspires, it's a difficult, even a dangerous, place to be LGBT. When, in 1976—thanks to Jo Davison, a lesbian biology teacher, and Bill and Brenda, two lesbian friends—I realized at age sixteen that I was sexually attracted to men, Hinton immediately became a place to escape. There was no way to be openly gay there. Homosexuals, if they were mentioned at all, were objects of scorn and contempt, to be avoided, driven away, or bludgeoned senseless. And so my queer friends and I stayed in the closet as best we could, read lesbian and gay novels, and dreamed of fleeing to college and, after that, to some exciting city where we might live in more welcoming circumstances.

When I got to West Virginia University, I hurled myself into the queer life there. My freshman year, the bar to go to was the Fox, where gays and straights mingled uncomfortably, and at least once I ended up backing my butch lesbian buddy Bill in a brawl with two huge queer-haters. My sophomore year, it was the Rendezvous, where intimidating drag queens like Miss Corley and Miss Leroy held court. Later, there was Angie's Den of Sin, as we called it, situated well beyond the outskirts of town, where patrons' tires were occasionally slit. Still later, during my WVU graduate-school days, there was the Double Decker, where I fell madly in love with Steve, a red-mustached, promiscuous bartender, and Paul, a charismatic user who resembled the young Ernest Hemingway. After I'd graduated and become an instructor at WVU, there was the Class Act, a basement bar entered from an alley—"an underground shame-hole," to borrow a phrase from *Absolutely Fabulous*. It's still there, I gather, under the new name Vice Versa.

Meanwhile, my attitude toward my hometown was gradually shifting. With queer friends and social spaces in Morgantown to help me make sense of my gay identity, it became time to come to terms with my Appalachian identity. I began to appreciate my kin more. I began to see things about Hinton and rural West Virginia that I missed and found increasingly valuable: the dialect, the traditional values, the good manners, the landscape, the food, the folk culture...and the country boys, the sort of men I'd first learned to desire and after whom I'd fashioned my own personal style (the boots-and-baseball-cap look I've jokingly come to call "redneck chic"). For years, I spent summers with my family in Hinton—partly for financial reasons and partly because I felt increasingly at ease there. Still, even then there were queer-starved summer-night jaunts with friends to the Shamrock in Bluefield, where Miss Helen, despite her wheelchair-bound status, guarded the door with a baseball bat, and the Grand Palace in Charleston, where statuesque drag queens shimmied and pranced.

I was never in my element in gay bars, despite my hunger for queer companionship. Though I enjoyed dancing with friends—songs by the Village People, Donna Summer, and the Pointer Sisters come to mind—I was far too shy and introverted to pursue men I found desirable, and only rarely did mutual attraction shared with a stranger lead to something more. And, as accustomed as I was to small-town life, the loud music and crowds in bars became, as I aged, less something to enjoy and more something to tolerate in order to spend time with other queer folks.

In August 1989, when I moved to Blacksburg, Virginia, to teach at Virginia Tech, my bar days pretty much ended. The nearest gay bar, the Park, was in Roanoke, a forty-five-minute drive away, and I had no interest in taking the risk of drinking and then driving home. I do have one amusing memory of the Park, though. In the mid-1990s, I shared occasional frolicsome fuck-buddy weekends with burly and bearded Keith and Tony, a Roanoke couple who savored erotic variety, and one Burns Night, the three of us went dancing at the Park. I wore my kilt, hoping to catch the eyes of handsome strangers who might take it upon themselves to discover whether or not it's true that nothing's worn beneath the kilt. But no! The men all seemed chagrined by my tartan garment, though all the women seemed fascinated. Luckily, I still had Keith and Tony to entertain me at evening's end.

When I met John, my present husband, in 1997, my interest in spending time in gay bars dwindled further. For a few years, we had a house in Charleston, West Virginia, and would, ever so rarely, have drinks at the Tap Room, another "underground shame-hole" where members of the leather and bear communities hung out. (For you heterosexual mainstream innocents, leather men are practitioners of BDSM — bondage/discipline/dominance/submission/sadism/masochism — and bears are burly, hairy, masculine, bearded gay men.) One evening there, in a contest emceed by drag queens, we got to see our buddy Ken win Mr. Mountain State Daddy, complete with studded black-leather sash. Another evening, an acquaintance infamous for stripping naked and dancing after he'd had too much to drink provided everyone with a sweaty floppy-genital show, one punctuated by many a horny patron's appreciative hoop and holler.

During our travels together, John and I have often visited the local gay bars (all tracked down beforehand via the Internet): in Key West, Provincetown, Vienna, Amsterdam, Copenhagen, and Bruges. We've frequented the Green Lantern in DC, where, on Thursday nights, shirtless men drink free. During trips to New Orleans for Saints and Sinners, the LGBT literary festival, we've admired go-go dancers gyrating atop the bar in Oz and leather-clad Daddies glowering in the dark corners of the Phoenix. In San Francisco, we've checked out the original bear bar, the Lone Star Saloon ("All these guys look like they're from West Virginia," John whispered to me), and the Eagle, where a handsomely goateed and shirtless youth licked and spit-shined my black harness-strap boots.

On June 13, 2016, the many gay bars I've frequented were very much on my mind. The day before, an armed madman murdered 49 people, most of them Latino, at Pulse, a gay nightclub in Orlando, Florida. In the aftermath of the massacre, LGBT friends on Facebook reminisced about their favorite gay bars, and articles appeared here and there — in print journals and online — about the importance of gay bars as safe spaces and community centers.

So many people seemed shocked and surprised at what had happened in Orlando. I was not. I've been steeling myself for violence ever since I walked into my first gay bar in 1977. Then I'd envisioned frat boys with baseball bats, not semi-automatics, but still, I'm always intensely aware when in a public queer space of a grim possibility: that space might be disrupted by violent, homophobic outsiders. This caution/paranoia exists partly because I grew up in a place hostile to homosexuals, and partly because Jo Davison, the lesbian biology teacher who helped me come out, told me horror stories about gay bars in her hometown — Columbus, Ohio — being busted by policemen who beat and intimidated the patrons. "They used rubber hoses, because those cause a lot of pain but don't leave marks. When you step inside a gay bar you've never been to before, look for the rear exit, so you can escape if the place gets raided," she'd advised.

I've been preparing for the worst ever since, at the same time that I haven't let fear curtail my freedoms, dictate my behavior, or hamper the sometimes ferocious frankness of my very gay and often erotic publications. Still, having drinks with John in late June 2016 at the Tavern on Camac in Philadelphia's "Gayborhood," or, in mid-July, at the London Pub in Oslo, Norway, I was more aware than ever that anything could happen at any time, that John and I might be ended at any moment.

II.

The Pulse shooter can rot in hell. For four decades, I've done my best to be brave in the face of homophobia, and no terrorist attack like that which occurred in Orlando is keeping this almost pathologically ornery and defiant West Virginia redneck/leather man/Daddybear out of a gay bar if I feel like lumbering into one for a martini or two. What is far more likely to keep me out is geographical distance and the strong preferences that have developed as I've aged. In other words, these days not only do I prefer to drink at home, I prefer to enjoy my queer spaces at home as well.

John and I have become inveterate homebodies. During the day, I'm either teaching at Virginia Tech, preparing for classes, or trying to write, and he's either working at his desk or traveling on business — to Texas, Tennessee, Oregon, South Carolina, and California. In the evenings we're weary, and we prize our quiet time together, which usually involves a couple of stiff drinks, home cooking, profound relaxation, and Netflix or DVDs. Sometimes we watch queer series like *Where the Bears Are* and *RuPaul's Drag Race*, or campy film classics like *Addams Family Values*, *The Birdcage*, *Victor/Victoria*, or *Hairspray*. Other times, we might watch the superhero/action films I relish. *Captain America: Civil War*, *The Legend of Tarzan*, and *X-Men: Apocalypse* are my most recent favorites, though *300* and the *Lord of the Rings* trilogy are always to-be-seen-again options. (Yes, fundamentalist Christians, these are the details of our sinister Gay Agenda. Scared yet?)

Every now and then, though, we're in the mood for queer companionship. When that happens, we don't drive an hour to Roanoke to gyrate at the gay bar (the Park is, amazingly, still there). I'm 57, John's 53, and we've been together nearly twenty years; the bass thumping and jostling crowds of such an establishment are not in the least appealing, plus the much-younger regulars would no doubt regard us sad old bastards with palpable contempt. (And, honestly, I've had enough of the millennials' electronic-gadget addiction, bad manners, political correctness, and sense of entitlement. The more I avoid them—the generation that makes retirement look sweet—the better, though certain venomous colleagues and Virginia Tech administrators make retirement look even sweeter).

"The Soul selects her own Society," wrote Emily Dickinson. It's a line I've often thought would serve as a fine T-shirt slogan for introverts like me. Spending time alone, with my spouse, or with small groups of close friends has always been more enjoyable than noisy public spaces with crowds of strangers. So when John and I start hankering after the simpatico company of other queers, instead of going out we encourage a select few gay and lesbian friends to join us for a weekend. Luckily we possess the resources to make such private gatherings possible…which is to say that we own two comfortable and roomy residences and possess the salaries sufficient to purchase loads of liquor and groceries.

Sometimes we invite said few to our house in Pulaski, "Tabbywood," a brick Georgian where guests can shower attention on our three cats (two plump and loveable tabbies, plus a fluffy gray and white vindictress who possesses a punitive bladder), relish the meals produced by our plethora of cookbooks, or admire my collection of daggers and swords, prints of Confederate generals, or pagan altar. (I am, admittedly, an odd amalgam of elements.)

More often, though, we invite them to spend the weekend in "Fabled Hintonia," as I've been grandly dubbing my hometown since my undergraduate days. These are the hedonistic gatherings I've dubbed "Big Queer Convocations," aka BQCs. I like to think of them as the Southern Appalachian version of Gertrude Stein and Alice B. Toklas's salons in Paris.

Our Hinton house was built around 1920. It's a solid wooden two-story structure not far from the Summers County Courthouse. Set beside a little park and near the edge of a cliff that drops down to railroad tracks and the New River, the house looks out over whitewater rapids and the mountains beyond. My family moved there in the mid-70s, and I considered it home from the ninth grade on through high school and college and long after. Several years after my mother died, my father sold the house, to my deep disapproval and displeasure. In 2014, the folks to whom he'd sold it decided to move to Florida, so John and I bought the place. Now it's the site for BQCs, during which much quaffing and feasting occur.

Creating a feast is something I'm skilled at now, but that hasn't always been the case. When I was an undergraduate, I hardly knew how to fry an egg. Though descended from a long line of fine country cooks, I had not yet inherited their skills. I was too busy growing a beard, studying Romantic poetry and dendrology, lifting weights, browsing through gay porn magazines like *Drummer* and *Honcho*, and trying to become tough and butch so that I wouldn't get my ass kicked by queer haters.

Luckily for me, several of my college friends knew their way around a kitchen and made sure my poverty-stricken self didn't starve. Allen fried me pancakes and cooked up big pots of brown beans. Brenda made beef stew and spaghetti and big Sunday-morning breakfast "glops": fried potatoes, onions, and peppers mixed with eggs. Laura created vegetarian stir-fries, taboule, hummus, and tofu dishes, all quite exotic to a small-town West Virginian like me.

Eventually, my enthusiasm for eating translated into a passion for cooking. During graduate school in the 1980s and later as an instructor at WVU, I worked up a handful of specialties with which to feed my queer friends: eggplant Parmesan, broccoli and bacon quiche, tuna casserole, omelets, and chicken soup with Bisquick dumplings. During visits home, I had my grandmother teach me Southern staples like piecrust and biscuits from scratch. In the 1990s, lonely and horny in Blacksburg, I began to go to Europe once a year over my summer break, and there I became fascinated with international fare. My collection of cookbooks waxed, and soon I was driving home to Hinton on weekends (since I had next to no gay friends in Blacksburg) and making my family British, Greek, German, French, Belgian, Mexican, and Italian specialties.

When I met John in 1997, two accomplished cooks came together. We've been preparing solid meals of great variety ever since, for ourselves and for the rare set of guests. Culinary skill is to be expected of us members of the gay bear community: we're big men who prize comfort and love to eat.

So the BQCs in Fabled Hintonia center upon food and fellowship. John and I arrive on a Friday, lugging boxes of groceries. We turn the hot water back on and adjust the thermostat. In cold weather, we bring in firewood from the wood box on the porch. We make sure that the guest beds are all made and towels are set out. Then I open up the cookbooks and start work on a menu I've been planning for weeks.

Around 4 pm, my sociologist friend Okey (also known as the fabulous and ferocious drag queen and Internet celebrity, Miss Ilene Over) arrives from Huntington, West Virginia, bearing huge bottles of wine, loaves of bread, and assorted cheeses. Around 5 or so, my political theorist friend Cindy appears, bringing desserts from Just Pies, a chain of bakeries around Columbus, Ohio. Promptly at 5 pm, John sets out the requisite appetizers—cheeses, breads or crackers— and I prepare drinks: wine for Okey, Bud Light for Cindy, and martinis for John and me.

Sometimes Cindy's partner Laree arrives from DC, bringing a plethora of gourmet treaties from upscale grocery stores. Occasionally, Mizz Patty—a queer-friendly straight woman from a small Nebraska town who's traveled the world and speaks German like a native—accompanies Cindy, bearing the ingredients required to prepare her specialty, baked grape leaves stuffed with goat cheese and sun-dried tomatoes. Other times, Cindy brings along her Ohio housemate Lee, a radical lesbian feminist, cat lover, and union worker.

One of the advantages of creating queer space in my home, rather than finding it in gay bars, is the much greater control I have over that space, and, like most American men, I'm a big fan of being in control. I choose the participants—folks I know well, care deeply about, and trust—and I choose the music. No thumping disco tunes or any frenetic drivel that passes for popular music today. Instead, our iPods shuffle through old favorites: John's Barbra Streisand and Bette Midler, my Joni Mitchell, Carly Simon, and Judy Collins. (I'm a big country-music fan, but none of my guests is, so I save that genre for solitary drives to work in my pickup.)

The menus? My guests often request those. I always ask them beforehand what they most hanker for. For dinner, favorites include Hungarian cabbage rolls, stuffed peppers, haluski (fried cabbage and noodles), pinto beans and cornbread, and homemade pizza. Sunday breakfasts are nearly always buttermilk biscuits and sausage gravy, though North Carolina liver mush, ramps and scrambled eggs, and Tex-Mex *migas* are tasty alternatives.

Before, during, and after eating, the conversation flows. Sometimes we read one another snippets from our latest works-in-progress: Cindy's MS about the US State Department's intervention on behalf of LGBT rights overseas; Okey's drag queen romance, *Make Me Pretty, Sissy*; or my upcoming gay vampire novel, *Insatiable*, in which my fanged alter ego takes on mountaintop removal mining. Sometimes we share funny stories, as in Okey's latest outrageous gem: "That restaurant server was so rude, obviously a homophobe, glaring at us, so when he gave me attitude, I looked up at him and said, 'Honey, would you like to butt-fuck an old showgirl?' He turned red as fire and never came back to the table! They had to assign us another server!"

Quite often, the conversation runs toward a gratifying bitch-fest/cussing session, long bouts of savage grousing that John quietly avoids. There are few pleasures more delicious than comparing notes with like-minded people who detest the same things you do. During the BQCs we enjoy said pleasure in spades, aiming our contempt at both the far Left and the far Right.

We excoriate Republicans, conservatives, and religious funda-mentalists; we joke about "nasty women" and "grabbing pussies." We deride a variety of millennials, among them spoiled, well-off students who feel "unsafe," fear "microaggressions," and demand "trigger warnings," or young politically correct queers. "Bless their hearts," I drawl, rolling my eyes and curling my lip. "After all the struggle and suffering that our generation endured, after all we accomplished, these brats are arguing about 'preferred gender pronouns?'"

With a second martini, my ire waxes hotter. I snarl about colleagues I loathe, the latest disrespect I've suffered at Virginia Tech, the editor who said he was tired of how I "fetishize rednecks." Cindy describes the latest bullshit that the transgender language police are pushing: "It isn't called a vagina any longer. They insist that we call it a 'front hole.' No F-to-M person wants to be reminded that he still has a vagina." Okey tells us about the latest homophobe he put in his place, the latest fundamentalist he told to kiss his queer ass. "Honey, when I first did drag, I carried a brick in my purse, and, the way the country's a'goin', I have half a mind to carry one again!"

After purging ourselves of bile, we move on to dessert and hysterical television entertainment—Brother Boy in *Sordid Lives* ("Do you see my pussy now?" and "Shoot her, Wardell! Shoot her in the head!) or Bubbles Devere in *Little Britain* ("Is she as…beautiful as they say?"). Sometimes, I play the guitar or the piano, or, more rarely, the Appalachian dulcimer. Three times out of four, Okey and I stay up late, talking about his difficulties as a gypsy instructor, my frustrated literary ambitions, and the neopaganism we share.

Then the short weekend is over, and we must leave our safe queer sanctuary and go back into an overwhelmingly heterosexist world where we feel little at home. Before we disperse, we compare schedules, already planning the next Big Queer Convocation in Fabled Hintonia. After our guests have left, John and I turn down the heat, turn off the hot water, and pack up leftovers and recyclables to take back to Pulaski. As we leave Hinton, a great irony occurs to me: that hostile, homophobic town I was so desperate to escape forty years ago so that I might live my life as an openly gay man has become the very place where I most enjoy gay and lesbian camaraderie. I will, I feel fairly sure, go back to that house and that town as long as I live, and I'll continue to create a haven there for my queer kin.

III.

I'm writing the final section of this essay on November 10, 2016, two days after Donald Trump has won the Presidency of the United States. As a gay man, I'm devastated, numb, nauseated, frightened, and furious. Trump and his running mate Pence have made clear their hostility toward LGBT people and LGBT rights. They have mentioned their desire to repeal same-sex marriage by stacking the Supreme Court with conservatives.

Like comedian Trae Crowder, I identify as a "liberal redneck." To my disappointment, though not to my surprise, one set of those I consider to be My People—small-town and rural folks, those who live near me in Pulaski and Hinton and in similar places all over the nation—is to a great extent responsible for Trump's triumph. That triumph spells dark days for another set of My People, gays and lesbians.

I'm trying to make sense of this situation. I'm trying to decide how to go on, how to grapple with a future turned very grim, how to continue without being devoured by my own rage and dread. Yesterday, I had only enough energy to lift weights in my basement gym, read a few pages from a new translation of the Norse *Poetic Edda*, and, in my husband's absence, drink heavily all evening and post as my new Facebook cover photo an image John sent me from Oregon, a hand-lettered sign that says "FUCK DONALD TRUMP."

Today, browsing more of *The Poetic Edda*, I'm thinking about what the past teaches us about coping with the future. For decades, I've been interested in my Celtic and Teutonic roots in Scotland, Ireland, and Germany, and I've been reading Norse mythology and Icelandic sagas. I've also been collecting swords and thinking about what it means to be a warrior and what I—a middle-aged author of the twenty-first century—can learn from long-dead Highland chiefs and medieval Vikings.

The concept of the clan is dear to me, and, as an Appalachian, the clan mindset comes to me naturally. My family and my (mostly queer) friends are my clan. If I am to resemble a warrior in any way, then my job is to provide for my clan and protect them, as much as is possible. My writing must be a kind of warfare: speaking as a gay man and a liberal Appalachian, no matter how frankly queer, angry, defiant, and erotic my words might be, no matter how offensive and unacceptable to conservatives and the mainstream.

Today, as I imagine America under Trump, I realize that not much has changed in my relation to and attitude toward the outside world. Things have just intensified. As I've said, I'm always expecting the worst and preparing myself to deal with it. As a queer and as a hillbilly, I've always regarded the larger world as hostile to me and those I love, and I've always fiercely cherished my clan and passionately hated my enemies. (I'm a heathen: I feel no Christian obligation to love or forgive my foes.) Now, after Trump's victory, the world simply feels more hostile and the things I love more fragile, more in need of defense. For the first time in my life, I'm seriously contemplating the purchase of a gun.

That deepening sense of the world's enmity will give me the drive to continue doing what's necessary, despite the sick despair I'm feeling today. I'll celebrate the natural world—the sugar maple's fiery orange, the tabby cat snoozing on the bed, the chickadee chattering in the spruce. I'll continue to publish in-your-face gay poetry, fiction, and creative nonfiction, small literary rebellions in the spirit of my Rebel ancestors. I'll arrange Big Queer Convocations as often as I can, in quiet, conservative Hinton, in Republican-poisoned West Virginia. I'll arrange for my people the small pleasures—music, talk, food, and drink—that have always helped beleaguered human beings endure hard times.

Next month, some of us will gather again. I'll honor Hestia by making a grand meal and starting a fire. I'll clean ashes from the hearth, lay on newspaper, kindling, and dry logs, and strike the match. My husband, friends, and I will drink and laugh and feast. I'll do what vigilant men have always done to keep their people safe: check the perimeter, secure the doors, pull drapes against the cold. I'll watch the flames and think of my forbears, scruffy Scots and burly Vikings gathering in long-ago crofts, castles, and halls. They're drinking ale and mead, adding wood to the fire, savoring bread, cheese, and roast meat. Some among them—the grizzled and the wary ones—are keeping their senses alert, weapons at the ready, acutely aware of the surrounding dark.

THE GRAVEDIGGERS
Robin Lippincott

The hole for the grave had been dug in the wrong place, and the family, when they arrived for the service and noticed, was upset. But the gravediggers had merely done what they were told to do, where they were told to do it.

It wasn't as if the hole for the grave lay a few feet from where it was supposed to be — which would have been bad enough — but closer to twenty yards: how could things have gone so wrong? That was what some members of the family wanted to know, especially when the precise location of the burial had been stipulated in writing, and paid for, so many years ago. How could there even have been a question, much less a mistake as flagrant as this one? Here they stood, on a bitterly cold day in January to bury a never-married ninety-eight-year-old relative whom all of them called aunt, under the big elm tree next to her brother and their parents.

The youngest gravedigger, a stocky boy-man with the face of a cherub, threw up his arms and turned away, expelling a cloud of white hot air, when he overheard the family's response and understood what had happened. Then he stood with his hands planted on his wide hips, glaring at them.

The other worker, who spoke with an Eastern European accent, was almost as tall and lean as one of the pine trees in the cemetery; he listened intently to what a few of the men from the family were saying.

Though the gravediggers wore only jeans and long-sleeve shirts — the younger man the flashy orange and white of a sports team, the other a brown sweatshirt — both men were sweating.

Their boss, the owner of the funeral home, was dressed in a black suit with a long, black dress coat and a black wool cap pulled down low on his forehead. He had the hard face of a loan shark as he quarreled with the family about the placement of the grave and where the hole had been dug; he was actually arguing with them, right there in the cemetery on the day of their beloved's funeral, mere moments before the graveside service was scheduled to begin.

The young gravedigger vehemently, if silently, egged him on, looking as though he might implode. The older of the two, who must have been twice his coworker's age, had a disbelieving look on his face: Yes, this man was their boss, but it was wrong to argue with the family on such a day.

Raised voices carried across the otherwise silent cemetery as the discussion heated up.

The gravediggers exchanged a look that seemed to ask if this could possibly come to blows. The younger man found himself wishing that it would, and that they might not have to dig another grave after all, whereas his coworker closed his eyes and hoped for a quick resolution. Some family members joined in on the argument, while others shook their heads in sadness and disbelief; still others tried to calm things down, to make peace. The Reverend, who reassuringly announced that he'd seen this sort of thing happen before, if only about once every ten years, was trying to get a word in. He would begin to speak, only to be drowned out by the arguing of the funeral home director and several male members of the family. Finally, he managed to command silence, after which he suggested that the service proceed as planned. Once they had left the cemetery, the Reverend continued in a calm, comforting voice, the grave would be dug in the proper place, their beloved aunt would be buried there, and the erroneously dug hole would be filled in. He promised to see that these things were done, adding that the body would never be left alone, and that he would personally come back in two hours and repeat The Lord's Prayer.

The family concurred that this was the best solution under the circumstances, also agreeing with the Reverend that this was neither the time nor the place to settle the score with the funeral home; that could and most assuredly would occur later.

The small group—less than fifteen members—huddled together in the cold amid the flurrying snowflakes while the Reverend remembered their aunt as someone who enjoyed people, and loved to dance. In fact, he had never met her. Only the eldest among them, the eighty-nine year-old sister-in-law of the deceased, spoke when the Reverend asked if anyone would like to make a statement. In what some family members said afterward they took as a remonstrance (others were less sure), she thanked her late sister-in-law for having created this opportunity for the family to come together. The Reverend recited The Lord's Prayer; family members placed flowers on top of the coffin, and then they filed out of the cemetery. Some had to return to work, while others went back to their homes, but a small group of five decided to go out for lunch together.

"All right, get this done," the funeral director said with his back to the gravediggers as he stalked off to his waiting car and driver, its muffler sending noxious plumes of white smoke into the biting air. No apology or consoling words of encouragement, just, "Get it done."

The gravediggers looked at each other, then picked up their shovels and walked over to the proper burial site.

"He *would* call in today," the younger one said. There was supposed to be three of them. Always, there were three.

"He's really sick," the other responded. "I talked to his wife this morning."

"Yeah, right."

"He could die. It's in his lungs." The older gravedigger shook his head.

The two men leaned on their shovels and glared at each other. The older gravedigger felt angry at his coworker for showing no sign of sympathy or caring for the man who had stood digging alongside them countless times, who was their comrade. "Why are you in such a hurry?" he asked.

"People to do, things to see," the young one smirked. And then he added, "And there's a game later."

"You've got time."

"I'm tired."

You wouldn't feel so tired if you were in better shape, the older gravedigger thought, but all he said was, "Let's get to work."

They started with the sod, which was always tough, breaking it up into about sixteen squares. Once that was off, they could set to digging.

The sky shone blue with occasional bursts of sunlight, though snow continued to fall in slow, almost dizzying flurries.

The gravediggers' shovels huffed at the unforgiving earth, which was always harder in winter and gave off little of its usual rich, loamy scent.

And now there were the roots of the hovering elm tree; the young gravedigger reached them first. He felt the unforgiving roots at the end of his shovel before he saw them, then groaned: he bet the family hadn't thought about *this.*

"Figures!" He slammed his shovel into the dirt and scowled. "It's all just too hard sometimes."

The older man scowled at his coworker. "What do you know about it?"

Both men had stopped shoveling.

"I know."

"What do you know? You're young. You were born in this country. You don't know anything." He stopped himself from continuing and looked across the cemetery, hoping for some kind of visual refreshment. The sprawl of most American cemeteries was so different from the smaller, crowded graveyards of Bosnia. The last time he had seen his homeland, there was snow on the ground. And also blood. It suddenly struck him that this blind, stupid stubbornness his coworker exhibited was the kind of thing that led men to fight wars. "Let's just finish," he said.

The younger man looked at him and nodded. "The sooner I'm outta here the better."

They picked up their shovels and resumed digging. And because the two men weren't talking, the older gravedigger started singing out loud, softly, the song he had been singing internally, to keep himself good company:

> The summer's gone, and all the flowers are dying
> 'Tis you, 'tis you must go and I must bide.

He had lost friends in the war back home. He always thought of them when he was working this job.

The younger man continued to ignore him as he went on singing.

> But come ye back when summer's in the meadow
> Or when the valley's hushed and white with snow
> I'll be here in sunshine or in shadow
> Oh Danny boy, oh Danny boy, I love you so.

It was a nice song that his wife had taught him when they first met, and he liked to sing it whenever he thought about his friends. He also considered his absent coworker now, hoping that he would recover soon.

As the two men neared the end of their digging, the older man noticed that the anger he felt toward his coworker had begun to dissipate, and he began to feel sorry for him; he was breathing hard, and sweating heavily. The older man suddenly had the thought that the younger one could easily have been his very own son. But alas, he and his wife had only the twin girls, both approaching their last year of high school.

"Almost there," he said, to which the younger man merely grunted. The level ground was up to his shoulders now. He was winded, and if he wasn't careful he could end up in one of these graves prematurely, the older man thought.

They were further back from the cemetery's entrance, finally filling in the erroneously dug grave, and almost finished, when the five members of the family who had gone out to lunch together returned.

"How'd it go?" one of them called as they approached the new, proper gravesite. They could see the freshly turned earth under the elm tree and just hoped that their aunt's coffin was buried under it. Once they saw the older gravedigger's face, they instinctively felt they could trust that the deed had, in fact, been done.

He walked toward them. He could tell by their facial expressions and body language that they were sorry for the extra work they had caused, even though it wasn't their fault, and also that they wanted to express their gratitude. While it wasn't necessary, he appreciated it, and was grateful for the conversation. He smiled at them, a smile that branched out from the corners of his eyes. He mentioned the big tree's roots giving them some problems but said that the job was done; and then he reassured them that the Reverend had indeed returned, as promised.

The younger gravedigger hung back, resting on his shovel, and did not speak to the family; but at least he was no longer glaring.

"Thank you," each of the family members said, looking into the eyes of the older gravedigger, and also at the begrudging, younger man standing in the distance, who nodded.

The old gravedigger watched as the five filed out of the cemetery now. For the first time, he could see almost the entire graveyard from his perspective, and he noticed that the ground was entirely white, as the snow continued to fall. The peacefulness of the scene allowed him to relax, finally, and also made him realize how tired he was. He looked forward to sleep, but first an early dinner, and then a nap, before going to his other job; he worked a second job as a night watchman so that his daughters could go to college and have a better life: they called it the graveyard shift. His wife worried that working so hard would send him to an early death, but he knew better: he came from strong, healthy stock; he could live to be ninety-eight, like the woman just buried. He looked over at her grave now as the young gravedigger roared off in his black pickup without saying goodbye.

The old gravedigger was determined not to fight this or any war, and so he said, "Peace be with you, brother," and then he let it go.

COTTAGE INDUSTRY
Laura Argiri

Snow is rare here, fragile as a wedding dress. I love snow — I've lived in places with the long white winters this place lacks — but here we don't get much. Looking out into the tangerine light of this January sunset over our silent street, I realize what else we lack: that *scunch* of feet on snow that lets you know someone's approaching. Fair warning — I like that too.

LaLoma and her mother and sister usually did approach on foot, from the nearby bus stop. They'd be on the front porch ringing the bell before we could retreat to the back of the house and pull the curtains to pretend no one was home. I hated that about them. When they did turn up, we stopped whatever we were doing and fed them their next meal, and Grandma found out what else they needed and gave it to them. They had aborted many of our shopping trips and treks to the park, blighted many a Saturday, and that was reason enough for me to dread them. Were they poor, I wondered, since that was why we had to feed them? Back then you could still see hunger in the slums and the sticks down here: slack-faced people whose joints seemed large under their pasty skin. But LaLoma and her mother and sister were tall and fat, LaLoma especially. Her mighty thighs seemed like weapons, her whole body a bouncy battering ram. She was always radish-red in the face, as if perpetually furious above her big smiles. She was ruddy when she turned up that winter afternoon, chap-cheeked and underdressed: just a jacket over her shirt and tight Capri pants, big bare calves, sneakers and socks.
"Got to let her in, she's family," Grandma said, as I scowled.
I'd put in my eight hours at school and meant not to spend the rest of my waking hours bored. I wanted to sprawl by the fire, read, and sink deep into my own head. I wanted to listen to *Swan Lake* on Grandma's new record player; I wanted to dream of tremendous winters in the Russia of my imagination, sledding and skating and sequined nights of snow, ballerinas swept up after their curtain calls into the czar's sleigh. LaLoma would linger until supper, after supper, and until she got what she wanted and the day was worn down to a numb nub. After LaLoma finally slouched off to catch the last cross-town bus, Grandma would be withdrawn and grim.
"But I don't like her," I whined.
"I don't either, but what can we do? They're our blood," said Grandma, and worked her way upright to hobble to the door.

Grandma was a cutting, unrelenting snob about some modes of misbehavior, despite her hardscrabble beginnings, and she encouraged me to be the same. She used the harshest terms: *worse than a low-down dirty dog. Tramp, lowlife, trash, slut.* Along with her contempt for her disreputable kin, though, was an unhappy loyalty. When they shambled up her porch steps, her expression did not say *Welcome*. It said, *What fresh hell...?* But she opened her door.

"Why did her mom name her LaLoma?" I persisted.

"It's a trashy name, all right," Grandma admitted. Trashiness and avoiding the slightest hint of it were hot concerns for us Milltown strivers. According to Grandma, trashy names usually involved some ignorant attempt at fanciness: all those LaWandas and LaRhondas and LaVernes and LaRues named in the optimistic postwar years by mothers who wanted to raise starlets. "June Louise never did know much," my grandmother allowed reluctantly. June Louise was Grandma's sister, the one who'd conceived and birthed and named the thunderous LaLoma.

I wasted my breath a little more: "LaLoma's mean." When I was younger, LaLoma had liked to point out violent deeds and the characters doing them on TV and tell me, "I'll make them come get you!" She'd smile. I knew TV movie events weren't real, on one hand, but I also knew her threat was a cruel, mean-minded tease. Normal grownups didn't go out of their way to scare children who weren't even bothering them. That one wanted to make a fraidy-cat out of me and make me scared of a television set.

"She's ignorant, I never said she wasn't. They all are. Now go put some cookies on a plate," said Grandma. When she had let LaLoma in and herded us all to the kitchen, she put the coffee on.

"So, what is it now?" she asked our guest.

"Does it have to be anything?" LaLoma shrugged and took two cookies. "Just wanted to drop in on my Auntie Sue Marie. I'm going to see someone on Vale Street, and you're on the way. You still got that crochet bedspread I like? Can I have that after you're dead?"

"I'm feeling just fine," Grandma assured her, and chunked wood into her woodstove. The hungry winter fire seized it.

"I said when you're dead."

"I'm not going anywhere anytime soon—I'm not the one running around outside half-naked and begging God to give me pneumonia. It's not even thirty degrees out there. Haven't you got some long pants to wear?"

LaLoma shrugged. "I'm not cold. Hot-blooded, that's me."

Maybe boiling blood explained why she was always so red. Her flaming face and blonde hair clashed. The blonde was real, sunny honey. That hair didn't seem to belong to her. It seemed that she ought to have gotten it some lying, sneaky way, but Grandma had confirmed that nothing from a bottle was involved. "That hair's Loma's little bit of good luck," Grandma had said. "Just about all the good luck she ever had."

Maybe her natural insulation kept LaLoma warm; she was even fatter than when last seen. I hated to be in the same room with LaLoma's fat, which looked contagious. The sight made me feel that something was expanding sneakily under my skin. I knew about periods and tits and the big butts of grown women, which they crammed into strangling girdles. I would have sold my small queasy soul to attain adult height and power without all those adult afflictions if only I'd known how to make the deal. It seemed like you could catch them, blood and bags of jouncing fat fore and aft, just from being in the room with that woman and her sweat. Now that I was taking ballet lessons, I knew how important it was not to be like that!

LaLoma probably knew I hated her, if not exactly why.

For my part, I knew that LaLoma's mother, June Louise, had once defrauded her own sister, my Grandma, by altering a check for a loan of fifty dollars. That sounds small, a scanty week's groceries for a little household in 2015. In 1960, though, fifty dollars was a substantial sum. June Louise had made it even more substantial by changing $50.00 to $150.00. June Louise might not have known much, but she knew how to commit fraud, and she knew that my grandmother wouldn't turn her in for it.

"You gotta put up with 'em, they're family," was all Grandma would say.

Now LaLoma's eyes were on me—like her hair, eyes I thought she shouldn't have had, slate-blue and gold-lashed. If she hadn't always looked like she was thinking about doing something hateful, I'd have admired her eyes. Was she mad at herself for the flopping tits, the curved jelly gut? She never tried to hide any of it.

"You still stuck up, Lizzie?"

"Yeah." *Stuck up* was LaLoma's term for people who did not like to be teased, called names, poked, pawed, or tickled. *And no one calls me Lizzie*, I thought. If I'd said that aloud, LaLoma would have battened on my name and crowed, "Dizzylizziebusytizzy, stuck up!"

"Want to go for a walk with me? I'll buy you a treat."

"There's no place around here that sells stuff for kids," I said.

"Go on," urged Grandma, the treacherous thing, probably wanting a tot of something alcoholic to enjoy alone. To celebrate not being hit up for a handout yet, perhaps, or get numb for when she did get hit up. "Take a little walk with Loma. It won't hurt you any."

So I did.

It was not a long walk, barely three minutes. Right before twilight, the evening light had caramelized on the horizon, and it was far colder than when I came in after school. Lamplight, whiskey-gold, bloomed in some of the little windows. Our shoes, small loafers and big sneakers, made sneaky, gritty sounds on the sidewalk.

There was no one around to see me poke the enemy with a pointed stick, so I did. "It's nasty how you come over here and tell Grandma the stuff you want when she's dead."

"Well, how's she gonna know if I don't say nothing?"

"You sound like you're going to be glad when she's dead. And I won't let you take her stuff." Without Grandma to urge me in the direction of charity and niceness, I didn't go there.

"You ain't gonna be able to not let me."

"Will too. I'll change the locks." That was what people did when a thief had gotten their keys, a fun fact from television. "She only lets you in because you're related, and she says you're pitiful." Grandma meant *pathetic*, a notion I couldn't connect with LaLoma. For a fourth grader, *scary* and *pathetic* have no overlap. "She says we have to put up with you. But when I'm grown, I swear I won't."

That was sass, and something more than sass. It should have made LaLoma hostile. The wheedling tone she took instead puzzled me. "Don't be mean," she coaxed me. "This is my friend Sadie we're going to see. Be sweet and I'll buy you something."

I was about to point out that the Dixie Drug was the only store anywhere near here, and not all that near, and that it closed at five, and that LaLoma's normal reason for visiting was getting some of Grandma's ready cash, not spending her own. But we were already at Sadie's place.

Sadie's house was small, like all the houses on Vale Street. Its tiny yard had the draggled grass and dead flowers we have here instead of snow, plus a concrete baby angel—one of those cheap yard-statues that go with genteel poverty. When we entered, though, there wasn't the camphorated reek that went up your nose when you opened most front doors in our neighborhood, Milltown. That was the mill smell, liniment—people who worked in the Erwin mill and basted themselves with liniment to tamp down the pain from continuous repetitive motion at the roaring machines. Inside, Sadie's home looked more prosperous than I'd have guessed. Her front room was warm and very neat, without scattered newspapers. Her couch and chair were rose velour. The ash trays were empty and clean, as if Sadie expected company. A frilly pink lamp and a curtain of rainbow beads over one door were the only memorable features. There were no Jesus pictures; most living rooms in our neighborhood had several. There were friendly winter smells of wood smoke and oil heat and an undertone of country ham and biscuits.

"Sadie, this is Lizzie," LaLoma told her friend, an unremarkable old woman in a flowery house dress and a cardigan. I'd seen that old lady in the grocery store.

"Elizabeth," I said. Grandma had told me mine was a refined name, a name for a lady, after a saint in the Bible.

"Here, take off your coat," said Sadie.

"It's okay. I'm not staying long." I didn't know why I was here in the first place, but I had no plan to linger.

"You'll catch a cold if you sit in a hot room in a coat," urged Sadie, and somehow I was shrugging out of my coat. She looked me up and down as if she found something fascinating about my clothing: red pullover, sweater tights for cold weather, scratchy skirt of gray wool. My hair was ordinary brown, but it was lush then, almost long enough to sit on. Sadie admired the only striking part of me and said she could tell someone took good care of it.

"It's Grandma," I said. "Grandma Sue Marie does that. She shampoos it every week and puts Avon conditioner on it."

Sadie's expression changed, as if something I'd said was a surprise, though not a good one. However, she smiled — "Oh, you're Sue Marie's grandbaby! Didn't know you right off. You've grown. I buy my Avon from your grandma," said Sadie. Then she offered me a honey bun and joined LaLoma in the kitchen. They spoke in secret voices, but the little house kept the sound close and clear. My skin felt strange, as if someone had seen me naked. I thought I heard, "old Clarence that runs the dry-cleaning shop" and "what he really likes" and "five hundred, and you can gimme twenty-five percent," from LaLoma.

"How old is that kid?" asked Sadie, impatient — perhaps disgusted.

"Twelve," LaLoma said quickly. "Lizzie's twelve."

"Nine," I told them. "And it's Elizabeth."

"Okay, so she's tall for her age!" LaLoma seemed to find something important in the ritual query about kids' ages. Sadie hadn't bothered with the other half of it, about where I went to school.

Sadie crossed her arms over her breasts and shook her head. "Nine! And she's Sue Marie Swain's granddaughter, and Sue Marie's right there on Swallow Street, and I've told you time and time again about not shitting where you eat. Sometimes I don't know what goes through that fat head of yours!"

LaLoma protested in a hiss of whispers. Her chins quivered.

The old girl still shook her head. "Nine! I wouldn't touch her with a ten-foot pole. Too young!"

LaLoma weighed in yet again. She wanted something badly, but Sadie was having none of it.

"You need money? Make some yourself. Not like you ain't got what it takes. I'll fix it up for you." Then came a fervent warning: "But don't you ever mess me up with Sue Marie, girl. If you ever get Sue Marie on my tail, that's the last day you'll work here, and that's a promise. I know Sue Marie from school — it took a fool to tangle with Sue Marie, even then. I remember when Tansy Smith called June Louise a whore. That wasn't right — your poor mama didn't sell her honeypie, she let 'em have it for free. June Louise never did have any business sense. But Sue Marie wasn't letting anyone insult her big sister. Sue Marie wasn't as big as a skeeter, but she scratched up Tansy's face and yanked out a handful of Tansy's pretty yellow hair from the front, where it showed. Served Tansy right. Even back then, Tansy prissed around with her nose in the air like she was better than the rest of us. But Tansy comes from mill people too, and that man she married ain't right in the head. Looks like a movie star, but that fella's got shit for brains. And if you don't have shit for brains too, you'll keep your hands off Sue Marie's granddaughter and not take her to any house like this one. Or they'll have to wash what's left of you off the floor with a hose when Sue Marie gets done with you."

"Aunt Sue Marie puts up with all Ma's shit." A sullen, defeated protest.

"Sue Marie's sorry for your mama. But I bet she ain't all that sorry for you, girl. Call me when you're ready to work, and don't bring kids like that one around here."

LaLoma wouldn't let the topic go. "Well, what kind you got in mind?"

"The kind with mamas like yours!" Sadie told her, and I did hear disgust then. "Ain't you got any sense? Sue Marie's got custody of that kid, she ain't letting that crazy daughter of hers raise her grandbaby, and she don't let that kid run loose like you and your sister did. She prob'ly makes her do her homework first thing after school. I heard she's sending her to dancing school. She has plans for that little girl. Look for the ones nobody's got plans for. You ought to know 'em when you see 'em. Now take Elizabeth straight back to Sue Marie's."

LaLoma took me straight back. "Sadie says you're not pretty, not good for anything," she told me on the way.

That wasn't what I'd heard, though I didn't argue. Now I know what there was to fear. Then I just felt fear, a cool, bright knife, and knew it for an accurate emotion. I thought it was stupid of Grandma to let LaLoma into her house, and that her crass nagging for that coverlet after Grandma was dead was the least of it.

Grandma brightened when I trailed in alone. "Did she go on home, then? Good. You can take off that skirt and hang it up so it don't wrinkle, then practice while I cook supper. Turn your feet out like Miss Rose told you. Hold your stomach in tight."

I wanted to say that the visit had been scary, but could not have explained why or even formed my questions in my head, and Grandma had small patience with vagueness and dithering. I took off my scratchy skirt and hung it up, put on my soft ballet slippers, and moved one of the kitchen chairs into the hall to use as my barre. I put on my practice record, and slow Chopin mingled with the kitchen clash and sizzle. I gripped the back of the chair, turned my feet out as far as they'd go, and started my pliés. A couple of years later, Grandma would hire a man to nail up an old stair railing for a barre.

Grandma's dead now, and Sadie is too. Like most houses around here, Sadie's house has been redone, its history gentrified out of sight. It has blonde bamboo floors, ceiling fans, clever compact cabinets, and a Bosch washer and dryer. The walls are painted in postmodern designer colors: Sky, Clay, Ice. The realtor's flyer, designed to make people feel brilliant for overspending, details it all in luscious language. The home stagers put in lamps and left them on at night while the house was for sale. People passing saw sweet amber light in the new windows and pooled on the new flowerbeds, the April-green turf. If you lingered in the twilight, you couldn't resist imagining yourself in there, sovereign of all that compact slicked-up deliciousness. That four-room house sold for $243,000. The new owner surely doesn't know that an old lady once ran a cottage-industry whorehouse there, behind a door veiled in twinkly beads. Yet I have to give Sadie credit for equal attention to the importance of appearances. Viewed from the sidewalk back then, her house had appeared as sad and respectably poor as any other on the block. Nothing about its outside would have interested anyone, even a paranoid vice cop.

Rather than getting lamed at the mill, like most of Milltown, Sadie had put her skills and the assets of others to work in less wearing ways. She probably got quietly, modestly rich and made sure that no one ever suspected as much. Nothing about that scenario would trouble me if Sadie's pocket prostitution venture had involved only consenting adults, but it hadn't. LaLoma brought little girls to Sadie, some disgusting man paid Sadie $500.00 for the chance to rape a child, and LaLoma got her cut. She and Sadie had been so easy with the topic that I have no doubt what might have happened to me there had happened many times to other kids, slightly older and not as lucky.

I go by that sleek, freshly Pottery-Barned little house often. Sometimes the owners' daughter is playing, safe behind the gated white picket fence. I remember what I escaped. The media's full of it now: pedophiles, child trafficking. That buzz started when Madeleine McCann evaporated from a resort in Portugal. And right here in Milltown, back when the Beatles still sang over the radio, how many times did LaLoma collect her finder's fee for a little girl Sadie didn't consider too young? While Sadie and LaLoma did their specialty business, I had been watching television, or playing in my fantasy snow in the Russia of my imagination, or yawning through my homework half a block away. What would my fierce Grandma Sue Marie have done if she'd known what her niece was up to with her neighbor? Would that information have trumped pity and blood and made Grandma call the police? I don't know.

Now Grandma's house is mine, and it's gentrified too, with all the conveniences between its vanilla-cream walls, and pretty birch flooring, and a real barre. I guess I'm gentrified along with it, as Grandma Sue Marie planned; I teach ballet at Rose's Studio of Dance. We teach all levels, from pre-dance and creative movement on Monday afternoons through pointe on Fridays. This is my niche. I am safe from the mill-future Grandma feared for me, as well as from dirtier dangers than any she imagined.

I can imagine LaLoma jeering: *You were s'posed to be hot shit, Lizzie, and here you are, teaching in that dumb hick town dance school! D'you tell all those little blimpo-butts they can grow up to be ballerinas?*

If LaLoma ever turned up here, I'd have questions for her too. I'd ask her how many little girls she'd found for Sadie to rent out to the local pervs. That may be one reason the overheated troll doesn't appear to claim that bedspread. There's also that I'd rip her a new hole to monetize if she set her feet on my porch, though I have no idea if she's still in town. Someone like LaLoma could be anywhere—dead, or still selling her crotch, or in jail somewhere under another awful name.

Feast of the Sun
Charles Dodd White

She hunts always at dawn, having followed the footpath between the tall chicory and wind jostled walls of river cane. Daylight is a perturbed omen in this first hour. Not the lusty blue of midday, nor the burnt ooze of eventide. Instead, a gradual slide from granite to calcite, everything above her a kind of mineral reckoning. She covers ground, counts off her steps against a mental map, figures distance and the likely carry of the rifle's report to her father's trailer. He left for work long before she took his scoped Marlin and stepped into the woods, but she will not risk anything unforeseen. This is her secret, and to surrender it before its time would upend the great care she'd taken, profane her earned truth.

At her hip rides the small trophy purse, unclenched and open as a mouth. She had washed it clean after each hunt, but still the scent of blood lingers. As she walks deeper into the woods, her fingers play absently at the slack pouch lips. These same fingers, so light at the touch, would be enough to drag down what tenanted the sky, to kill with the absolute steadiness of hate.

She comes to the river ford, grounds the rifle butt in the sand and watches the water roll. The dam has not yet been let go, and the current smooths itself over the rocky bed, clear and governed. At the bend of the river a fishing cabin above the water, but there is no one visible on the overhanging deck and the interior lights are not on. She raises the rifle above her head, like she's seen soldiers do in her history book, and steps into the water. It needles her skin, but she warms to it quickly, moves along the flat stones, cautious of the slick edges, remembering the previous crossings and how she had once fallen in. The time the rifle had gone in too and she had scrambled after it before it was lost in the river's quick shedding. She had turned back that morning without making it across, broken the weapon down to its bare components and salved them with a clean coat of gun oil to prevent rust.

Once she reaches the opposite bank, she slings the rifle and turns to follow the stand of mixed hardwoods buffering the paved road. She stays to the cool folds of shade, walks up the soft runners of moss, until she sees the swathe of cleared land on the other side. She hurries over the asphalt and vanishes into the leafy blackberries, the reach of white pines. With her small Tasco binoculars, she glasses the tall steel towers of the power line but sees no shapes among the high keeps. She tightens her hands to the rifle stock and waits.

Within an hour, the hawk appears, crests the far tree line and lights in the drooping wire of the tower's left branch. It rolls its scapulas once before settling into its perch like a fang upon a thin smile. Her heart rises to her temples as she lifts the rifle, anchors it in the vee of a sapling to steady her aim. Through the scope the hawk jumps into detail. The imperfection of his feathering. The sidle of his eyes. She clicks the safety off and releases her breath to still the crosshairs over the hawk's breast.

The .22 snaps and the bird no longer lives. That simple. That complex. She stands and pushes free of the undergrowth, vines ripping, and lays the rifle at the clearing's edge. Through the tall grass beggar's lice attaches to the cuffs of her upturned jeans.

At the base of the tower she finds nothing. She cuts a larger circle for signs of the hawk, but he is nowhere on the ground. She shelters her face against the burning sun with the edge of her hand as she gazes skyward. Far up, in the girding, the carcass hangs, like a reprimand to the symmetry of the tower. She looks back at the road once before swinging herself up to the first horizontal crosspiece. The metal is surprisingly hot to the touch, but she wills herself to endure it so that she has time to consider each subsequent hold before committing her weight. The ground wheels out beneath her feet with each new ascension. It is its own kind of dangerous gymnastics, scaling the bright side of death.

When she reaches the hawk, she is faced with the effort of dislodging it. In its fall, the bird had half entered a span of small iron guards where the power cable connected, and as she pulls at his tail, the feathers come loose, but the body does not. With no closer foothold, she has to reach high and pull down. Her foot slips and the fear of overbalance swings up through her belly like a sharp blow. With her pulse on the run, she fishes out her Case knife from her hip pocket and pinches open the blade. The bird's head twists in her hands. The edge makes the neat detachment. She places the head in her blooded purse, leaves the rest for the buzzards.

Once home, she circles from the brow of the hill above the trailer, seeing Evelyn's Subaru parked in the gravel drive, the driver's door open, one sandaled foot dangling out. She curses and backs off for the bordering hedge of rhododendron, stows the rifle and hawk's head in the concealing arbor. Then she goes down to deal with another of her father's serial mistakes.

"Hey, Winter," Evelyn says, twisting out one of her hand-rolled American Spirits. She licks the paper once and seals it with an expert slide of her pinky finger. She holds it out. "You want one?"

"I'm not old enough to smoke," Winter says, watching this woman through a filter Evelyn couldn't understand, coming as it does at the end of so many similar episodes, the long refracted history of mother figures, each new issue a cheaper counterfeit than the last.

"Hell, girl. You're sixteen. I know I was into plenty by the time I was your age."

"I don't want cancer anyway. You go ahead."

Evelyn makes an attempt at a smile but fails. She sits a while, smoking and finding no place easy to set her eyes.

"My dad's at work. He won't be back until after three."

"Yeah, I know. I told him I was coming up here to look in on you. Maybe have a little girl time. With school out and all, I just figured you might get bored. Want to get out and do something."

Winter goes up the three short steps of the deck and moves some of the tomato plants into the morning sun patch. Evelyn clumps up behind her, blowing smoke. In the hard light, Winter can see the shadows drifting across the stained boards like thin abstractions.

"I guess I could use some shoes. These are starting to look a little ratty."

Evelyn smiles like her teeth are too precious to be covered, just pleased to be in Winter's good graces. *How predictable they always are, thinking that if they can get into favor with me, Dad will follow.*

After checking to make sure the trailer is locked, Winter climbs into Evelyn's Subaru, nudges aside a Ziploc bag of CDs and a couple of James Patterson mysteries checked out from the library. The dash is pale with dust, and she can smell the fulsome scent of patchouli. Evelyn gets in beside her, plays a minute on her smart phone, then cranks the engine. It squeals in need of a new fan belt, though Winter doubts Evelyn has the first idea what that is or how she might fix it.

They drive into town and park on Main Street a few spaces down from the front entrance to Peeble's department store. It is an old place full of second rate clothes and lawn furniture and the inside smells like a grandparent. Winter had hoped for one of the tourist driven shops with Colombian sandals, fleece hoodies, and The North Face backpacks draped from wall hooks, but clearly Evelyn is bound to a stricter budget. They go straight to the back, dig through the bins of water shoes, flats, and hooker pumps that look like they'll bust a heel if you stare at them too hard. Winter picks up a pair of spangled stilettos with cherry bows, swings them loosely by the strap from her fingertips.

"Honey, don't you want something a little more..."

"What?" she challenges. "Less trashy?"

Evelyn crimps her mouth. "I was going to say practical."

"These are fine. I like the way they look."

"Don't you want to try them on first?"

She glances at the sole and then starts for the cashier. "Naw, they're my size. Let's go."

She doesn't wait to see if Evelyn will follow.

Outside, the air is heavy, unseasonably hot. Despite the morning hour, middle-aged women and men donning jean and khaki shorts stand on the sidewalk, gazing past their own reflections in the glass facades of antique and curio shops. Some slurp at Styrofoam cups of lemonade or sweet tea. Tourists descending on the self-conscious quaintness of Canon City, a township no one would ever mistake as urban despite its moniker. Winter clutches her plastic bag of shoes under her arm and surges past them.

"Hon, where you going? The car's back this way," Evelyn calls.

"I need to eat," she says, not troubling to turn her head when she speaks. *If this woman can't keep up with me, it's her own goddamn business.*

They turn in at a diner with a chainsaw carved bear set on a pedestal out front. Still too early for lunch, the few customers sit over plates of eggs and toast, drinking coffee in steady markings of time. A booth full of sunburned men in brand name fishing shirts and caps glance up when they enter. Winter feels their eyes slide past her skinny body and light on Evelyn, taking her in like potential recreation. *All tits, tan, and bracelets, a kind of maternal porn fantasy come into the real world.* Maybe that's what her father saw too, just a body to fill an appetite, though even as she thinks that she realizes it to be untrue. Not him, not the man that chases after truth and meaning like they are important creatures on the edge of extinction. Not the Idealist.

Winter sits with her back to the wall under a television where CNN silently scrolls the news via subtitles. She consults the menu, speaks her order to the waitress when she comes, then sits for a few silent minutes, glaring. The food comes.

"So, you planning on marrying Dad?"

Evelyn tenses, places her fork across the thin edge of her plate. "You like to bite, don't you?"

Winter shrugs.

"Just asking a question."

"No, I think you're doing a little more than that."

Within a few minutes of pushing around at food she has no appetite for, Evelyn raises her hand to attract the waitress' attention and sends her away for the bill.

"What, you not eating?" Winter asks, feigned innocence.

"No, I'm quite done."

On the way back out to her father's trailer, Evelyn doesn't try to engage Winter in conversation. The silence agrees with Winter. She is happy to make Evelyn pay for wedging herself into her life, into their lives.

Once home, Winter watches the Subaru grind out of the drive, flipping stones, ripping tails of dust. In the silence that follows, she closes her eyes and builds up her surroundings by memory, erects the shaded dimensions of the woods, invests them with light, heat. Perhaps this is a kind of meditation, though Winter prefers to think of it as an anchoring, sinking herself into the particulars of where and when she was to keep this place as hers for a while, removing the threat that living could so slyly exact, moving, as it did, without remorse. When she opens her eyes the sun soaks back in. She remembers then what she'd left undone.

She goes out to the hedge and retrieves the rifle and trophy, brings them both up to the porch where she sits under the bench umbrella where it is cool. She wipes down the rifle with a rag and places it back in her father's bedroom closet, catches sight of herself in the mirrored doors. She likes the way she looks holding the rifle, serious and ready. She turns to profile, hoists the stock over one shoulder, then faces back, drops it in a horizontal line across her waist. Not so skinny looking now. Not so plain. She thinks of Cal.

She goes back to her room and sets the new shoes and the trophy purse on her dresser. At her desk a laptop is open. She sits down and stirs it to life with a keystroke. She pulls up Facebook for a minute to check messages from friends out of state. There is nothing new, so she clicks over to Cal's page and looks through his same five pictures, the most recent of which was uploaded six months ago. It is of him standing cross-eyed beside a street sign that read SLOW CHILDREN PLAYING. She stares at the image for a long time, trying to see past the teenage posturing. She has had glimpses of the real person beneath that counterfeit when they'd walked the trails behind his house, his "keep" he liked to call it. He was always concerned that she be at ease around him. If there was a single thing that Cal couldn't tolerate it was that others be uncomfortable, physically or otherwise. That was the reason for his continual stabs at humor.

Winter had learned to study people's habitual actions, how to sound out the parts of them they believed best concealed. Perhaps it was a survival tool, but whether acquired or innate, she was expert at reading another's deference. She knew that Cal was shy about the privilege he'd been born into, generous and loving parents who were well-educated and successful, free of the petty country resentments and judgments she had so often seen and despised in the many small communities she and her father had fled from over the past decade. His consideration had surprised her, frankly. When she had moved in to this new place, she had wanted to loathe everyone for their pettiness and prejudice. Instead, she'd found that the more she understood others, the less she could predict what made her want to be loved by them.

She closes the laptop without sending a message, opens the trophy purse and carefully lays the bloody head of the hawk on a doubled over sheet of newspaper. It begins to draw its own thin pattern across the print: a figure half realized. She narrows her eyes, pulls the head away and slips her fingertips through the spotted gore, traces a grotesquerie she could call familiar. Then she wads it all up, carries it outside to the plastic garbage can and hides it all under the stew of leftovers, broken down cardboard. The shoes too she carries out, shoves them past the gummed carrots and decapitated head.

All of it excess that needed to be carried off.

ACE OF SPADES: SEPTEMBER 15, 1973
Randall Horton

An aging clapboard house leans against the corner of 8th Avenue, simulating a low note suspended in the curve of a saxophone. The house is viridian and most of the exterior paint is chipped, withering to the sundial of time. The infrastructure sags in the middle with the burden of a heavy trumpeted blues, a blues lived by a certain kind of folk in this town. The kind of blues played with a metal slide — wailing in a whiskey still voice on long summer nights behind the backdrop of a jaundiced moon. Sometimes the only relief is a rigid shot of Kentucky Tavern or the snapback of a can of Budweiser or Schlitz. Ten years ago, the cornerstone of this American way of life was rocked to the foundation by a dynamite blast from the basement of Sixteenth Street Baptist Church. Only eight blocks from the point of detonation, this structure has witnessed serious interactions concerning race. The people who frequent this shot house are scarred from years of having to explain, defend, and get along. They live in a city trying to heal the lacerated wound of indifference. The city is still divided on the inside, and on the outside, people get along for the sake of trying — trying to reconcile, get over, and move on. Something easier said than done. And here, in the bootleg house of Pearl Lee, who inherited the house from her mother and mother's mother, resides a communal institution, a meeting place to unwind, relax and have a good time. Here, in Birmingham, a bootleg house can be a person's best friend.

Earlier today, The Jukebox Man drove up in his spanking brand new '73 Bonneville to load Pear Lee's jukebox with black vinyl — .45 discs. In many ways, even though The Jukebox Man is an interloper in this community, meaning he "ain't black" — he determines the rhythm of their blues or the octave of voices in card games by the records he selects for the machine. Like tonight, Catbird, with his string bean frame drooping over the glass casing, slips a quarter through the slot and selects a double play of Gene Chandler and Johnny Taylor. He then two-steps with an imaginary dance partner, right hand around the imaginary waist, the left elbow slightly raised, almost pantomiming — and he turns and dips until he floats into the kitchen.

"Hey Pearl, you betta' call the am-bu-lance, 'cause we 'bout to kill something up in here tonight. Watch out now!" Pearl Lee cannot hear Catbird, as she is up front in the big-room. Although Catbird does not work a legal job or cut-a-slave, he stays dressed sharper than a hatchet after the grindstone: Florsheims with silk socks, two-piece dark seersucker suits, and a Dobbs, forever tilted on the back of his forehead. Catbird is a numbers runner by trade; he simply refuses to work for Mr. Charlie, thinks a job ain't nothing but another form of owning.

"Catbird sit yo ol' wrinkle ass down. We got one more hand to go and you wanna get up and play some goddamn *running to the end of the rainbow* type shit. Hell, we 'bout to have yo ass at the end of a rainbow in 'bout five minutes." The voice comes from Sledge, who thinks to herself, *What the hell Catbird know 'bout some damn blues?* Shit, she lived the blues everyday of the week she woke up and dragged her tired ass down to Deluxe Beauty Shop by 8:30 a.m., a shop she did not own, and by the time she paid the chair fee, all she could do was take care of her rent and come down to Pearl's for whiskey and a laugh.

For Sledge, the thing about digging fingers into a wooly head for a perm or a curl, was not so much the act itself, but what came with the act. She heard more *my man done left me*, or *the rent due and I ain't got two nickels to rub together* problems than she wanted to hear. When a woman sat in her chair, Sledge received an offering of slow strummed realities fretted from hard living.

"Catbird, I ain't playing with yo toothpick looking ass. Why every time we play cards on Friday you gotta act a natural fool?"

"Sledge, why I gotta be acting? All I'm trying to do is have a good time, suga. Can't a man enjoy himself every now and then?"

"Man, you been enjoying yourself since you popped out yo mama womb. Before you step them Florsheims in hell you probably gone ask Lucifer if he got a dollar for a shot of red." Defeated in his defense, Catbird sits down. He stills managed to let out a "You damn right."

There are two other people at the table, Bookie, who is Catbird's partner, and Dot, Sledge's partner. Before Dot begins her deal, the familiar slide of bedroom slippers gliding across a pale blue linoleum floor signals the arrival of Pearl Lee from up front. Pearl Lee is a rather large, big boned woman, with a steel gray afro and piercing tar-liquid eyes. She enters the kitchen and begins a verbal assault on the man who shacks up with her every night, just because a woman in her line of work needs a man around for the physical stuff.

"Bookie, how in the hell you gon' pour shots and play cards at the same time? Paperboy say he wanna pint of gin and two beers brought to the back room where him and that gal Florene at. Man, seem to me, the older you get, the dumber yo black ass get."

Bookie could be called dumb, but that might do him too much justice. He left the corn and cotton fields of Boulder Gee, Alabama, back in '40, with only a third-grade education to draw words from.

The thing Bookie can do well is work a manual labor job, the one trait he inherited from his daddy. Hard work it was to rise after the moon disappeared into the crevice of night and before the solitary break of sunlight swept across the red clay roads that led to the field. When Bookie turned twenty, he left for Birmingham, stayed for a while in Tuxedo Junction, which is not too far from downtown Birmingham, drinking and jazzing with the hipsters. Time has not been good to Bookie. An old man now, he still works hard, but has moved no further along in life.

"Now hold on, Pearl Lee, you know I'm keepin' an eye on thangs. If a rat move, I know what hole he went into. I don't know why you be all on my back bout lil stuff. I'm gon' take care ya, baby. One hand to go and Dot dealin' right now. Shit, if we win, me and Catbird got a fifth of that good red comin'."

"Fool, I don't care nothing bout no liquor! In case yo dumb ass don't know, I run a damn shot house. And yo ass drinking for free." No one at the table says a word. Pearl Lee means business when she starts cussing.

"Don't worry, Pearl Lee, his behind be up in a minute," Dot said while scooping the pile of cards she'd just dealt herself, arranging them in like order, with a Kool Filter King dangling off the edge of her lips, the slow glow of red burning brighter when she inhaled, the soft ashes at the end hanging on for dear life. She is Pearl Lee's best friend, has the upper hand when it comes to any kind of sentimentality or compassion concerning Pearl Lee.

"Damn it, I'll do it myself." Pear Lee goes inside the kitchen pantry, pouring the half pint and grabbing two beers from the Frigidaire. She leaves as she came, sliding her slippers across the floor.

Dot is the wild card within this bunch sitting at the table. The first time she came to Pearl Lee's, B.B. King's "Down Home Blues" was jumping out the jukebox on a Friday night. Her husband Gene brought her so she could see where he came every payday for the past five years. The entire house welcomed her with good music and good drink. Dot is educated with a college degree from Alabama A&M and has a good teaching job in the school system. This kind of life used to be foreign to her; always thought she was too sophisticated to hang with these folk. But when it came down to it, she realized she was just as down home as the rest of them; had experienced the same kind of blues, the same joys. Pearl Lee took to Dot so much that they were almost like sisters. She was around the place so much now that her husband stopped coming.

Card games at Pearl Lee's involve a lot of overhand card smacking and shit talking. These are the most serious engagements one can walk into. The rivalry is furious between partners and oftentimes battles take place along the lines of gender. This one playing out right now is down to the last hand: first one to seven books wins the game of Whist. For the winner there's a bottle of state store whiskey at stake. But there is something else going on in the shotgun house directly behind Pearl Lee's house. The house is rented by Mrs. Two-Bit. Her place is small and doesn't do the business that Pearl Lee does. When Two-Bit's husband Frank retired from U.S. Steel, she decided to make a little extra money by selling liquor to supplement his pension that takes care of them both, plus Two-Bit gets a chance to have company every now and then.

"Two-Bit, gimme another shot of whiskey," the man sitting in the kitchen ordered.

"Man why you dranking so much tonight? What? You gon' spend the whole paycheck here? Take that money home to your wife and kids." Two-Bit sits in front of the one window in her living room. If she angles her head just right, she can see who comes and goes out of Pearl Lee's house. Two-Bit is also known as the 'Mouth of the South,' and tells everybody's business when she can get her ears and eyes on it.

"Two-Bit, why is you worried about my family, woman? I'm spending hard earned money here tonight, that's all you needs to know. I spend the money and you pour the dranks, that's how it 'sposed to work." The man's name is Gene. Gene bangs his glass on the table, signaling for Two-Bit to get up and pour another drink.

"Stop making all that damn noise. You know Frank in the back room asleep." Two-Bit gets up and lays a half-gallon on the table. "Here's the damn bottle, you gon' pay for the whole thing." Two-Bit returns to the window. She has a small transistor radio tuned to an Atlanta Braves game. She listens and looks between the radio static.

Gene's mind is still on the "noise," a noise that will not stop banging in his drunken head. He had hoped consistent shots of gin would evaporate the noise—make it melt away from his consciousness. But it is still there, along with the vision, the one vision a hard-working man never wants to see; the kind of images that can twist a man's insides tighter than a tourniquet, a vision that drops the heart heavier than an eight ball in the corner pocket.

Gene couldn't believe what he saw and heard. It was something inconceivable. That day, he just happened to come by Pearl Lee's house during lunchtime from his job down at Acipico Steel. Pearl Lee was not home and when Bookie saw him coming up the back steps, Bookie's eyes bulged a bit and his speech began to stutter.

"Wh…wh…what you do…do…do…doing here this time of day, Gene?"

"Man, what the hell wrong with you? You done forgot how to talk now? Gimme a drank. Mr. Charlie down at the mill been riding my back all week bout putting out more work. Man, they act like I'm a machine or something. I took lunch early today, my nerves shot, man. There gotta be a better way to get bill money."

When Gene passed Bookie and sat down by the jukebox, he saw something familiar on the table: a set of keys with a plastic baseball on the ring. The lettering on the ball itself read: Barons. The same kind of key chain he bought his wife at a minor league baseball game last year. Gene picked the keys up and looked at Bookie. Bookie looked like he was about to run a stream of piss down his overalls. The harder Gene looked at him, the harder Bookie sweated.

"Now...now — now...hold on G...G — Gene, it ain't what you think going on here. Sh...sh...sh — she left them keys here this morning before she dropped Pearl Lee down to the courthouse to pay them fines the police come in and give her the other night."

Gene got up and went in the middle bedroom, grabbed a chair and propped it next to the wall where he and Bookie would sometimes watch people who came in to rent rooms to have sex. Gene would then go home and make love to his wife. Bookie stood in the frame of the door, unable to get a word out as Gene stepped up on the chair and placed his eyeball on the small hole in wall that had been carved with a pocketknife.

On the other side of the peephole, lying on the bed with the body of man on top of her was Dot, his wife, the mother of his children, the woman he brought his paycheck home to every week. Her legs said eleven and two, and the man in the middle was loving her like a freight train. Gene saw the orgasmic look on her face as his wife's body trembled until she convulsed uncontrollably. Gene turned from the peephole — an anvil formed in his throat; he could not swallow his own saliva no matter how hard he tried. And when he tried to catch his breath, the voice of his wife echoed through the keyhole once more, driving the stake of betrayal further into his heart, and all he could feel were the strings of Leadbelly plucking in his veins. He looked at Bookie with wet eyelids and ran from the bedroom, crashed through the backdoor, the screen door swinging in the wind. That was the last time Bookie saw him. Bookie never said a word to nobody, no even Dot. Gene never said a word to Dot.

Sitting at Two-Bit's table right now, with the burn of whiskey in his throat, these are the sounds that haunt Gene. He has never confronted Dot about that day, about her infidelity. He has been living with this knothole for almost a year. The last drop of liquor leaves the shot glass and into his throat. His tongue smacks his palate. He digs in his pockets and leaves a fifty-dollar bill on the table.

"Two-Bit, I'm gone. I'll see you." Two-Bit gets up and takes the money off the table, realizes it is a fifty. She goes back to her window with the bill in her hand and looks at the silhouette of Gene through screen.

Inside Pearl Lee's, the game is down to the last play of cards. The men and women both have the same number of books made: six.

The next made book determines the winner and will bring the smoothness of Johnny Walker Red and the right to talk shit for a week until the next card game. Everyone at the table is tense. Even Pearl Lee has left her bedroom up front for a minute to see how this last hand goes down.

"Come on man, it's your play." Dot addresses Catbird. At this point, there is no bluffing or whimsical deceit. One card will either win or loose. Catbird rubs the tattered grey stubble on his chin and slaps his lead off card on the thin kitchen table. The card spins north by east, revealing the ten of hearts. He then yells, "Teach me how to swim, I can drown with the best of 'em!"

"You gotta brang ass to get ass you old muthafucka!" says Sledge with a flick-release of a defiant jack. Bookie then draws from his third grade education, throws out a trump card — the six of spades — without eye contact.

Bookie yells, "That's right, you hair grease smelling heifer! I drank Johnny Walker Red. Sledge don't worry, you can keep that ass — that wrinkled thing be safe with me, baby!" Before the riff of laughter envelops the kitchen, Dot slaps the last card on her forehead. She rotates her neck 90 degrees for Bookie and Catbird to view.

"How 'bout both of you old crusty muthafuckas kiss my natural black ass, next!" Glued to Dot's forehead is the ace of spades. There is the beginning of a smile. But this formation of a smile is immediately replaced. The moment her cheeks begin to part, the tracery of a bullet discarded from a .38 Special pierces through the black miniature spade on her forehead and bursts her brain into a sea of blackness, she enters that void of the unknown, the uncertainty, but Gene hopes that it is hell. He hopes his wife rots in hell.

"Holy shit!" Catbird yells, watching blood seep through the hole in Dot's head. Dot slumps over and her face smacks the table harder than any card played tonight. In the doorway of the kitchen, the raised right arm of Gene is still pointed in Dot's direction, smoke from the barrel rising toward the ceiling. He has parted the onlookers deeper than Moses did the Red Sea, only Pearl did not flinch or run out the room. She eases her hand on top of Gene's arm and presses the gun barrel downward. Bookie, Sledge and Catbird are still at the table, watching the blood as it begins to coagulate on the table. Pearl Lee looks at Bookie. The next play on the jukebox is B.B. King's "The Thrill Is Gone."

I BECOME A SOLDIER
David Hunter

It was late in April of 1965. Pope John Paul VI was on Peter's throne; cosmic background radiation was discovered and eventually established "the big bang" as the prevailing theory of cosmic origin. A Harvard professor named Leary was making the transition from educator to guru with a hallucinogenic chemical called LSD.

The above events were either unknown or considered inconsequential to me. I was excited by being in love; by a war smoldering in a place called Vietnam about to burst into flames; about a little book called *In His Own Write* by Beatle John Lennon; by the music of the Beatles, Bob Dylan, and by the fact that I had turned eighteen.

Being of legal age — to fight wars, but not to vote, drink alcoholic beverages or get married without permission — was by far the most exciting thing that happened to me in April of 1965. I was old enough to leave home and nobody could stop me.

I stood on the sidewalk in front of the of the imposing gray marble U.S. Post Office on Main Street, Knoxville, Tennessee, my stomach knotted in anticipation, the way it always was as a child on Christmas Eve. At that time, the military recruiters were stationed in the basement of the main post office.

It had been the ambition of my short life to join the ranks of war heroes; put in my combat time; then retire to write books on the scale of *For Whom the Bell Tolls* or *From Here to Eternity*, and to collect my Pulitzer, maybe even a Nobel Prize for literature by age twenty-five, while I was still young enough to enjoy success.

I was sure God was going to compensate me for my chronic depression (as yet undiagnosed); weak eyes, a big head, an even bigger nose, severe acne, for having stopped my growth at five-and-a-half feet and for a total lack of skill at any athletic game except boxing, which gave no varsity letter when I was a student.

My eighteenth birthday had arrived three weeks earlier, and my father, aware of my intentions, had kept me busy at a small boat dock he was leasing over on Melton Hill Lake, north of Knox County, while he worked days as an ironworker. He had been busy somewhere else that morning, so I had taken my opportunity. I would have enlisted earlier, but my parents refused to be a party to my military ambition by signing the papers.

Taking a deep breath, I went in and quickly descended the steps into the bowels of the building where the recruiters were located. I paused at the Marine Corps recruiter's door and longingly looked at the young man talking to the crew cut Marine recruiter behind a desk. The Marine Corps had always been special to me because my father had been a Marine. However, only the U.S. Army allowed enlisted men to fly helicopters through their Warrant Officer flight school program.

The Army recruiter's door was open, but I started to knock anyway, just as a sergeant, middle-aged and leathery looking, sitting behind a desk boomed out, "Come in and sit down. Tell me what I can do for you." Military recruiters are soldiers who find their true vocation of direct sales after beginning a military career. Everyone I ever met was as genial as a used car salesman. I went in and took a seat in a straight back chair by the sergeant's desk.

"I..." My courage seemed to fail for a moment. "... I want to enlist." I swallowed hard. *There, I said it out loud.*

"You've come to the *right* place. What would you like to do in the Army? We have all kinds of programs."

"I want to fly helicopters." I was shocked at my own audacity.

"That can be arranged — if you can pass the tests and the physical. But if you can't get that, helicopter crews have gunners and mechanics."

"I'd like to try for helicopter pilot."

"All right, I have a little screening test..." the sergeant was interrupted by another young man who walked into the office, looking around with what appeared great trepidation. "Sit down, son and tell me what I can do for you."

"I want to join up." He was about my age. His dress pegged him as a country boy in my eyes, unsophisticated as I was. He was wearing a flannel shirt in warm weather, and scuffed work boots peeked from under his denim cuffs.

"What would you like to do in the Army?" The sergeant asked.

"I just wanna be a *rag'lar* soldier," he said. His accent put him in one of the outlying counties from Knoxville, Union or Claiborne, maybe.

"So, you're interested in the infantry?"

"Just want to be a *rag'lar* soldier," he said again.

"I was just about to give a little screening test to this other recruit. Why don't you two sit at that table over there." A thrill went through me when the sergeant said, "other recruit."

A couple of minutes later, Lowell Snyder and I were filling in multiple choice blocks with a soft lead pencil. It took me about ten minutes. It appeared to me that the only thing being tested was whether I could read the screening test. A grammar school child, I thought, could have passed it.

When I looked over and saw that Lowell was chewing his pencil, deeply in thought, I decided that I had missed something — that I had fallen for a trick to test my alertness. So I went over every question again, with the same results. Twenty minutes later, Lowell laid down his pencil and shook his head ruefully. "That was *hard*," he said.

The recruiter, who had been reading a newspaper while we took the test, came over to the table with a template and laid it over my test. There was a black mark in every space.

"You made a hundred, Goin. We don't see that very often." My heart swelled at his words. "You just might have what it takes to be a pilot—or at least an officer, somewhere in the Army." He laid the template over Lowell's test and winced. Then, as I watched in amazement, he proceeded to erase incorrect answers and mark in correct ones.

"Well, you both passed. Can you two be at the recruiting office on Central at seven in the morning for the physical and written tests?" We both nodded in agreement

"Snyder, go home and get a good night's sleep. Goin, hang around a minute. I need to speak to you about something."

Lowell Snyder left smiling. When he was out of earshot, the sergeant closed the door, sat down at his desk and fixed me with a serious gaze. I squirmed a little.

"Goin, was your father in the military?"

"Yes. The Marine Corps. He was at Iwo Jima." I hoped my father's branch of service would not be held against me.

"Well, old Lowell's daddy was a war hero. It'll kill the old man if his son can't carry on the family tradition. And I don't think he can pass the tests tomorrow."

It didn't cross my mind to ask how the sergeant had learned this, since we had all been in the same room and nothing had been said about war heroes. I guess I just presumed that all recruiters knew about all war heroes.

"You can do that boy—and your country—a favor tomorrow," the sergeant said in a voice that was dead serious.

"How can *I* help?" My mouth was dry, very dry.

"I'll arrange for a friend of mine who works at the induction center to make sure you sit by Snyder. He'll turn his head when that poor, old ignorant farm boy copies off your test. You get my drift?" The recruiter winked.

"What if somebody else notices and...." My head was filled with visions of a military career ending before it had begun.

"Don't worry. It won't be the first time. Why should a man, a war hero's son, be kept out of the service just because he has a little trouble reading and writing?" I didn't say anything, so the recruiter went on. "*Good!* It's all settled. Go home and get a good night's sleep. All you have to do tomorrow is slow down a little as you take the tests. I'll arrange everything else."

*   *   *

The U.S. Army induction center was across the street from Sears on Central Avenue. I had looked at it for years as my father and I drove past it on Saturday mornings on our way downtown, just waiting for the day I would walk in and start my *real* life, putting childhood behind me. But I was scared, scared I would fail the written tests or the physical. I was trembling inside when I took my seat in a plastic chair with chrome legs, along with a hundred or so other young men.

A bored private first class came in and barked at us to be quiet. We were lined up and taken to a room with neat lines of chairs at long tables. The first of hundreds of forms on which I would put my signature and vital statistics was put in front of me, and within ten minutes the battery of tests was in progress. I had hoped Lowell Snyder would oversleep but there he was, right beside me. The Spec. 4 (specialist fourth class) handing out the tests sheets quietly said something to the country boy. I presumed the fix was in.

The first battery of tests wasn't much different from the multiple-choice tests I had been taking all my life. I have always been a good test taker. I have always been able to sit down with a multiple-choice test and do well on subjects with which I am totally unfamiliar. Part of it's a gift, part of it is the result of omnivorous reading from the age of eight. Through grammar school and high school, I averaged reading at least one book a day, and usually more.

The only problem I had that morning was the tediousness of moving slowly enough so that my unwelcome protégé could painfully and slowly copy my tests. As I turned to the last page, I saw that Lowell had no pages left. He sat staring ahead for a moment, like a rabbit caught in the headlights of a car. He had somehow started on the wrong page, which meant that *none* of his test scores would be better than he would have gotten from random guesses.

He was out, and I wondered what the recruiter would have to say about my failure. It didn't matter, though, because I never saw either Lowell or the recruiting sergeant again.

As it happened, I was a terrible soldier, not good at obeying orders — poor eyesight prevented me from becoming a helicopter pilot, but I was door gunner for a year in the Republic of Vietnam. When my enlistment was up, I cheerfully went home.

I *did* see Lowell's picture in the *Knoxville News Sentinel* several years later. He had been killed while serving as a Marine during the Tet Offensive in Vietnam. Presumably, he had done a better job of copying answers the next time he took the test. Or maybe they had lowered the standards by the time the Marines began to use draftees for the first time since World War II.

I read the standard boilerplate used by newspapers to describe dead hometown heroes. By 1969 when I read the few lines, unless a dead or missing in action soldier was a family member, it was so routine that hardly anyone gave such stories a second glance.

ALL OF MY TREES TO DIE FOR
Lynn Pruett

"They eat toads, mice, rats, eggs, fruit and the rotting flesh of small animals," Cecile, Othel's wife, read from the computer's encyclopedia. Her pillow was couched between her knees. On it, the computer glowed like a favored pet.

Othel sighed. He was creating a nest for himself under the quilt and top sheet. A foul odor had floated up from under the house after supper, though Cecile insisted she smelled nothing unusual. Othel suspected a skunk. "Must have been the fruit salad your sister brought over what attracted the skunk. Poor fella." He pulled the quilt over his face.

"I am not sleeping with my head under the covers." Cecile flipped the blanket off Othel.

"Nothing gets past you." He closed his eyes. In the morning he would crawl under the deck and see if he could find the skunk, dead, he hoped, and turning into the rotting flesh of a small animal.

He could hear Cecile clicking past screens, reading more and more about rodents. Her mind would be working hard to find a Biblical analogy for the plague of dead skunks along Highway 30, something she could make into a lesson for her column in the Christian internet newsletter. Othel was awed by Cecile's mental pursuits. She had mastered the laptop and sent her messages out into cyberspace where thousands of people "hit" on her, as he understood it.

He pulled the quilt easily from under Cecile who gave a slight squawk as she tilted then righted herself like a seagull riding an ocean wave. She was the same slim size she'd been when they married, though what had been firm and pleasing to grip then was loose and soft and in need of inflation.

"I've got it, Othel. We Christians give off the aroma of Christ."

"The aroma of Christ? What the hell is that?"

"Othel, do not say that word in our bedroom."

"Yes, ma'am." During love making, he was not sure if she said *Othel* or *Oh, hell,* and if the latter, if she was mad or glad or asking to be forgiven. It was still a routine Saturday night activity between them, for which he was happy. He pulled the quilt over his head and held it tight. He felt her tug and he tugged back. If the quilt wasn't anchored at the bottom of the bed, his legs could kick free. But as it was, he was trapped by his own smell and her vicious grip.

"To fellow Christians, it's the fragrance of life and to nonbelievers it's the smell of death!" she shouted, though the quilt muffled her voice.

"The smell of death is what drove us to bed in the first place," he shouted back.

They lay there stunned, one on top and one below the red quilt. Their hands let go. Cecile moved the laptop out of the bed and curled into a bony ball on top of the covers and shivered. Underneath, the close air was no longer bearable.

Othel ran a stump grinding business called Stump Busters, a name his grandsons had suggested. About 7:30 a.m. a call came from a woman who lived on Campground Road. She was a *visiting* writer, a renter, but was somehow responsible for the upkeep of the yard. He said he'd be over in eight minutes.

The house was at the far end of the road, nearly three windy miles from the turn-off. A car with Kentucky plates was parked in the driveway next to the oddly-angled house, which resembled a building a child might make from blocks. The roof's two sections should have met at the peak but it appeared that one had slipped. Amid a descending garden of rusty-leafed azaleas and green gardenias, the downed cedar tree balanced on its own dead branches.

A lady sprinted up the steep driveway and back down again. Again she appeared in her molten gray spandex tights, arms pumping, pulling her nicely ample rear up the hill and then running away from it on the down slope. Othel appreciated how women kept their shapes longer these days. Despite living in the fattest state in the country, Mississippi, some women didn't give in to statistics. This woman was a mix and match. Her face and torso were narrow as a deer's but her rump was round and muscular as a thoroughbred's.

She approached Othel, her breath shooting white out of her mouth as she gasped, red-faced, under a bleak gray cap. "You got here soon."

"It's early in the day, and cedars aren't worth much but to make fence posts."

She shrugged. "A dead tree's a dead tree."

She was probably in her forties, not younger, as he first guessed. He remembered Cecile in her forties, the years she was a plump munchkin he liked to squeeze. The last hurrah of hormones before she assumed the natural aged shape of her gender, with its lumpish abdomen, sagging chest, and birdy legs. He called her that now, Birdy Legs, in moments of affection.

The woman pulled off the cap and shook her thick shoulder length hair like a golden curtain that made her suddenly beautiful. Her flushed cheeks and green eyes sparkled as if she was fresh from the slopes.

"Maybe we can do a lot of business together," he said.

She did not laugh and enjoy his gaze in a mutual exchange of delight, acknowledging that she was attractive and he thought her so. A flirtation always gave him a lift. The spark was not dead despite his wrinkles and paunch and thinning hair.

"Your five hundred trees," he said, opening his arms wide to encompass the woods around them.

"You want all my trees to die?" She hocked and spit near his boot.

He turned away, hit in the gut by the difference between what he felt and how he looked. He wanted to grab her shoulders and shake her and say, *You don't understand. Until you've lived it, you don't understand it. Until you read it in a younger person's eyes, inside you are hale and handsome, the same person you always were, but outside you are something tattered and even disgusting for still appreciating youth and beauty.*

He strode to his truck, her furious words glancing off his back, and climbed into the quiet haven of the cab. A man drove a green van into the driveway and parked, then lifted his hand in greeting. He wore glasses, which ticked Othel off for some inexplicable reason. The thickset man emerged, carrying a bag of groceries on one hip. A computer case dangled from his other hand. *Useless*, Othel thought. *A useless man.* Though it was dangerous to do on a blind curve, he backed the trailer down the steep slope and into the road and drove toward home and Cecile.

A couple miles later he obeyed the *Watch Children* sign and slowed down. Three small children were playing outside in the cold. The big oak in their yard was split, one section standing tall, its brim of branches spread against the sky, the other cracked like a bent fan in the dirt. A girl about five, wearing pink polka dotted pants under an enormous gray sweatshirt, jumped up and down on the broken branch. Her sneakers flashed red lights when her feet touched the wood. Two small boys in green, unzipped windbreakers and red knit caps danced in the leaf fall.

Othel sighed with involuntary despair. His two chunky grandsons loved to watch wrestling on TV, bowls of melting ice cream in their laps, while slick grown men in tiny leotards man-handled each other. Last Saturday, Othel had offered to let the boys use the chainsaw to cut up a tree they'd burn at Christmas but they were too weak to hold the chainsaw steady.

The children abandoned the tree and ran to the steps of small brick house and stopped. Tremors ran from the girl's pointing finger to her feet. "The spider's coming down. The spider's coming down."

The boys stood as if paralyzed. Othel could only see the backs of their heads and could only imagine their glazed eyes and open mouths.

"He's going to eat us!" The girl led the charge around the house, her feet sparking the ground as she took the corner, the two boys hollering, their round faces intent on escape.

The front door swung open. "Y'all!"

A woman in fuzzy pink pajamas stood there, a normal-shaped woman, Othel noted, with hips and thick thighs stretching the fabric taut. He climbed out of the truck. The woman started as she spied Othel. Her lids closed over her large brown eyes, leaving only a slit to peer through. "My children screaming at you?"

"They're screaming at a spider," he said, and laughed. "It's fixing to eat them."

"A spider." She shuddered.

"I'm here to chop up that tree," he said.

"You from the county?"

He nodded, not quite a fib.

"Where's your orange suit?"

"I'm not incarcerated," he said. "Yet."

"Me neither," she said. "Yet."

He laughed and she smiled and her eyes opened and his spirits lifted. He might just chop up the whole tree for her and the children, not just the broken half.

"My chainsaw could scare the children."

She waved her hand to dismiss that concern. "They need their snack soon."

He turned his attention to the tree. Along the split ran a black burn. It had been hit by lightning. In the standing half, the char crooked like an accusing finger at the house. On the broken half the strike had raced along the edges, blackening knots, but leaving the heartwood clean. Othel worked for an hour cutting first the branches and then the trunk into logs, sweating as the sun rose higher and drove the chill to the edge of the woods.

In the strange silence that blanketed the yard after the chainsaw was put to rest, Othel rested. The color of the day could not be described nor could the time nor the sun be pinned down. The wood was chopped, the broken tree was now a standing tree, the splintered limb excised as if it had never been there. Othel was warm but the air deliciously cold. He was inert but felt like he was moving, or rather that space was moving around him. He was at the edge of one thing and the beginning of the next, in a state of perfect contentment. He dared not shift an inch, and felt the earth's minute movement on its axis.

A child's shout nudged his senses to notice that his sweat had frozen, that he was shivering, and, in fact, was cold and hungry. He saw that the logs he'd cut lying in the front yard were an invitation to thieves. He gathered an armload of wood and carried it up the path to the house. He leaned on the doorbell with his elbow.

There were three windows cut like stair steps in the door. The woman's face appeared in the middle rectangle. "Just pile it round back," she said, through the glass. "I'll bring it in later."

"It should season some first." His raised voice hung for a moment like a small private mist.

"Are you a Christian?" she asked.

"My wife is the only one who can wear that badge around my place," he said. "She's a Christian with a capital C."

"Oh." She pushed the door open a crack. "A good neighbor's a good neighbor." Her voice ascended in a tinkly laugh, sounding too high pitched. "You want to believe something good happens at your front door but can you trust it?"

"You ought to thank your neighbor what lives in that funny house way down on the curve. She brought me out this way today and didn't have any work for me so you get my time."

"My neighbor?" she said. "My *neighbor* way down the curve?"

"I'll take the wood around back."

He was loading the chain saw into the truck when the front door opened.

"Want some coffee?" the woman said, then hesitated, glanced at the house across the street, then gave a quick dart left and right with her head as she pulled a green vinyl coat around her. Beneath the coat, an ugly gray skirt charged with static electricity clung to her hearty legs.

"No," he said. "I'm good."

"Where have you been?" Cecile said. "It's past noon. I am about to pass out faint dead from that awful odor." She stood at the top of the front steps, above the pink-bloomed camellias, in a white stretch pant suit that made her look like a hard-boiled egg with filmy, fluttering appendages.

"I'll fix it, Birdy Legs," he said, still cheery from his good deed of the morning.

"You'll fix it?" she asked.

"Yes, Cecile," he said, "even if it means taking the aroma of Christ from our house."

She directed her Scowl of Contempt at him.

He chuckled as the door slammed shut, then went around back to the shed and donned the bee helmet, the stiff leather gloves, and picked up the rake.

He had built the deck a number of years ago, a semi-circle of now grayed wood that required an application of mildew remover each summer. Even if he didn't find all the animal remains, the annual bleaching would render it harmless. The trap door had never fit right and rather than disturb it, he crawled under the deck. The hard-packed clay rang cold as concrete against his knees as he inched along, careful not to bump his head or shoulders on the crossbeams. He came upon the skunk's body near the opening to the crawl space. Pleased that the task had been easy, he dragged it out with the rake. As soon as sunlight hit the matted hide, he knew it was not the source of the smell. It was merely an old traffic casualty of flattened fur. He put it in the trash bin, turned and sniffed the air, and almost threw up.

Something else, more freshly dead, still waited under there. Othel sighed and picked up his rake and affixed his bee helmet, then took it off, and secured an air mask, its elastic tight across his ears. He crawled through the dimness and poked his head through the gap in the foundation. In the patchy light lay a shape larger than a deer. His heart beat fast. A pale human hand, its fingers open in greeting, reached toward him. Hunched in the opening, Othel sucked against the white cone. Air was hard to come by. Drowning in his own breath, his reflexes working against each other, to gag or to breathe, he ripped off the helmet and the cone and inhaled the stench to the depth of his lungs, grasped the open hand and pulled, surging forward through spider webs with their scampering shadows, toward the light of the backyard, its shimmering shriveled grass.

He coughed on the chilly clean air and turned to look at the man he had found under his house. The man was not hiding; he was not wounded; he was not moving. He was the smell but Othel was too shocked to retch.

The man's open eyes were as blue as the sky, simple reflectors now of the vast beyond. Freckles appeared as a sprinkling of black pepper across his cooled white skin. In life, he would have been ruddy-complected, Othel thought, as a spider climbed the pale curly hair of the man's freckled wrist. He was dressed in dirty khakis and a red and green plaid flannel shirt. The man resembled Othel ten years ago.

"Mother," Othel called, his voice high and reedy. "You better come out here and bring the Good Book."

Cecile appeared like a pale column of smoke, her white hair a small puff above the fiery red of her face.

"He's shot, Othel," she said.

"How do you know? I haven't even looked close." Othel pointed at the man, his hand suddenly slack, bumping against his hip. "How do you know?"

"You must bury him, Othel."

"Bury him? The sheriff, his kin...." He stuttered. "Bury him?" he asked again, his brain stuck.

She drummed her fingers on the deck rail. "Othel, you are my best friend."

Her eyes were as glazed as those of a chicken hawk. Though a strange laugh eeked out of Othel's mouth, his liver quivered. "You know him?"

"Awfully well." She flipped back a strand of white hair, a girlish gesture, familiar and odd, of a different place and time. From her mouth tumbled a long list of facts: He is good-looking, five feet eight inches tall, he likes to do crosswords and hunt pigeons and watch birds down on Dauphin Island...

"How do you know all this?" He heard himself say, his voice gone absurd, latching onto the most peculiar and concrete items. "How do you know he likes banana pancakes with peanut butter?"

"The internet," she said shyly.

"The internet? You found this dead man on the internet?" The woods around him closed in then receded with each of his quick breaths. "He's missing?"

She rolled her eyes, waiting for Othel to catch up.

"Were you, were you?" The shock hit Othel like a hard block of wood flung into his chest. He whispered, "Having an affair?"

"Virtually, until he wanted to meet me at a hotel." She sniffed. "But I thought here would be better. When I opened the door, he was there as he is but..."

Through the veil of shock, what she said did not register. Yet Othel's mouth asked on, his brain acting like a detective while his heart slammed his stomach threatening to force breakfast all the way up and out onto the lawn.

"Wait," he said, turning away. "Wait."

The trap door. She had shot him and pushed him through the trap door, had probably scraped the dead skunk off the side of the road and planted it under the house.

He faced the woman who had been his wife. Who had shared a past fast disappearing in the tin whine of the winter air.

She locked her eyes into his, defiant and ashamed, and whispered, "I was not what he expected."

Othel regarded her wiggling chins and watering eyes and heard her high whiny voice and knew that he was the only man who would ever love her, and knew, too, what the dead man thought when Cecile greeted him, puckered up, ready. He wanted to ask, *What did you say to him? What did you expect?* When women prolonged youth these days, didn't they know what they were up against?

The wind moved, a warm and sudden stench rising against their skin. Likely, another organ had burst on the lawn.

"Bury him, Othel."

He's dead, thought Othel. *He humiliated her and he is dead.*

"I'll fix it, Cecile," he said. "Go, go make some tomato juice." He asked himself, *Tomato juice?* And then, *Where is God now?*

He watched his boots cross the crunching grass, kick open the shed door and catch it on the rebound. Hot white clouds shot from his mouth, obscuring the shapes of his tools in the cramped building. His hands felt the cold canvas and the heft of the tent as he wrenched it off a splintery shelf. Defending a wife was old in his bones, an ancestral duty spouted from pulpit and stump, enacted with violence against enemies, real or imagined, generation after generation. This was work he could do, with his hands.

He flung the tent's ground cover down next to the dead man. He grasped the body under the armpits and dragged it onto the stiff plastic. He could see dried blood where the bullet from Cecile's small pistol had entered the man's shirt. An excellent shot it had been. Precise, close range. She'd carried on an affair with this man on the internet, perhaps even while Othel lay under the red quilt, and she'd invited him to their house.

As he tried to push the man's splayed legs together and cross his arms over his stomach, Othel understood Cecile's utter humiliation, and he felt the urge to shout and kick the corpse. Cecile still saw herself as the trim and vivacious teenager she had been when his heart had turned over for her. She had always acted the flirt. What had she felt when the mirror of the man's eyes had been held up, when the rejection came for being too old or ugly, for being who she was and could not help being?

Othel laced a cord through the cover's metal rings. There were gullies way back in the woods, carved before the Yocona River was dammed and diverted, before the road was crowned and ditches dug alongside it. A riven landscape of beetle-dead pines where flesh did not last. He drew the chord tight. The body shuddered and a cold whistle of pain shot through Othel's bones.

"Othel." She was at the back door.

His name O-thel, like *Oh, tell*, like *Oh-hell*, but really *O-thell*, the soft sweetness of her young voice when she had accepted his hand, the air full of gardenias. He held the scent of his name long after she had retreated into the house, straining to recall the wonderment of the long O on her lips, the pink oval that began his name.

The Hook Up
Chris Offutt

I rose early and took a hangover shower, sitting on a plastic milk crate in the tub, letting water drill the back of my neck. It'll get better, I told myself, it always does. A cigarette settled me enough to shave. I tried not to look at my face in the mirror, just watched the razor move over somebody else's skin. My memory jolted like a truck on a rutted road. I didn't remember getting home. Blackouts are supposed to be a bad sign, but all it really means is short-term memory loss. I didn't mind that. There aren't that many good things to remember. What I really needed was a six-pack of dog hair to feel better.

The sun cut into my eyes like the lash of a whip. I drove through Louisville's traffic to Thornton's for an Ale-8, then hit 65 south. The interstate median was strewn with trash. A lone cloud hung in the sky like a sentry for the sun. I used to love driving through hot summer days but now I'm putting in seventy hours a week and don't love anything. No overtime, no perks, not even my own business.

To recruit in high schools, I wear my battle dress uniform, but today is Saturday and I'm setting up at Walmart. Class Bravo Greens give a workingman appearance. Walmart attracted the backbone of America, and I sat by the door and say hi to everybody, pitching God and patriotism to the older generation, knowing it'll trickle down at the supper table. The store didn't mind my presence. The manager brought me a free meal and water. I ate to be polite, but the quality of food is the same as the store's products. I couldn't finish the sandwich.

Every hour I went inside for some A.C. The hangover began to lift like removing heavy gear piece by piece. Every single product in the store was made in China. They're cheap and wear out quicker, sending people back for an inexpensive replacement. It's a big tough cycle, like soldiers heading for the sandbox. Everyone I know is back from Iraq and Afghanistan, or on their way to Syria. After nine-eleven, we attacked the wrong country and now we're protecting people's rights to buy Chinese crap.

A truck radio tuned to WAMZ drifted country music from a window. I hated that shit, but I waved to the driver, who had the longest sideburns I ever saw. They were like hair stripes running down his head. The rest of his face was an unmade bed.

"Proud of you, son," he said. "Keep our country safe."

"Thank you, sir," I said. "Just doing my part."

"My nephew's over there."

"God Bless him."

Recruitment was down in all branches of the military, even those wack Marines. The Army raised the enlistment age, lowered the education standards, increased the sign-up bonus, and ignored legal convictions and emotional problems. We sponsored Halo tournaments and advertised in comic books. But national numbers were still the worst in twenty years. The only thing helping us out was a bad economy. Kids either go to college or join the service. My job—help them decide which. Due to better armor, their chances of survival were better than any other war. Flip side is they're more likely to lose a limb or sustain brain damage from a head wound. I don't tell them that. No branch does, and neither does the liberal media.

Two weeks ago my boss, Master-Sergeant Jackson, put the word on me: if I don't get more recruits, he'll transfer my ass to South Korea. He's a pissant. His nickname is Inaction Jackson. A lot of recruiters break the rules. They conceal criminal records and medical histories. They give people cheat-sheets for the test, tell guys how to cleanse their bodies of marijuana, and even falsify a high school diploma. But I don't believe in that. I stood in front of Walmart birddogging young men and women heading into the store. I'm a sideshow barker. I can make an Eskimo crave ice and a dog want fleas. I can talk a virgin into giving it up for free. I am a good soldier. I follow orders. I make my quota.

"Sign here," I said. "Get your thirty-thousand dollar bonus. Buy a car, buy your mom a Sunday dress, buy your baby new shoes. We'll take care of you—food, clothes, and a bed. Like to blow shit up? Sign here. Want to get away from your family? Sign here. Want to slam the door on home and prove to your mama you're a man—sign here. Got no money for college, yo? Let me hook you up with sixty-five grand. Sign here. Yes ma'am, there ain't no glass ceiling in the army, sign here. Hey fellas, join with your buddies, and see your girlfriends on the weekend. Want to get paid to learn computers? Sign here. What's your dream job—I guarantee we've got it. Like to party? Soldiers drink cheap, and none of that over-21 bullshit. Like the ladies? The sexiest chicks wear army green. Dude, what have you got to lose? Sign here."

By the end of the day, I'd sweated out last night's whiskey, talked my voice half-hoarse, and got three boys amped-up to enlist. I felt pretty good about that. Two of them are video-gamers who will be outstanding at piloting drones.

I packed up and drove home, wore down as scraped clay, my clothes plastered to my body from the humidity. I needed a combat nap. I'm a young man of 23, but I believe in resting up to get trashed later. I believe in being practical.

At age 17, I was a high school dropout in the hills with a dead brother, no dad, and a mom who smoked crack. The only available job was in a cave, picking mushrooms out of horseshit trucked in from Lexington. The smell was terrible and the wage worse. The owner didn't care. He just made the same joke over and over—I got a low overhead. Get it? After three days he offered me a promotion to crew boss. By then I realized that all the other workers were developmentally disabled, severely so. I quit and joined the United States Army. Frankly, I flourished.

I loved military life—the structure, the camaraderie, and the weapons. I went to jump school, made my wings, and was sniffing around after Ranger school. But politics came into play and the worst soldier I ever met took my slot due to his daddy being a veteran and old buddy of the C.O. I was offered a promotion to recruiting sergeant, which sounded good at first—better pay, live off base, more freedom of operation. Part of me wanted to pay the army back for how it had helped my life. I believed that other young men might benefit the same way. But I didn't know that the pressure to recruit would increase one-hundred fold, while the number of volunteers would drop. Fact is, I hoped for a draft. But as long as they can use the Guard and Reserves for three tours, the politicians wouldn't do anything to risk a vote. That meant recruiters picked up the slack, and so rich kids wouldn't fight.

I took a three-hour nap and woke up ready to rage all night. With my pockets full of cards and pamphlets, I stopped for a beer at a hipster joint. Sitting at the bar is a girl whose head actually jingled from multiple piercings. She had a face like the inside of a tackle box. Her hair hung in a slab of white-girl dreadlocks, and I wondered if it came from a mail-order kit. Just add water. She was talking loud on a cell phone.

"You think I'm boring?" she said. "Then you can move out of my boring apartment!"

She snapped the phone shut and turned to me.

"I'd rather be called a drunken slut than boring. Do you think I'm boring?"

"No way," I said. "You are definitely the coolest. You in school?"

"Bellarmine," she said in a tone that made me know I was supposed to be impressed. "Where do you go? U. of L.?"

I told her my occupation and she was smugly outraged. She probably had the same response to meat-eaters, bigots, and NASCAR fans.

"Those aren't wars," she said. "They're invasions and occupations."

"Job's a job," I said. "You ever have one?"

"I did volunteer work with Habitat for Humanity this summer."

"People like me protect your habitats," I said.

"People like you attack habitats."

"Not everybody can be a Trustafarian."

"That's not okay," she said.

"No, but it's not boring, either."

I left the table and walked past the bad-but-original art, the mismatched tables, and the retro posters, wondering why the hell I'd gone there in the first place. I didn't fit in with civilians, and I no longer lived on base. Recruiting is an in-between life, like a ghost in a movie who can't stay in the grave or join the living. Like being gay in a small town. Maybe the dreadlock-girl was the same. It must be difficult when the only form of rebellion is mud in your hair and metal in your face. Nobody has it easy, I told myself. She sleeps safe because of men like me. Politicians want war but don't trust generals. Civilians want security but dislike the cost.

I sat in my car listening to Tupac spit those hella rhymes, then drove across town to the Hook Up. At eleven, the night was just getting rolling. Two massive doormen checked my I.D. and waved me in. Cigarette smoke floated in layers, lit by the changing stream of colored lights. No one cared if you were soldier or civilian, black or white, straight or gay. I lost myself in the pulsing lights and roaring music — disco, hip-hop, and the occasional cheesy Village People song. The crowd was a mixed hip bag. Lesbians staked out their own zones, gay men cruised, straight couples were raving on ecstasy, and the bi-curious furtively lurked the perimeter, hoping they wouldn't be recognized by someone from church. Generation Z suited me down to the ground. They were my meat and potatoes. But who was I among them? A spy, an interloper, the guy who used their flaws against them.

I ordered whiskey from a guy with forearms so heavily tattooed they looked like overlapping pages in a comic book. I sat on my stool and marveled at the skeezy and the crunk. A guy wearing a pair of gardener's knee-pads gave me a longing stare, and I warned him off with a shoulder twitch. I may not be a stud, but I hit the gym three times a week.

I distributed a few business cards on the bar and eased through the crowd, placing pamphlets on tables. The place smelled of sweat and the ferocity of sex. Dim lights left dark corners where people moved in secret. A woman stared at me, and I recognized her military bearing. Soldiers are like that. We know each other, and if there's trouble we gravitate together. Rank didn't matter; it manifested. I ignored her and she returned to her personal business with a female companion, scrawny as a famine victim. She was pretty through the eyes, but I despise the emaciated look. It killed me that young women puked their way to the grave while others had liposuction. Bald men got hair transplants, women got boob jobs, and everybody tried to counteract the sag of gravity. Body modification meant people treated themselves like wood on a lathe. But that's freedom, and freedom is what I'm charged to defend. Freedom to dye your hair green and stick a bone in your nose. Freedom to frequent the Hook Up or attend a Fundamentalist church.

The pulsing music was giving me a headache, and I went outside for air. The sudden silence was sharp as a hammer blow. I stepped to the side of the building, feeling abruptly lonely. It's one thing to feel that way alone in your room, but much worse in a crowd. I missed the camaraderie of army life—sleeping in a barracks, eating as a unit, working with a team. As a recruiter, I was on my own all the time. Sometimes I woke up unsure of who and what I was. I'd joined to get away from home but was still in Kentucky. In a year I could change jobs, and I worried the Army would keep me in recruiting. If a soldier doesn't have some juice up the ladder, he'll wind up stationed in hell.

A man stepped from the shadows and asked for a light.

"Sorry," I said. "Don't have one."

He shrugged and offered his hand.

"Bob," he said.

We shook and his other hand wrapped mine in a powerful grip. I pulled back but he wouldn't release me. I sensed someone behind me.

"Your wallet, faggot," Bob said. "Give it up or we'll gut you."

He had the showy build of a weightlifter, and a neck like a bucket of lard with a face on the front. The steroids made him slow, typical street meat, a tough guy until you popped him in the throat or the nuts. I went for the throat and Bob crumpled like a puppet with the strings cut. Something struck me hard in the back of the head. I staggered and twisted, lifting my arm to block a second blow from behind. A man slammed a length of two-by-four against my triceps. Most people retreat from an attack, but I ducked the lumber and rammed him. He was a big bastard who back-pedaled rapidly until hitting a parked car. I gave him a chance.

"Turn loose of the board and leave," I said. "You can't win this."

He stared at me, his dilated pupils shiny as new dimes, tweaked to the max on meth. He swung the two-by-four. I waited until its arc had cleared me, then kicked his kneecap with just the proper force to crack his patella. He'd walk again, but with crutches for a month.

The meth made him impervious to pain. He shifted his weight to his good leg and swung the two-by-four again. I'd had enough. I caught his wrist and twisted it until he dropped the board, then hit him twice in the stomach and four times in the face. I'd have hit him again but people were yelling and the area was suddenly filled with light. I turned warily.

The two doormen glared at me. Each held heavy mag-lites. I touched the back of my head and found blood. My arm hurt where the two-by-four hit.

"It's cool," I said. "I was just leaving."

"I don't think so," the doorman said. "The law is on its way. We're not putting up with gay-bashing anymore."

"They attacked me."

"Don't look that way to me," he said. "And I don't know you."

"You must be new," I said.

"Don't get smart," he said. "We've had enough fuckers like you starting trouble with customers."

The weightlifter was struggling to breathe. The tweaker moaned and spat blood. Standard operating procedure for me was to keep my mouth shut around civilians. I sat on the car trunk to wait. I'm good at waiting; all soldiers are. It's our primary skill after fighting. We wait and wait. We eat and sleep when we can. We fight on command or when attacked.

An ambulance and three Metro Police cars arrived. The EMT's loaded the two guys in the ambulance and treated my head wound. A cop took me to the VA Hospital. Three hours later I had a clean X-ray, three stitches, and a terrible headache. I also had overnight accommodations in the Jefferson County Jail. There were fourteen men in a ten-bed pod. Cigarette smoke was worse than the bar. The whiskey was wearing off and the hangover was coming on. I found a corner and sat cross-legged facing out. When I was a kid, I wanted to play pinball at a diner, but my grandfather wouldn't give me a quarter. He said anything that backed itself up against a wall and took on the world couldn't ever be beat. That's how I treated jail time.

The cops released me Sunday morning. My back hurt like a toothache, my neck was stiff, and my head throbbed with every movement. I took a cab to the bar and got my car. That's the way it is with civilian police—they lock you up for getting assaulted, then turn you loose on foot. At least I was out. Maybe I'd switch to the M.P. unit after recruiting. The pay was good. The only drawback was having to arrest those trained to fight and kill.

I ate aspirin and stayed in bed until Monday, then drove to the recruiting office. I was bouncing back. Whiskey's no good, everybody knows that, but my life wasn't much better. Liquor helped a little. I sat in the office and stared at paperwork.

At 1100 hours, in walked Master-Sergeant Jackson, my direct superior. I'd expected his arrival because the local precinct had an unofficial agreement to notify command in the event of a soldier's arrest. I didn't expect him to be accompanied by a Major. I came to the position of attention. Major Whitley at-eased me and we sat stiffly in the hard plastic chairs.

Jackson asked what happened. I explained the situation, stressing that I had used no weapon, although the second man was armed with a length of lumber.

"Brawling's not the issue," Jackson said.

I waited, refusing to ask the obvious, and studied the Major. He was African-American and squared-away as they come—trousers creased sharp as blades, gleaming boots, hairline high and tight. He wore steel glasses and one of those neatly trimmed go-to-hell mustaches. At his level, there's a lot of competition to command a battalion. It's a crucial career move and politics figure in—the right wife, the right mentor, no public screw-ups. He was clearly a player. The fruit salad pinned to his chest told me he'd distinguished himself in the Sandbox.

He stared at me a long time without blinking, and I wondered if he'd practiced that in a mirror. He spoke through a clenched jaw.

"Your personal life is no concern to me," the Major said.

"Yes, sir."

"But it is to my army. You were arrested at an establishment known as a meeting point for homosexuals."

I didn't answer, just waited for him to continue.

"Were you aware of the clientele when you went there?" the Major said.

"Yes, sir."

The tension rose like floodwater. We were all treading the delicate ground of military policy: Don't ask, don't tell. Jackson was staring pointedly at a spot on the wall just past my ear. He'd be no help, the prick. His motto was kiss up, blame down, get out in twenty.

"Was there a specific reason," the Major said, "for your presence there?"

"Yes, sir."

"What was that reason, Sergeant?"

"I was carrying out duties as a recruiter, sir."

"Are you telling me that you were actively attempting to recruit homosexuals?"

"No, sir." I said. "I made no inquiries along those lines."

"Why that particular location?"

"Sir, I go where young people congregate. High schools, trade-schools, poolhalls, clubs, and bars. The Hook Up has a high percentage of army-age individuals on Saturday night."

The stitches on my head were irritating, but I was determined to remain still. I resisted the urge to glance at the clock. The sound of laughter and car horns came into the office from the street.

"Pending the results of a formal review," Major Whitley said, "you are hereby relieved of duties."

"Sir," I said. "I have three appointments this afternoon. Two men already signed letters of intent."

"Sergeant Jackson will take those."

"Sir, I believe my presence will be more effective. I have a personal relationship with each man."

"That's exactly what we're worried about."

"Sir?"

"Last year," Major Whitley said, "more than a hundred recruiters were brought up on charges of raping recruits. Another three hundred were found guilty of falsifying records, coercion, or outright breaking the law. Command does not want any more impropriety, and your story stinks to high heaven. You're facing a reduction in rank and pay grade."

We looked at each other for many seconds. Now that he'd gotten the worst part out of the way, it might be possible to talk soldier-to-soldier. He was a lifer. I planned to be. A black mark on my record would follow my entire career. I had nothing to lose.

"Sir," I said. "My recruiting statistics are the highest in the state of Kentucky. They are in the top ten percent of the nation. My methods are effective and legal. They will withstand scrutiny. I am not aware of any statute that forbids where I recruit."

The sun glinted off his steel glasses. His eyes narrowed as he tried to stare me down, like drilling holes in my head. I didn't flinch, breathing long and slow. We both knew an enlisted man could outwait an officer. The key to understanding chain-of-command is that it works both ways—up and down. I decided to take a final risk.

"Sir," I said. "I do not want my rank busted. I do not want a letter of reprimand in my file. If anything of that nature happens, I am prepared to reveal myself as gay. Whether I am or not doesn't matter. But the army will be forced to discharge a top recruiter."

I kept my face impassive, vision locked on the Major. I wanted him to understand my words were neither bluff nor threat. I concentrated on not blinking. Master-Sergeant Jackson spoke into the silence.

"As your direct superior, I order you to retract that statement."

I didn't look at him. He was just covering his ass in front of an officer. He was a tool who took credit for my numbers, and I knew of four criminal acts he'd performed to clinch an enlistment. He knew I knew. I could ignore him forever.

"There's no place for gays in the military," he said. "Not ever."

The major slowly swiveled his head to stare at Jackson. His shoulders strained at his uniform. He was in his forties, wiry, tough as woodpecker lips.

Jackson was a fat white man who took blood pressure pills and ate candy.

"You're dismissed," Major Whitley said.

Jackson shot out of his seat as if it were on fire, saluted and left with visible relief. I faced the Major alone, prepared to receive his full wrath and fury. I'd gambled and lost. I was well and truly fucked.

"Not too long ago," he said, "the army had the same attitude towards black men. That turd isn't fit to clean my boots."

I said nothing. To agree was to disparage my superior officer, a bad move.

"There's gays in the army," he said. "Always have been. Most serve with distinction. Last year, 49 soldiers were discharged from Fort Campbell for being gay. Overseas we lost what we needed most — skilled speakers of Arabic, many of them homosexual. I don't agree with the policy, but the Military Code is clear."

"Yes, sir."

"The nature of war is changing," Major Whitley said. "Small teams of Special Forces took Afghanistan with very few casualties. Then the politicians gave the country back to the Taliban. Typical bullshit clusterfuck. We withdrew regular troops and now we're going back with Delta and Recon. Same with Syria. But the ranks of Special Forces are below capacity. And we need them the most."

His tone was optimistic and weary, not unusual in a soldier, but his honesty was surprising for an officer.

"You're smart," he said. "Your record is exemplary. You can fight and you already got your jump wings. You're capable of lateral thinking. Your methods are unorthodox but effective. That means resourceful. You just showed me you are willing to negotiate calmly and without fear."

He stepped close to me, his voice lower but no less hard. His chin thrust forward like a flash suppressor on the barrel of a rifle.

"You want this mess of yours cleared up?" he said. "Put in a request for Special Forces candidacy. There's an open slot in next month's rotation. On my desk tomorrow at 0800."

He went to the door. I stood and saluted. Before leaving he turned and spoke.

"Take care of that head-wound, son."

"Yes sir," I said.

I sat at the computer to download the necessary forms. My head throbbed and my arm hurt, but no mind. I felt real good. I was headed to Fort Benning.

He That Hath Ears
Cynthia Rand

One day, during the summer of her tenth year and while digging in the bank of the small stream that divided the lower meadow, Aleatha found a vein of the purest grey clay. The clay shone so pale it was almost white. She brought some to her lips to taste it and was delighted to find that, although soft in texture, it tasted like cast iron. This would be perfect for Ray. Holding it in the palm of her right hand, she shaped it and squeezed it, until its coolness gushed between her fingers. She dipped the lump into the cool waters again to keep it wet, then plunged her left hand into the side of the bank and pulled out more clay to add to the firm lump. While standing with her feet planted in the stream, she rolled the lump of clay in her palms and stared at the mica that flashed amidst the red garnets around her toes. The flecks of light danced through the traveling water and caused her to think about miracles.

She recalled Sunday School lessons and many sermons. Her faith was much bigger than a mustard seed. If Mama found out, Aleatha would be in for the butt whipping of her life. Mama had grown real tired of Grandmother Arrowood dragging in one faith healer after another, all arriving with vials of anointing oil and speaking in tongues. It wasn't that their mother didn't believe in Miracles or Holy Oil or Spirit Tongues, but she voiced her own strong belief that her son ought to be able to grow up without thinking anything was wrong with him because of his ears. It was The Lord's will for the child to be deaf, and they should all accept him and let the child be happy. Aleatha kept her mouth shut, while questions tumbled around in her heart about Jesus and miracles.

Aleatha felt that one more miracle for her little brother was all that she would ask for, and then she would stop asking. God had granted her that first one. Ray received sight. It had happened while her brother was still a baby in Mama's arms at the Church of the Nazarene under the praying palms of Elder Ma King. He had been born blind and had been made to see. The miracle was one she had prayed for and all had rejoiced that Ray's eyes could now see. Aleatha had thought that was the end of miracle asking. She did not want to hog up all the miracles for herself. Then one Sunday after hearing a visiting minister preach on the endless abundance of God's love and healing power, Althea decided to ask for one more miracle. For Ray.

The garbled noises that now came up behind her didn't frighten her. Ray's ears knew only the sound of silence, but he was not mute.

He came stomping and slushing through the ferns and weeds and lilies, marching and hollering in cacophonic syllables, sometimes shrill and high and sometimes low and deep. He stomped down the hill to the edge of the stream. He pretended to talk to her, she pretended back. It was their private game — this joke of imitating people's expressions and gestures with gibberish sounds. Their favorites to imitate were Ricky Ricardo and Lucy, Spock and Captain Kirk, Gilligan, Charlie Chaplin, and their favorite TV preacher on the Jubilee show from way down in Louisiana, and certain newscasters, and a couple of eccentric relatives. Now he switched to Grandpa Walton, with quizzical eyes, swiping an invisible mustache and rubbing his chin with one hand, while the other hand raised the walking stick and pointed it to the bucket.

Aleatha placed the lump of smooth clay into the old, rusty bucket and signed a question to him, "Do you want to hear?" He hesitated and clutched his walking stick that he didn't need but carried everywhere to bang on trees or poke into old stumps discovering what would come slithering or buzzing out. He created noises that he could not hear because he was curious. He snuck up on the cows in the upper pastures, and then banged his stick against abandoned plough tines. He would laugh as the cattle stampeded around the ridge, their hooves thundering through the ground to his own feet. Now he struck the stick into the rocky side of the stream.

Aleatha repeated her signed question.

"Yes, I do want to hear. Yes!" He signed back to her in ASL.

"Do you remember the story where Jesus put clay into the deaf man's ears?" Aleatha signed.

"No." Ray shook his head.

"Do you have faith that God can heal your ears so you can hear?" Aleatha signed, "Do you want me to put clay in your ears and ask the Lord to heal you?"

No hesitation came with his blonde head nodding up and down, his navy blue eyes shining, "Yes. Yes. Yes. A trillion and one times yes."

"Come over here…look at this! I have found clay. See? We can put it in your ears and pray for you to hear. I have faith. I have faith as big as that mountain!" Aleatha signed and turned and pointed at the high, blue mountain behind her. Then Ray picked up the bucket and studied the clay for a moment.

Aleatha turned back to the earth and showed him the spot where she had pulled forth the pliable clay. She reached in and brought out more of the smooth globs. He climbed down into the chilly ankle deep water beside her and chattered happily in garbled gibberish. He reached in and pulled more from the earth's yielding side. Aleatha grabbed the rusty pail as she listened to his high-pitched shrills. She wondered what his voice would be like if he could speak. Would he sound like their father, whose voice was deep and bear-like? And what would Ray do with his voice if he could talk. What would he become: a preacher, a news reporter, or a teacher? Would he like to sing? Would he sound like Elvis or John Denver? She decided he would probably become a teacher since he loved his books, or maybe a comedian because he could make the funniest faces. When they tried to lift the old bucket by the slim wire, the fragile handle broke away. Aleatha laughed and signed,

"It's too full, too heavy. Don't need this much clay for your two little ears."

Ray looked into the full bucket of clay and laughed a nasal bubbly laugh that turned into a snort. He shrugged and thought for a second.

"We can make pots and bowls?" He asked with his hands.

She signed back, "Yes, let's make pottery, but let's do your ears first."

Aleatha told him to wait there and she would go get her Bible. She wanted everything to happen the way it had happened in the scriptures. She did not want to mess this up. She scooted under the barbed wire fence that separated the pasture from their tree filled yard, then ran, faster and faster, ducking through the sheets hanging on the clothesline that seemed to gleam with holy light, careful not to dirty them as she passed. She jumped onto the back porch, then darted in and out of the house, her Bible in the crook of her arm.

"Where are you going?" her Mama called, not turning from the dishpan at the sink.

"We found clay... I'm in a hurry!" Aleatha shouted back.

Her mother dropped the dish that she had been washing back into the pan, wiped her sudsy hands on her faded roses apron, and ran out to the porch.

"Where did you find clay?" her mother shouted.

Aleatha slid under the barbwire fence again and stood up and pointed,

"Over there, under the leaning tree."

"Watch out for snakes over there... and be careful. Is Ray over there with you?"

"I know, Mama, snakes. We'll be careful. Yes, Ray is with me. We're digging clay."

"Aleatha! Is that your Bible you are carrying? Don't dare get it dirty!"

"Yes, ma'am." Aleatha ran down through the meadow toward the tree and the stream. Ray was already shaping clay into lopsided bowls and lifting them up to place them on the wooden planks of the slender foot bridge to dry in the sun. She placed her Bible on the planks and leaned down to rinse the grey clay from her hands in the clear cold water of the stream, then dried them on her blue cotton blouse. She took the Bible and flipped through to the New Testament.

Ray grabbed the holy book from her and started his pretend preaching game. He preached his heart out with sweat and passion using all the faces and hand gestures of a preacher who knew how to move a congregation with soulful words—only Ray's words were like the sounds of yipping foxes. *Just wait*, Aleatha thought, *you want to preach, you will have the words soon. Very soon.* She imagined teaching him how to sound words the way she had learned at school back in first grade with phonics.

She asked for the book back, saying "Please," with her hand on her heart, and so he handed it over. She motioned for him to come with her, and together they found a grassy patch on the hill above the moss. She flipped through the New Testament and came to the passage. Her finger gliding under the words, read the verses in Mark. She slammed the good book shut. She had misremembered. The healing for the deaf man had not been done with clay but spit. All of this excitement over healing clay and now this—just spit.

She handed her little brother the Bible and put her head down, but Ray opened it back to Mark and found the verses. His finger traced under the words and stopped on spittle. With his asking face he pointed to that specific word.

She spit on her hands and showed him. He wrinkled up his nose at the thought of spittle and then he laughed through his nostrils.

"You are not Jesus." He signed.

"But I have faith…faith bigger than the mountains." Aleatha still wanted a miracle for her brother.

Ray again began searching in Mark for something else. He found the word clay and then he showed it to Aleatha. She leaned into the book and ran her finger along the verses whispering the words. Then she signed to Ray,

Aleatha asked.

Then, she watched him scramble down the hill now to the clay-filled bucket. He brought out two handfuls. He held them up to Aleatha. *Try it,* he was saying with his eyes and nodding. *Try it.* Aleatha kissed the cover of her Bible and whispered, "A little help about right now would be good, ok Jesus?" and jumped down into the stream to face her brother.

She shaped the clay into two small, pliable pieces then carefully filled and pressed it into all the curves and swirls of her deaf brother's ears. She covered his ears with her palms pressing them, and with her heart pumping wildly, shouted "Be open!" Then with her head lowered, she asked the Maker to bless her brother's ears and let them hear. When she was finished praying Ray looked at her with raised eyebrows.

"Now we have to wait." She spoke without signing.

He raised his eyebrows.

She would not be deterred. This could be one of those to wait a while for miracles.

"Miracles might take time. Clay needs time to pull out the silence."

Ray nodded slowly and then scooped more clay from the bucket and began to play.

Aleatha and her brother rolled and pinched and made tiny pots and bowls while they waited for the clay in his ears to dry. They shaped people and animals, slick figures standing, running, and walking. Aleatha gave them acorn tops for hats and reeds for clothes. She created miniature cats and dogs and cows and horses. Ray made a house and barn with walls of clay and no ceiling and moss for carpet.

They were lost in their play, standing in the creek, reaching into the side of the earth for more globs of clay as they needed it, and after a few hours of Ray occasionally tugging or scratching at his ears, Aleatha heard their mother calling them in for supper.

She dipped her hands into the clear water of the creek to wash away the residue of earth and signed to Ray, "Mama is calling. Time for supper. I think we should take the clay out of your ears now so you can hear. You ready?"

Ray nodded, his blue eyes shining with great hope.

He wiggled the damp but drying goo in his ears with his fingers and pulled out the heavy earplugs shaped like the inside of his ear. He placed them in his sister's palms and she lifted them up and placed them on the wooden plank bridge alongside the tiny bowls and pots and creatures. She turned to face him.

"Can you hear me?" she asked him with her voice.

He signed, "What?"

Disappointment washed over Aleatha. She stared at her bare feet, frozen toes shining alongside sparkling mica in the floor of the creek.

Ray rested his clay-covered hand on her shoulder.

Aleatha wiped her eyes with her shirttail and began to sign a storming flurry of held-in wishes for Ray's life, "I love you. I love you the same whether your ears hear or not. I just wanted a miracle for you. I wished for you to hear words and all kinds of music. Hundreds and millions of songs I wish you could hear. I want you to know the sound of a Beethoven symphony and Elvis's songs, and The Beatles, and Dolly Parton's song 'Coat of Many Colors', and Johnny Cash singing 'Ring of Fire', and Reverend Grant's gospel choir that visits our church when he comes to preach. I wanted you to hear the crows cawing and the dogs barking and the jets in the sky and the helicopters that fly in over the mountain, and Papaw's Volkswagen, and the sirens from the fire truck, and fireworks on the July fourth, and Christmas Carols and the tune of Happy Birthday, and all of the songs on the radio, and the booming organ at church, and what people are really saying on TV, and Mama's voice reading bedtime stories."

His signed, "It's ok. That stuff doesn't matter to me." He shrugged his shoulders but smiled and signed again, "You tried, but you are not God. It doesn't matter. I am okay."

Aleatha couldn't hold back the river of water now streaming down her face. She lifted the hem of her blouse to cover her face and pressed the fabric into her eyes. Ray leaned down into the stream, and she could hear him splashing around washing his hands real good. Eventually she felt his cold fingers tapping her elbow.

"Zud-Zud." He spoke the only other specific word he could say with his voice, besides the word Mama. Zud-Zud was his way of saying Sister, and it was his nickname for Aleatha.

She let go of her shirttail, uncovered her face, and stared at him. Through her blurry vision she read Ray's signs to her that tumbled forth in fast motion: "It matters to *you*. But me, I just hear *different from you*! I *can* hear. I hear the sound of rain when I feel cold drops fall on my face, I feel the *sound* of the water rolling around us now at our feet, and I can hear by feeling the music with that drum beating from the visiting gospel choir! I hear snow in winter when I taste it on my tongue. I hear the way you love me when you try to make miracles out of clay and faith, and I hear it big when I see your eyes raining down tears into this stream."

Aleatha nodded slowly to her brother, a slow but sure nod that showed him she now understood. Then she knelt down into the water feeling the sharp garnets prick into her knees. She dipped her hands into the icy stream and splashed a shock of water to her face.

"Mama is still calling us," Aleatha signed up to him. "Are you hungry?"

"Yes," Ray nodded.

"Race you to the house?"

"Yes!"

Then he plucked up his walking stick and pointed to her Bible on the hill. She scrambled up to fetch it and held it close to her heart and turned to see Ray sneaking off with a head start. His sneakers tromped through the marshy lilies, while the slick mud pulled the heels of Aleatha's bare feet, holding her back. They rolled under the barbed wire fence, then dodged the crisp sheets on the line that now held in a day's worth of sun. They scrambled up through the mossy yard. It was Ray who first set foot on the porch. He won for the first time and turned to flash a proud smile back at Aleatha.

It was then she first knew how gladness and sadness could live together in the same heart.

MUSHY GAY SCENARIOS
Erin Reid

Amber Bock was not named after beer, but none of her drunkard friends believed her. At The Piston & Valve, their own small town Alabama gay bar, "she" was ordered at the counter all night long. "You sure taste good, honey," they'd say. "It was named after me," she'd retort.

The irony of the matter was that Amber didn't even drink beer. She didn't like it. And she didn't particularly like gay bars, not that she'd been to that many. Her family would be horrified to see her in a place like this. She had to block out their sincere faces, full of concern, in order to even show up. Drinking helped.

Her favorite was a Cosmopolitan, she hated to admit. So girly. But she liked the sweetness and the feel of the martini glass. The aesthetic. The Piston had its own aesthetic, and it didn't include stemware. Here, Amber got cranberry juice and vodka. Plain, in a thick squat glass. As much as she felt distaste at the smoky air and sticky floors, she couldn't help coming back. She never came alone, always with Jess and Jenna. The Js. Her bodyguards. She never wanted to look like she was trying to pick up a date.

She liked to sit near Nick, the bartender who had this friendly shine about her face. Her eyes crinkled when she smiled, and her dimpled cheeks spread out wide. She had an aardvark tattooed on her left wrist, which was oddly reassuring. Nick's husband Dougie was just about the only straight male regular. Amber talked to him a lot. He wore a flannel shirt and dirty old work boots. He talked about football and his dog, Motley. Amber couldn't really think of what they had in common, but she guessed he reminded her of her brother, self-assured, comfortable in his skin. He didn't have to agree with a person to get along with them.

Dougie always drank ambers. He often raised a pint and said, "Here's to you, Amber Bock." She loved this gesture. She secretly hated her name. "Amber" sounded like someone cute in a mini-skirt and heels, someone who accessorized. She would've liked to be named Jo. It was her fantasy as a child. Jos were universally splendid. Jo March, the boisterous, brilliant writer. Jo Polniaczek, the wisecracking, motorcycle-riding Brooklyn tomboy. Little Joe, the cowboy, grinning impishly on horseback. She had imagined herself a cowboy, swinging her booted legs easily over a tall horse and punching out rustlers. Once she'd tried to punch out Buddy Bracket, the curly haired bully who tormented the first graders. All she remembered after was stinging, her cowboy shirt unsnapped, and Buddy's sniggering face.

Brawls rarely happened at The Piston, but when they did, she kept her distance. The Js said Bama butches had some fight in them, but usually for a good cause. It was still an amazement to her that she, born and raised in Southern California, had ended up in Alabama at all. People at The Piston, just getting to know her, would say, "So, let me get this straight. You left *California* to come to *Alabama* to go gay?" They'd hollered with the irony.

She never told them that she grew up in her own tiny town, populated largely by members of a closely knit church who didn't drink, smoke, dance, or even eat meat. She could have said, "Think, *Footloose*," and made everyone laugh even more, but she didn't want them to see that in her. She was afraid they already did.

One night, Dougie called over, "Hey, you got to ask Nick for this beer they got in." A sweet nectar of a beer, syrupy, and refreshing. She let Dougie buy her one and then another. The Js slipped away since she had a new guard. Amber wasn't worried. Dougie usually stayed all night. Curled up under a fluffy blanket the next morning, she had the uncertain recollection of laying her face on a cardboard coaster and looking up fuzzily at a woman's broad mouth.

"I'm Lotta," said the mouth. Amber felt a warm trickle of drool sneak past the corner of her lips and slide down her chin.

"What's my name?" boomed the mouth, who now had a broad face to match. She barked the question like a drill sergeant.

"She's taken," said Jenna, sliding neatly between them. Amber felt Jenna dab her chin with a napkin. Jess pressed into her from the other side. Amber felt pleasantly sandwiched, even as the room spiraled about her head.

"I'm Lotta," barked the woman. "What's my name?"

"Goodbye, Lotta," said Jenna, who managed to speak in a way both final and also flattering. She may have even squeezed her arm. Lotta's chair scraped away. Why could Amber hear a chair leg scrape over the music that pounded the room like a fist? Jess hummed along to "I Will Survive," almost like a feminist lullaby in Amber's ear. Jenna ordered a shot of bourbon.

"We're your vajayjay posse," Jess said as they stood close. And they were, ever since they bonded in the frozen food aisle over the one box of Morningstar Farms veggie sausage. Amber was astounded by their friendship; she worried they would one day wake up and be gone.

"Why do I go to that place?" she moaned in the morning. She stuffed her mouth with scrambled eggs and fake meat. She was sitting upright on the Js' couch with her legs stretched out under her blanket.

"Because you're a good person," said Jenna. Jenna had the habit of running a hand through her short cropped hair. For a moment the long strands in front disappeared under her palm and Amber saw her full strong face. She was handsome, beautiful. She wore a white undershirt and jeans and sat reclined in an armchair with one leg kicked over the armrest. Looking at her, no one would imagine that she had been raised in curls and ruffled dresses, bobby socks, Mary Janes, the whole bit. She even had a prom photo—herself in a dress, sky blue sateen with a v-dropped waist and a ruffle, a wrist corsage, big Southern hair. She was something of a skinny bombshell. She dated lots of boys—and apparently she also made out with girls in the locker room, behind the bleachers, in her mother's car. It was a tragedy when Jenna came out. Her mother had not yet forgiven her—not so much for being gay, but for cutting off all that blonde hair.

Jenna touched the back of her head. Amber watched her long curving fingers and wondered if she was feeling short hair or long. Jenna sipped her coffee, held by cupping the rim, not the handle. It gave her drinking a decidedly rugged appearance. But her wrist and fingers made such a lovely line. Graceful.

Jess walked in from the kitchen with a pipe wrench in one hand and a yellow plastic pitcher in the other, a retro coffee pot, glass lined. Amber imagined she could see steam rising from the open top, although she knew that couldn't be true because it was warm in the room.

Jess said, "You know we all go get smashed there so they'll stay in business. A town's got to have a gay bar." She added more coffee to Amber's mug. She wore an orange striped apron and Sponge Bob pajama pants. Her curly hair was pulled into two pigtails. For her attraction to animated character prints and Punky Brewster hair, she was brisk and airy in her mannerisms. She had a solid way, and her voice had a raspy timbre, as though she had been a smoker from birth, although she did not smoke at all. She hopped about in fluffy slippers. She waved the pipe wrench for emphasis. Amber realized that she had probably just fixed the leaky faucet that had dripped all through her dream memory as a broken waterfall.

Jess had the easiest way about her of anyone Amber knew. She seemed just natural. Not constrained by so much culture, family expectation, doctrine. If Amber tried to imagine a hang-up Jess might have, it could be a slight mournfulness that she didn't have any hang-ups and therefore was something of an outsider in the "share your childhood traumatic gay coming of age" stories. When Jenna and Amber would sit in silence after reliving together communities that held them perilously close, Jess would busy herself with some chore or other. But then she'd cock her hips and say, "It's a good thing you two heartbreaks have me, so you can have a model of healthy lesbian identity and family life." They sneered mockingly. But they knew it was true, and they were grateful.

"What happened to Dougie?" asked Jenna. She shifted herself upright in the chair, looking a little miffed that he had fled his post.

"Probably had to pee," said Jess.

"Probably Lotta took him out," Jenna smirked. "Dougie's got nothing on her."

"What's my name?" barked Amber. The Js laughed together, the same laugh, low, rumbling.

"Well, Lottas need a place to meet women, too," said Jenna kindly. "That place is seedy, but it's the option, you know?"

The three women nodded silently. Amber wondered how, in this day, gay people could need such a place in order to meet other gay people. Of course, in her town, there had been no way. She didn't even know "gay" existed, except that her brother played a savage game called "smear the queer," and people said things about Liberace and Little Richard. There was that magazine cover she'd seen in the store — k.d. lang in a three-piece suit, leaning back and smiling as Cindy Crawford held a razor to her lathered cheek. Amber had stared at it a long time with no words for what she saw.

She lifted the blanket and surveyed her clothes now — black pants and a black turtleneck, scattered with hair from the Js' two cats. They'd slept on her all night. Her hair was probably tangled, and she wiped at her chin to check for drool residue. She tucked back into the blanket and suppressed an almost overwhelming desire to pull it over her head.

"It's no wonder you got the treatment from the drill sergeant," said Jenna. "You look like the Russian mafia." Amber had the notion that all-black made her disappear a little, be less conspicuous in public places, and slim her wide hips. But probably it made her stand out. Most people in Alabama did not wear all black, unless they were in a funeral procession.

"I thought she looked like a priest," said Jess meanly. She plopped herself on the couch and patted Amber's feet. "Isn't that the idea, Reverend?"

"Why aren't you at church this morning anyway?" asked Jenna. She combed her fingertips through the bristly hair over her neck.

"Sunday off," she said.

"The place gonna fall apart without you?" asked Jenna.

Amber thought of the small cinder block building, the two rooms allotted to the children and teenagers, the earnest, hearty queer Southern Protestants who paid her 20 hours a week to bolster the nontraditional spiritual lives of their offspring. It was a great irony that she'd ended up working at a church anyway — after her own defection — but it made a sort of sense, because in this one, she could be herself in most every way. She'd actually always loved church, the singing especially, but she hadn't loved the "programming." The "my way or no way" part.

At The Heart of Christ Church, there was no single way of thinking. Maggie, who would be teaching the little ones today, would be using the new felts that Amber had cut. A young Jesus in sandals and with brown skin and a curly beard. A Mahatma Gandhi, bald, smiling peacefully. A Buddha in a seated position. A Rumi with a quill pen and a scroll. A Teresa of Avilla in rapt prayer. Lucy the first woman holding berries. Che Guevara, with his red star. And Sojourner Truth, who stood taller than them all and wore a delicate white cap. These were the first in her series of felt figures—"Spirit Posse," the great teachers and activists of the world, Jesus' global apostles, or, depending on your theology, a wise pantheon of which he was a part. She was sad she hadn't been there to see them appear on the board for the first time and hear how the children made them talk.

"Don't those church types mind you carousing in bars with the likes of us?" asked Jess. Jess looked at her curiously, and Amber realized she'd tuned out of the conversation.

"They'd be all over you heathens," she said. "All over." The phrase could have two meanings. She wondered which one the Js would take. They both cackled like they particularly enjoyed her remark. Jess snorted. Jenna got up from her chair and sat on the end of the couch behind Amber. She patted her back.

"You love us heathens, don't you, honey," she drawled. Amber set her empty plate on the coffee table and reclined her head onto Jenna's lap.

"It's ironic, you know," said Jess, who started to rub Amber's feet. "You go to a bar where you'd never date anyone you meet because you're the kind of girl who would want to meet a nice girl in a church. But you work at the only gay-friendly church in town, and you can't date anyone because you're on staff. How crazy is that?"

"Tell me something I don't know," said Amber dryly.

"You should get a dog and hit the dog park scene," said Jenna. This was one of the Js' favorite conversations—how to find Amber a girlfriend. "Or you could take a class at the university and have an affair with one of those Women's Studies professors or some baby dyke undergrad."

"Please," said Amber. But she was laughing.

"I know!" shouted Jess excitedly. "We could take a road trip to Atlanta, and go eat at that restaurant owned by one of the Indigo Girls."

"Yeah," said Jenna. "And you could meet some hot waitress and have a great weekend, and then you could see each other like once or twice a year. That would be perfect!"

Now Amber realized they were making fun. She got their tactic— to show the absurdity of her solitude.

"I'm an outlier," said Amber seriously.

"No you're not," Jenna said, her voice abrupt, and serious. She looked a little embarrassed, like she hadn't intended to be so forceful, but she seemed moved with conviction in some deep place. Her voice had a slight tremor.

"You could find anyone you want if it weren't for that big 'Closed for Business' sign on your chest." She paused and then she seemed to decide to go all the way. "And it wouldn't matter if you lived in San Fran-fucking-cisco because you'd take the goddamned sign with you." Jess chuckled nervously, but she was nodding.

Amber rolled onto her side and pressed her cheek into the rough fabric of Jenna's jeans. She wrapped her arms around her knee like a toddler holding her mother's leg. Jenna smoothed her tangled hair from her face.

"I'm not closed," she said finally. "People just don't come into my shop."

"People don't come into your shop because you're closed," said Jess. "People can tell these things. I'm telling you, if your door was cracked open an inch, they'd be all over you."

"How can you think you're just not wanted?" asked Jenna, still patting Amber's hair. "That's so sad. That's totally not fair to you."

Amber was silent. She closed her eyes. Her chest felt tight inside and she was suddenly angry that the Js would ruin her mellow morning. She unthreaded her arms from Jenna's leg and clutched them to her chest. She was in a full fetal position now, which, no doubt, did not help her case.

It was true, she hadn't dated seriously in a while. Hell, she'd never really dated at all. Max had been a fluke, a four-year fluke of proximity. Veronica had been an awkward, intense, short-lived mess. Billie had been nothing, loved from a distance, longed for. That was it. That was her complete history of what she called "mushy gay scenarios." Scenarios. Not relationships.

She loved her tiny apartment, its walls covered in Jackson vine, her hidden front porch. The quiet joy of sharing a space with no one. She loved her work at Heart of Christ. She loved her friends. She could not imagine setting up house. When she lay in bed alone and felt the longing well up in her like a whirlpool, sucking her into herself, sucking all the energy out of her limbs, she wanted right then for the comfort of another body. But these times passed, and she was fine.

"Relationships are for straight people," she blurted, surprising herself, trying to be funny, but sounding only strange and forced.

"And what are we?" asked Jenna. She jabbed Amber's arm with a pointed finger. The gesture left it unclear exactly which "we" she meant. Amber didn't use the words out loud, but she thought, *This is a messy gay scenario.*

She pinched her eyelids tight. She said nothing. Her mouth felt hollow. She held her breath and released it in jerky rasps. She tried to be inaudible. She just needed to give them one sign. Just a small signal is all it would take. But she was immovable. Her curled hands cramped.

And then Jess was stretched out over her, stretched out, and tucking herself neatly behind in a perfect spoon. And Jenna was leaning over down to her mouth, whispering at the corner of her lips. Amber reached out her tight fingers and brushed them back and forth, back and forth, in Jenna's bristly hair. It was surprisingly soft.

I Have Not Yet Returned
Katie Winkler

Sam, Jr. took the biggest, most wicked looking blade out of the butcher's block and tested it against his finger. He knew the blade wouldn't draw blood, but it emphasized his point. Sam made most of his points in the kitchen. He grabbed the hunk of smoked Boston Butt firmly in his hands. The sharp blade came down with a firm "whumpf" against the stained, wooden chopping block. "Admit it, Sis," he said between chops, "you don't want to go visit him."

"It's not that I don't want to go see him," I said. Sam paused in his work and smirked. "It's just that I don't think he wants to see me right now. He seems to respond better to you."

Sam started back chopping. "He won't even know you're there."

I flung my hand toward him. "There you go," I said, defining the matter.

"There you go?" He waved the knife, painting the air with it. "So, because he won't recognize you, won't see you, you shouldn't bother to go see him?" He brought the knife down hard on the meat. *Whumpf.* "The truth is, it makes you feel uncomfortable."

"And it doesn't make you uncomfortable?"

Whumpf. "No, it doesn't."

"When did this big change come about?"

Whumpf. "It's never made me uncomfortable."

"Right."

Whumpf. "Because I admitted it from the get go."

"Admitted what?

Whumpf. "That Dad is, you know, crazy."

I stared at the meat. It was hacked to bits, just the way I liked it. I looked up at Sam. His handsome face, so much like his father's, was flushed with heat. "I don't think you should talk that way about Dad," I said.

He dropped the knife on the counter and wiped his meaty hands on his once white linen apron with its faded "Hug the Chef," across the chest. He scraped the meat onto the big porcelain platter embossed with a chicken. "If the shoe fits," he said, carrying the meat to the table.

I was angry, yet I followed him into to the dining room, sat down and ate. There's not much, even a father who might have diabetes-related dementia, that could stop me from eating my brother's barbecue. After we were through, Sam brought out the lemon ice box pie, the kind Dad liked so much and still ate some of, despite the diabetes.

Sweet enough to make your teeth hurt.

My mother had made the best lemon pie I'd ever eaten. She made it with real lemons, plus the zest, sweetened condensed milk, fluffy meringue and those little vanilla wafers lining the bottom and circling around the sides. No other crust. Back when she was alive, I'd seen Dad eat a big slice of that pie, but now he says, "I'll just have a little sliver, just a sliver. I can't have too much sugar now, you know."

I looked up at Sam, who was cutting himself a fat piece of pie. "They don't serve Dad anything remotely like this at the hospital. Strict diabetic diet, they say."

I didn't say anything, just twirled my fork around the last piece of pie, mixing the soggy sweet wafers with the pie and meringue. It wasn't Mother's, but it wasn't bad.

Sam held up his fork. "Just like Mom's. That damn hospital should let Dad have some pie. Just a little sliver wouldn't hurt."

"I don't know," I said. "I think Dad's problems are related to his diabetes," then adding as I popped a glob into my mouth, "and Vietnam, of course."

He just looked at me.

I looked at him. "They've got to be related."

"What does it matter what it's related to?"

"But he always has an episode when his diabetes gets out of control."

I jumped when Sam's fork clattered on my grandmother's china plate. "An episode?" He stared at me, his hands on his hips. "He thinks he's Jesus Christ! You call that an episode?"

"He only said that once." I paused, pushing my fork once again into the soft goo. "Besides, I think Dad could have been speaking metaphorically."

"I think you're as loony as he is," Sam said, bringing his elbows to the table and folded his arms across his chest. He looked like some sort of, I don't know, Buddha—a Bubba Buddha.

My fork clattered this time. "You should show more respect for your father than that. And for me."

He pushed his chair back, picked his plate up and started to pass me by. Then he leaned down and whispered, "Yeah, well, I go to visit him, don't I?"

I didn't tell Sam where I was going that next day. I just went.

Dad's room was on a geriatric ward on the top floor. The hospital put the older psych patients there, and I wondered how the old people who were just old felt about that. I wouldn't have liked it. No, I didn't like it. Did not like it at all. Just because a person's old doesn't make him crazy, does it? Just because Dad's body was giving way and affecting his mind while doing so, didn't make him insane. I had read that it was even common for veterans, people trained to kill, to think of themselves as a Christ, a healer. It's not even crazy when you think of it. It certainly didn't make Dad...what Sam said. It didn't. Did not.

I waited for a while at the nurses' station, longer than I needed to, but I had forgotten how to buzz into the rooms, had forgotten the procedure for getting through the security. Alzheimer's patients, you know, try to run away. Dad wasn't an Alzheimer's patient. His blood sugars had gotten out of control and affected his mind, and he was there on the ward to get things straightened out.

That's all.

Dad ended up here because he hadn't been sleeping well, and so my brother insisted on taking him to the hospital. Sleep deprivation does funny things to a person's body, they had said. Does funny things to the mind, especially the mind of a veteran. It's all linked, I thought, waiting for them to come back to the station and help me to get in and visit my father because I couldn't just go back there, walk back there, walk into his room and visit him. I had to be let in.

The body, the mind, and the spirit—all one. I had heard that and believed it. When the body is affected, so is the mind. Body, mind and spirit. "We are a trinity, we are," That's what Dad always said.

I sat down in an uncomfortable chair in the small waiting room. It was stiff and narrow. I sat hunched and awkward. A magazine, several years old, lay open on the side table beside the chair, and I picked it up to flip through it, gazing at predictions that hadn't come true.

When a nurse finally came back to the station, I waited, finishing the article, even though I knew how it would end. Finally, I rose and walked over to the window, resting my fists on the ledge. Her back was to me. I waited patiently. She turned and seemed startled to see me there, giving a little jump.

"I didn't know anyone was here," she said, placing her hand lightly over her heart. She was jumpy. I supposed from working in a place like that.

"I've come to see my father."

"Oh, you must be Mr. Krone's daughter Kim."

The place was getting creepier all the time.

"How do you know that?" I said, sounding rude, I'm sure. My mother had taught me better.

She cleared her throat, and I dared her to say that there was a strong family resemblance. "Your brother said you'd be visiting soon," she said.

"Oh, he did?"

"Yes, he added your name to the list."

"Oh, yeah, he did. I knew that," I said, nodding my head too vigorously. She stared at me, and I tapped my fingers on the table. "Could I see my father now?"

She smiled. "Did you sign our book, here? We do need to keep good records of visitors, you know."

I pushed my palm against my forehead. "Silly me."

"Perfectly all right. No one expects you to remember all these little procedures."

In my mind, I dared her to say, "Especially when you've only visited one time before," but I didn't really say it. I signed the paper and pushed hard on the door. It wouldn't give. Then, I remembered. She had to let me in. I waited until I heard that irritating buzz and pushed the door hard. It came open easily. The nurse popped her head around the door. "Room 505, remember?" I hadn't, but I nodded my head nevertheless.

Walking down the hallway was my least favorite part. Walking in and walking out were equally as bad because in the hallway there were patients who were not quite right, and I so much wanted to be in the room with my dad and not have to confront those people.

Halfway down the hall, I saw him.

He was dressed in the dark blue silk pajamas I'd spent an hour in the mall finding. I sent them by my brother, and now I wondered why Sam hadn't said anything about the size. The pajamas were way too big, so they hung loosely over Dad's gaunt frame. If I had known, I could have taken them back, traded them for a smaller size because I always keep the receipts. I don't know, I always thought Dad was bigger than that. He had been bigger in his younger days. A football player.

For some reason, I looked at Dad's feet and saw he had on cotton twill loafers. Then, I looked up. He was hunched over like an old man, but his shoulders were wide. He looked down at the floor and shuffled along, holding onto the wooden rail that lined the hallway. He reached up a bony hand to run his hands through his head of thick white hair.

"Dad?" I asked, suddenly overjoyed to see him.

He looked up and stared at me a moment. I wasn't sure he knew me. Then he smiled, showing the strong white teeth I did remember. "Kimmy," he said, his voice strong, not a bit shaky at all. "Kimmy, come here and give your daddy a hug." He held out his arms, and I came to him, like a five-year-old girl, practically running down the hall. Glittering white.

He hugged me then pushed me back. "Where's your brother?"

I looked at him, annoyed. "I came on my own, Dad. Sam's at work."

"Work, work, work," Dad chanted. "He works for me now; did he tell you?" He turned from me and grabbed hold of the railing with both hands, leaning back.

I didn't say anything.

I was afraid to.

I hoped he would go back to his room.

I hoped he wouldn't mention Sam again.

"Let's go back to your room, Dad," I said gently and tried to steer him back down the hall.

"Don't touch me," he said, jerking his arm from mine. "No one should touch me... for I have not yet returned."

"Dad," I said firmly, "I won't touch you, but you need to go back to the room."

He nodded and turned to go, shuffling slowly like before, his hand on the rail, lightly on the rail. I passed him so I wouldn't have to watch him shuffle. I heard him behind me. "Bam. Bam. Bam. Bam," he muttered, and I closed my eyes as he started to giggle.

Gratefully, we reached the room; the muttering and giggling stopped. Dad plopped down in his stiff, hospital issued recliner and gave a deep sigh. I sat primly on the edge of the only other chair in the room, not knowing what to say.

He gazed at me a few moments and started giggling again. I wished I could go and get something to eat. I'd had no appetite before I came; now I was voracious. I thought of Sam's country barbecue. It had tasted so good.

But he was still giggling. "What's so funny, Dad?" I said, exasperated.

"BAM, BAM, BAM, BAM," he said and I got up to leave. "You know what BAM stands for, girl?"

"What?" I said, turning towards him, not really wanting to know.

"It means Broad Assed Marine." Dad stamped his feet on the floor, just like when I was little and he'd tease my mother. He'd tell his corny jokes, slap his thigh—stamp his feet. "You're getting to be a BAM, honey. Just like your Mama."

"Dad! How can you say that about Mama?" I tried to be mad, but couldn't because I knew the old Dad. He only teased people he loved. I looked up with that fake, firm smile I'd seen Mama use with him a thou-sand times. "I hope I inherited more than just a fat ass from her."

He looked at me the way he used to, the way he did when he told me mother had died, passing out of the pain of the cancer that had eaten up her body—the way he did the day I left for college. "Oh, honey," he said, his voice quavering, "You sure did get her pretty eyes and her big heart. Besides, I always loved..."

I smiled and reached to put my hand on his, but he pulled back, looking at me, eyes wild and big. "Don't touch me." I jerked my hand away and stood. "Stay away. It will burn. I'll burn you. Burn you." He pushed back hard in his chair, pushing against the pillows behind his head.

"Dad…Dad… Dad," I repeated like a mantra. "It's okay."

He lurched from his chair and lunged forward. "I am Samuel Maybin Krone. My name is Samuel Maybin Krone. Samuel Maybin Krone." He balled up his hands and pounded his fists in the air.

"Dad?"

"Samuel Maybin Krone."

"Dad."

"My name is Samuel Maybin Krone the First." He turned to me and pointed, his finger hovering in the air, shaking. "You are…you are…Oh… I'm Samuel Maybin Krone."

"Dad, it's Kimmy." I was crying now because I was alone — because he was. I got up to meet him, my arms outstretched, needing to touch him, to hold him close, so he would know me. "It's Kim." I grabbed at his arms.

He shrieked and turned his back to me, hunching over and hugging himself. "No one should touch me!" Now it was a cry. "Not yet!"

I came to him from behind and wrapped my arms around his waist, leaning my body to fold over his. He didn't shriek but whimpered and shivered. "Oh, Daddy," I said. "Oh, Daddy."

"Jesus!" he said, but it wasn't a curse. "Jesus Christ! I'm the Christ! No one should hold me…" He breathed heavily but didn't fight anymore. "For I have not yet…have not yet returned to…my father."

"I know, Dad," I said, resting my head on his bony back, filling full and satisfied. "This world is enough to make anybody crazy, isn't it?" I smiled. Just felt like smiling. "It's going to be okay."

The nurse came in with a tray, so I stopped hugging him and helped him to sit in his reclining chair. He kept rocking. I couldn't make him eat, not even the sugar free vanilla pudding. He kept rocking. Leaning down to wipe some drool from his chin, I said. "It's okay, Dad," He didn't look at me but somewhere off in the distance, and kept rocking. "Okay," I said.

Then, I sat beside him, picked up an old magazine and began to read, as my broken, beautiful father rocked back and forth, searching for himself in the darkness.

RIDE THE PETER PAN
Allison Whittenberg

There were times when it seemed like all the beauty was sucked out of my life. This was one of them. It was cold and damp, early spring, and I was Greyhounding from my old life to my new, from North to South. I was 24, master degreed, unwed, and pregnant.

All around me, I saw failure. As each passenger climbed aboard, emptiness filled the bus. I saw the unshaved and the unshowered. The angry and confused. Widows, retirees, practically invalids dragging their duffle bags. Beside me, a degenerate unwrapped his plastic wrapped sandwiches. I stared out of the windows like a peeping Tom. Riding the bus never meant passing City Hall, never going by the nice restaurants or boutiques melting into friendly pedestrians strolling past. No businessman with wedding bands checking briefcases. No, I saw a squeegee man dirtying clean windshields.

I wished I'd taken the Peter Pan, a special line that showed escapist movies. I'd taken that before when I was only going as far as NYC. I saw a flick about moving an elephant cross-country. It wasn't a box office smash, but for a bus ride it was perfect. Here, there wasn't even a blank screen. I could have gone for another feature length; too bad that line doesn't go down South.

A man with eyes like the sky was doing the driving. He loud-talked to the passengers in the front couple of rows about how fake pro wrestling was. He asked the question, "How come every time they hit each other, they stomp their feet?"

Back in high school, I was valedictorian. A decade later, long after "Pomp and Circumstance" was played, I found myself a loser. Just another confused minority waif riding public transportation bouncing the back of her neck against a greasy headrest...

My wish was for a miscarriage. I know that was a horrible thing to wish for.

I had used up all my distractions. I put on my headphones and heard only a staticky cassette tape. The magazines I had brought, I had read too quickly. I had put away the novel I had brought miles ago. I just couldn't get into it. It was just words on a page. *Now what?*

There was a woman with chicken wings in her shirt pocket. Her fingers smudged the window.

I'm going to kill my baby. Strangle it with my large intestine or with my hands like the Prom Mom. It was a fleeting thought. I blamed it on the bus. Some people get motion sickness; I get homicidal thoughts.

If only the Peter Pan would go way down to Georgia. Maybe I should have flown or rented a car. Truth is, I didn't have the presence of mind to do either. I needed to let someone else do the driving. Let someone else make the stops and turns. I was so angry. Angry at rape, domestic violence, the porn industry, sexism, fascism, racism, ismisms. My life wasn't supposed to go like this. I was the smart girl.

I should have watched my drink.

I should have reported it.

I should have taken the morning after pill.

I shouldn't have been in denial.

RU486 could have stopped this from being compounded. *How am I going to look at this product for the next 18 years? How? What am I going to do? Where am I going? I know where I'm going. Macon. But where am I going?*

I was going home. I didn't even have a job waiting for me. I had two grand saved; that's all.

My legs were cramping from a rocky night when I tried to turn the seat into a sofa. I snuggled in the best I can.

I had no plans other than to live with my mother. My mother was loving and nurturing, but not understanding. She couldn't understand this; I couldn't understand this.

A few rows behind me, that Lolita pop music was playing. Someone else turned on a hip hop station and overpowered it. This all could have been understandable if I dressed like that navel-centric nymphet, but I didn't. I never did. Even on that night, I had on my work clothes at the party, navy skirt, light blue turtleneck. (When groping for cause and effect, fall on stereotypes.)

I had thought I knew Warren. We had talked before about peace, public education, and reparations. My life was going so well. I was saving to buy a condo, something tasteful with modern furniture. It would look like the furniture storeroom at Ikea. *Now look at me, boomeranging back to my same humble beginnings, to the grey borough I grew up in. I have lost control. My power is taken. My destiny. Couldn't he at least have opened up a condom package and put it on?*

The woman in front of me was babbling about how thick her son's neck is. He was in the Navy and that Navy wanted to kick him out because he'd gotten fat. They had been taping his waist and throat to find the density.

My rapist wasn't big, but he did overpower me.

My rapist didn't look like a rapist. He was tall, slender, a runner's build, dark, bookish eyeglasses...kind of like me only male and a pervert.

I only had one glass of wine.

Date rapists aren't any different from rapist rapists. In a lot of ways, they are worse. They gain your confidence, then betray you.

They Milli Vanilli their way into your life. They don't carry a knife or a gun. Just a drug. And surprise.

I remember my stockings pulled down around my ankles so I couldn't move my feet and run. The wheel of my mind takes in the way he braced my arms, so that I couldn't move my arms and clock him. The way he got inside my mind so even my voice didn't work. Why didn't I scream? I lived in an efficiency on the third floor where the walls and ceilings were as thin as loose-leaf paper.

I worked in the politics of shame as a counselor at a women's shelter where the politics of silence was busted every day. I should have come forward. Instead, I did what I urged others not to do, I swallowed it down… yet the projector kept whirring and clacking.

There was a woman on the bus with her hair so uncombed she had dreads from the neglect. Her carry on was a shopping bag full of pain. I was just like her. Up until the rape, my life had been so fine-toothed combed. Pregnancy dictated to me that all my dreams were gone. Even my distant ones of going to Africa, eating raw cashews in Nairobi, tracing my roots…

The bus driver stopped just past Columbia. He told us to get a smoke or a coke. The previous day, I had thrown up twice. Today, I was hungry. I went to the restroom to wash up. The smell of joints hit me as did the sight of women brushing their teeth and washing up. Not just bird baths. Not just splashing under the armpits, spritz to open the dry eyes. These women had their tops off and their pants down. They were buck-naked crowded by the drain.

I left the restroom and cleansed my hands with a moistened towelette I had stored in my carryall bag. I ducked into the terminal coffee shop and sat at the counter.

A waitress made her way over to me and grunted at me.

"Do you have any turkey?" I asked.

"No."

"What do you have?" I asked.

"Burgers. What did you want? A club?"

"No. I wanted a Rachel."

She looked at me blankly.

I explained. "It's like a Reuben, but you use turkey."

"We don't have no turkey."

"Do you have bacon?"

"Do you want a BLT?" she asked.

"No. Bacon cheeseburger."

"We don't have no cheese."

I squinted. "No cheese? No bacon?"

"Nope. So what do you want?"

"An abortion."

She gave me a blank stare.

"I'll have a burger," I swallowed hard and said hoarsely.

"You want fries with that?"

Soon, the moon-faced waitress slid the plate my way.

The bun was cold, and the burger looked like an SOS scouring pad.

I just didn't get it; I had done everything I was supposed to do right down to only using my first initial on the mail and the phone book. How did I get raped?

Some fellow with a head full of shiny Liberace hair—every strand in place—sat next to me. I eyed him. He was a brown-skinned man, chubby, I don't know why I thought Liberace. I should have thought Al Sharpton.

"How's your burger?" he asked.

I said nothing.

"My name's Brian." He smiled. I noticed that he was missing a side tooth. "You know, you are exactly what I'm looking for."

I thought for a moment; exactly what was I looking for? A life of fox furs, red sequined evening dresses? White candles in silver candlestick holders? The man kept smiling at me, showcasing his missing molar. I told myself to give up. Life is not going to be gallant.

He chewed his burger favoring one side. "What's your name?"

"Ann." I lied. It was really Arna. This is what I always did. I never gave strangers too much information. Even in singles clubs, when asked for my phone number, I would give only the last digit. I was always cautious, watchful.

"Ann. I like that. I like women like you. I like a woman whose breasts are where they're supposed to be and have a nice small waist like you have."

I turned away from him and placed my napkin over my burger.

"I have a truck," he said.

I put a five-dollar bill on the counter.

"You want to go for a ride in my truck?" he asked. He smelled oily and close.

I stood up. "How old are you?"

"I'm 42, but I don't want no has beens. My daddy had kids up until he was 60.... I don't date women over 21, 22."

"You don't."

"Naw, I don't want a has been."

"Do you have any kids?" I asked.

"I have grandkids," he answered.

"You have grandkids." I absorbed and repeated.

"Yeah, but that's my daughter's business."

"What happened to your wife?" I asked.

"What wife? I've never been married..." He leered. "Yet."

I made a fist. "You're a 42-year-old grandfather. Why don't you date grandmothers?"

"I done told you I don't deal with no has beens," he told me. "Have you started your family yet?"

"By family, you mean a mother and a father and a child, right? If you mean that, the answer is no." I made my voice as icy as Massachusetts in December. I kept my cadence proper and dry.

"You know what I mean. You got any shorties?" he asked, still snaggle toothed grinned.

"The answer is no."

I turned to leave. He reached for me.

"Get your goddamn hands off of me."

The entire clientele craned their necks at me. An older woman next to the door looked over her glasses at me. The waitress cupped her hands over her face.

"I went to Smith!" I told them, then I gave Grandpa the finger.

I gathered my coat around me, clutched my bag and walked toward the pay phone. I had promised I'd call my mother when I got close to home. I pulled out my card and pressed the digits. Ma answered on the first ring.

"How's your trip going?" she asked.

"All right," I answered. This was my biggest lie yet.

"It's a cast of characters ain't it?" she laughed. I loved her laugh. It was full, colorful, and Southern.

"How far are you along?" she asked.

"Right outside of Columbia."

"How far are you along?" she asked again.

"I'm right in Sumter. Outside Columbia, I'll be there in another two hours."

"No, Arna, how far are you along?"

"You know? How could you know?"

"I just do. Something about the way you told me out of the clear blue that you were moving back home. You love Boston."

She didn't sound angry or disappointed. She sounded psychic.

"Everything is going to be all right. You're not around any smoke, are you? They say that now. That ain't good for the baby."

"I'm only two months in, Ma," I told her.

"It's too bad you have to travel pregnant. You have morning sickness and jet lag."

I smiled. It felt strange to smile. "Ma, you can't get that from a bus because you feel every mile."

"Buses ain't so bad anymore. Don't they show movies?"

"Certain ones do. Greyhound has a spin off. Peter Pan. I'm just on the regular one."

"Well, you'll be home soon. We'll all be there to pick you up."

"I don't have a job lined up."

"You're a mother now. That's your job."

"But I had a career."

"You find something down here. You've always been smart."

"Ma, I let a dumb thing happen."

"You're the first one in the family to ever go to college, Arna. You'll find something down here. We got everything Boston's got. Just a little less of it."

I saw a mass of people heading toward the bus. "Ma, I have to go."

"See you soon."

The bus was just about to pull off as I climbed back aboard. The driver asked me if I knew The Rock.

I crossed my fingers and said, "We're like this."

There was a reshuffling of the seats, and I found my middle of the bus seat gone. I went to the back.

It's always those honor students, 16-year-olds who don't want to disappoint their parents who hemorrhage from grimy abortions. Ma took the news better than I thought.

My mother had emphatic ears. She didn't wear makeup or nail polish. She had basic hobbies; she liked to sew and cook. She was lucky; she didn't go out to the world to discover herself. She was married at 15. I was the exact middle child of seven. Maybe Macon wouldn't be so bad, it's not like I had a job on Wall Street. There are shelters in my hometown or at least people in need of shelter.

A voluptuous big-hipped woman sat next to me. She had swollen ankles. She was one of the nude women I saw in the restroom.

I guess I wasn't put into this world to be pampered; I was put in this world to be squeezed between a window and foul smelling misery.

Back home, kids ride their bikes and chase each other up and down the sidewalk. Just thinking of that made me feel warm enough to ignore the draft that was coming from the metal vent alongside the window.

I will not end this life.

If it's a girl, I will cover her pigtails with red and purple plastic. If it's a boy, I will teach him to be kind.

The bus started up, and I got a mild case of whiplash caused from my neck bouncing against the headrest.

There are times when it seems like all the beauty is sucked out. This isn't one of them.

ABBY
Anne Whitehouse

The stainless steel mirror glints as I grasp it. It goes straight up to the high board, and I am climbing with a rocking motion, my arm muscles tensed and steady. The bathing suit sticks to my skin, for I am wet, dripping wet, and I know if I don't hold on tight, in a dazed second, I might be splayed across the concrete. It happened to my sister's friend, and she was in a cast all summer. That's why my sister won't go off the boards, why she averts her eyes as I climb.

Secretly I too am afraid but won't confess it. When I reach the top, I release the breath I have been holding without thinking, and begin to walk out on the board, my fingers tight on the rails. Its surface is rough so I won't slip. I look below me, beyond the board's edge: the pool shimmers in the sunlight, yet it's farther away than I thought. The dark blue stripes painted on its bottom waver as I try to hold them in my gaze. I think I am seeing them from an immense distance. I reach the end of the rails: a tongue of board, and then air. I bounce lightly, testing the spring. Other children in line below yell at me to hurry. "Go ahead, take your turn," and the lifeguard's whistle is shrill, as terrifying as a scream. "Ten minute break," he calls, "everyone out of the water."

If I go quickly, he won't notice. I run and jump out, far and high. I know the instant my feet leave the board for empty air, I will close my eyes. I don't see myself falling or the water spraying out in tiny drops as I break the surface, but I feel the rush, always a shock, as I sink, and the bubbles graze past my skin. I fall farther, I almost touch bottom before I begin to swim for the rope underwater, my legs flapping like fins.

When I emerge, the pool is empty. Again the lifeguard's whistle barks. "Break," he yells, just for me. Lifting myself out onto the brick gutter, I dangle my legs in the quiet water. Now the blue stripes are as straight as the lanes on a blacktop. I inhale the intense smell of chlorine and of the pines growing up the hill behind the chain-linked fence.

During the break, adults are allowed in the pool, but this time no one goes in but my grandfather, and he doesn't swim. He lies on an inflated raft, silent, beatific, wearing green-tinted sunglasses and a baseball cap to protect his bald skull from sunburn. He likes me to swim under the raft but not to disturb him, and sometimes, when he is tired of floating, he lets my sister and me take the raft while he reads in a shaded lawn chair. We both try to get on at once and overturn it, we yell and paddle. It is our boat. We have gone the whole length of the pool in it. Then we have to give it back so my grandfather can let it dry before he lays it across the back seat of his car and drives it home. He keeps it inflated so he won't have to blow it up each time he comes here.

I jump off the high board until the cold water hurts my nose and my head. I am afraid to dive. Once I landed on my stomach; it made a sickening sound and was red for two days. Another time my legs curled over like when I do a backbend. Even I who couldn't see them knew how they flailed like two lost disconnected fins trying to straighten before they sank. So now I jump, but someday hope I will dive, aiming for the surface like an arrow and like an arrow, sever it without a ripple.

Sometimes Peggy comes to the pool and brings her friend Karen. They have dark curly hair and deep tans. We play freeze tag with them or swim through each other's legs. My grandfather watches from a distance. He doesn't like commotion. Sometimes we race across freestyle or float like dead men. I can hold my breath the longest. Or we play underwater tea party, sitting on the pool bottom and sipping from make-believe cups to a pretend conversation like ladies at a country club. Then we try to guess what we said, but mostly we are wrong. I love the way the bubbles of gurgling sound look as they float upward. We usually end up laughing. Once my sister began to choke, and I had to help her to her feet, into the air again, and slap her between her shoulder blades while she raised her arms above her head.

The best times are when Abby comes. She is Karen's sister, and I love her, but this is a fierce secret no one knows. Abby is deaf. The lifeguard's shrill whistle, the cries of toddlers in the wading pool, and their mothers' reprimands are nothing to her. Abby is smaller than us, and Karen must watch her. When I first saw her, I didn't know she was deaf. Peggy told me later in a whisper as if she might overhear. But Abby knew I was staring at her because she tried to hide behind my grandfather's raft, propped up against the chain-linked fence to dry.

All the time, I try to imagine what it would be like to be Abby. First I stuffed cotton in my ears and walked dreamily around the house, but that only muffled my sister's questions, my mother's derision. I could still hear her running the vacuum cleaner; I could hear the air conditioner switching on and the steady hum of the refrigerator. I walked out on the patio, and the hot moist air enclosed me. I wondered if Abby lives in utter stillness or if she always hears against the background of her mind something like traffic swishing down our street, a noise at once overlooked and insistent.

Mr. Ferguson at the drugstore has a hearing aid, and when he doesn't want to fool with customers, he switches it off. I've seen him do this. I've snuck back behind the high pharmacist's partition to find him engrossed in one of his hunting magazines. Then I put my hands over his eyes and make him guess who it is. Even if he knows, he pretends he doesn't, and afterwards he buys me a Coke from the machine in the stockroom. "Our secret," he says, a finger over his lips, but I don't know if he means the Coke or the glossy magazines with pictures of elk, moose, and deer.

But Abby's world is as different from Mr. Ferguson's as it is from mine because she has never heard a human voice. She sometimes makes strange sounds like gurgles and she laughs and cries. Karen told Peggy who told me that in the fall Abby is going to a special school in Atlanta just for deaf children. She already knows how to make sign language. She runs the quickest of all of us; she is as fast and silent as a cat. Sometimes I go to Peggy's and we all play hide-and-go-seek, but no one can ever find Abby except sometimes Karen.

After the day she caught me staring at her, Abby tried to avoid me. Maybe she thought I was too curious or she was afraid of me. But recently, when Karen was buying snow cones at the pool's snack bar, Abby let me hold her. I wrapped my arms around her wet waist and she didn't even squirm, though as soon as she saw Karen coming, she broke away. So I try to watch her without her knowing it. Just now, swimming for the rope after the break has been called, it comes to me that I feel already, that I have always felt, close to what it is like to be Abby.

Underwater, everything is different. Even in this pool, where there are only other people, I watch from below their legs waving like ribbons. Sometimes I watch divers enter deep water: a long shaft of whiteness parts before them. And then the water is blue again, perfectly blue, more blue than the sky which even at its clearest is always streaked by the ghost of a cloud. Once my family went to Florida on a week's vacation, and each morning I woke with the beach outside my door and the sheer, shining gulf. I put on a mask to go into that water, for the salt hurts my eyes even more than the chlorine. There were jellyfish and shells on the bottom and swaying plants, and then a wave would break and take me with it. Other times the surface was smooth as a looking glass, yet gazing into it I did not see myself.

There is sound underwater but not as we speak it. Our language gets mangled like the conversation at our bottom-of-the pool tea parties. But dolphins sing to each other there, and whales. It is at the moment I reach for the rope and surface to the lifeguard's second whistle, hair and eyes streaming, lungs bursting, that the comparison flashes on me, that I have imagined being Abby. Plunged underwater, sinking until the mass of water slowed my fall, I began to swim. The shock of my leap was still in me; it had changed me, so easily did I move through the slight currents. Then I broke through them and came to air. My breath released from me all in a rush. I did not keep the sensation of being Abby.

Abby is the best diver I have ever seen. After the break is over and the pool is ours again, I see her arriving with Peggy and Karen. She dances down the steps, she is so glad to be here. She is wearing a red one-piece suit of silky nylon, like members of the swim team have, and her legs against he concrete steps are as thin and brown as bamboo. Peggy sees me and waves, and I walk rapidly — it is against the rules to run — to greet her. "I knew you would be here," she says, "because I called your mother. Where is your sister?"

My sister is talking to my grandfather. We all go over, Peggy, Karen, Abby, and me. "I can crack my fingers, I can crack my ankles and my wrists, I can even crack my knees," my sister is telling my grandfather as she sits cross-legged at his feet. He is in a lawn chair, and this time his baseball cap has a shaded green visor but he also wears sunglasses, just to make sure.

"Better watch it," he says, "if you crack your fingers too much, they will look like mine," and he holds his up to show us his knuckles swollen from arthritis.

Abby is restless; she shifts her weight from one foot to the other and pulls on Karen's arm. "She wants to go in," Karen explains and then signs to her sister. They head for the diving area across the pool from us, where the deep water is. We all watch, even my grandfather.

Swiftly Abby climbs the ladder, whereas I, unsure, must put both feet on a rung before I try for the next. She walks out to the end and back. No one tells her to hurry. Even if she could hear them, it wouldn't matter, it wouldn't change anything. Holding onto the rails, she lifts her light body into the air and then down, and then she runs the length of the board, and bounces, and jumps out far and high, the plane of her body horizontal to the water; arms outstretched, she is poised for that motionless instant — and then her arms form a V over her head and she curves down, straight down into the water, severing it with the sharpness of her confident accuracy.

Only then do I realize that I have been holding my breath too, as if I were Abby. She swims all the way across the pool, over to us, and when she gets out, my grandfather begins to clap, and, realizing, abruptly stops, frozen. But Abby delights in our smiles. She waves and flashes, into the pool again, into the sparkling water. In his benevolence, my grandfather offers us his raft though it is already dry. All five of us try to get on at once; then Karen, my sister, and Abby sit astride it, spreading their legs across its width while Peggy and I pull them around the pool.

When the lifeguard calls the next break, my grandfather gives us money for ice cream. They sell vanilla cones topped with chocolate and nuts that come already wrapped. Sometimes the nuts stick to the paper, and you have to eat them off. We lick ours slowly, without saying much, as the sun dries our skin and bathing suits and hair. Later Abby dives again and again. Karen goes after her, and although she is good, your eyes don't rivet on her as they do on Abby.

My mother takes us all home in the station wagon. Before we sit down, she makes us spread our towels across the seats. We are tired; my sister dozes in the front seat. Abby rests her head on Karen's shoulder.

The station wagon has a window in the roof. I lean my head back on the seat and watch the clouds cover the sun and the sun escape, and the anticipation fills me, of all the summer that still remains for me. Will I overcome my fear? I will never learn to dive like Abby.

Suddenly Abby starts in the back seat: out of a dream, a cry, and Karen shushes her, strokes her head softly and her useless ears. In the fall Abby will go to Atlanta. That is what Peggy said, and Peggy knows because Karen told her. But it is June, and three blank pages of the calendar's sheets stretch before us, with no school, no Sunday school, no scout meetings or lessons to be filled in. Just the sun getting hotter and burning the dew off the grass, and the pungent scent of the pines growing up the hill. And all the days at the pool where time is measured by the lifeguard's whistle, except for Abby who will never hear it, even if, in that distant unimaginable school, she learns to speak.

Raymond and the Mountain Militia*
Meredith Sue Willis

The two greatest gifts Jesus gave Raymond Savage were what happened to him in prison and his wife Dinah. In prison he was led to salvation by an old black con with ten teeth who called himself the howling wolf of Jesus, and he howled Raymond right into Salvation. Dinah lifted him up in everything. Sometimes her faith was not as clear as his, and she worried about a thousand things that Jesus had assured Ray would be taken care of, but she was the mainstay of his life. He felt sorrow for her concerns and doubts, but trusted that one day she, too, would see through clear glass. She had accepted Raymond, even when he said, "You know I did time in prison."

She said, "And you came out a new man, Ray. That's enough for me."

She didn't ask the details. He prayed over that, and in the end, Jesus agreed with Dinah. She had the basic outline, that he'd got mixed up with some bad actors back home in West Virginia, but that an old black man in prison had prayed him straight. Jesus told him to reveal the details on a need-to-know basis.

So Ray said to her, "I can have a foul temper, but I never took a man's life, and I never struck a woman."

Dinah smiled that smile of hers that was just one watt short of a revelation. "Well, Raymond, I already knew you had a temper, and I already knew you were a good man."

She took him the way Jesus took him, failings and all. Dinah and Jesus said, "We're here for you, Ray Savage." He felt their love like a trampoline catching him when he landed and sending him back up high. That's what Jesus can do for you! He ran the image through his mind, preparing a sermon. Or a good woman, if you can find yourself a good woman. Or vice versa.

Because of his temper, Raymond was pretty sure Dinah assumed he'd done his time for assault and battery. And when he was young, he did spend a couple of nights in jail after drinking and fighting, but Jesus told him that was all material for reaching out to those hard-headed men who were still in darkness. He imagined having a church of his own someday, with a cross on the side of a tower shaped like a lighthouse, for those men like lost seamen in a storm.

What got him into prison—and not some local lock-up but the federal penitentiary—hadn't been anger and it hadn't been drugs, it had been stupidity. He had been in the dark, which means—he tried it out in his mind as another line for a sermon—that you don't care enough about yourself to turn on the lights and see Jesus.

The thing he hadn't told Dinah about in detail was the Mountain Militia plot. It had been in the mid nineteen-nineties, and Poke Riley had got him the job driving trucks, hauling boxes. Poke also did time for stupidity.

So when Poke showed up now at the service station where Ray was repairing tires part-time, all these years later, with a business proposition, Ray knew it was time to tell Dinah the whole story. He was going to have to say, *I need you to know how I know this man Poke Riley.*

He figured Dinah was going to say, *Skip the story and stay away from the man.*

He and Poke went back way before the Mountain Militia. From home in Cooper County. They had been in high school together till Poke dropped out, and then, later, they used to hang out around Kingfield. Poke always had plans. Once he was going to tie flies for fishermen and sell them mail order, and then he had an idea to make high quality moonshine and sell it to students at the university who thought it was cool to buy illegal liquor. Then he had a job as a night watchman and dealt pills, and for a while, he ran a gambling scheme using West Virginia University team point spreads.

Raymond liked Poke personally, in spite of all the nonsense and even the Mountain Militia. So he was fine when Poke showed up and started talking about the old days. He still had the big laugh, big belly and that pony tail like a rockabilly guitarist which he never was. They agreed that they'd both been young and stupid for getting involved in the Mountain Militia thing.

"I've got a real good job now," Poke said. "Salary and all expenses paid, seriously. And the proposition for you, Ray, is totally legitimate." He told him he worked for a rich business man. The man had dabbled in growing marijuana at one time, Poke said, but now it was all legitimate investments. "I'm not going to lie to you," said Poke. "He's an oddball, but nothing illegal. And this man is looking to hire a preacher." Poke said he'd been visiting back home and heard Ray was a preacher now. "You know me, Ray, why put an ad in the paper when I know a man from home? It's all about who you can trust, am I right?" The rich man, according to Poke, was starting a media center up on a mountain in Pocahontas County. He had a lot of ideas, but he wanted a religious program for his radio station or podcast or whatever. "So I thought of you, Ray. Come down to Mountain Dome, and get interviewed. It's a real opportunity."

Nothing illegal, Ray would tell Dinah. And could hear her saying, *And how do you know that, Ray?*

Bobby Mack was working for the business man too, Poke admitted, and that made Ray a little uneasy, and he said so. Ray wasn't prejudiced against small men, but Bobby Mack always had a beat-down ratty look that made Ray think of Judas Iscariot.

The marijuana made him uneasy too.

Poke said, "Look here, Ray, I only mentioned the weed so you wouldn't hear about it elsewhere. I want all the cards on the table. My boss has been out of that a long time, and even when he was in it, he was diversified. And it's all going to be legal in ten years anyhow. My boss, he understands people have done things they maybe wish they hadn't in the past. He plans for the long haul, you see? He likes people who've made their mistakes and learned from 'em. That's why he took on Bobby Mack and me."

Ray believed in second chances too. We all deserve a second chance. What is Born Again but a second chance? That was the thing the old black con always said: "Jesus loves the Second Chancers." So Ray prayed about the opportunity, and Jesus didn't say yes, but He didn't say no.

Ray and Poke and Bobby Mack had been on the periphery of the Mountain Militia Patriot thing. Ray had certainly never meant any harm to his country, that was one thing he was sure of. They never had much to do with the gung ho ones. Ray went to a couple of meetings, but that was all. They said they were going to stop the New World Order, and later on, he had found out that meant not only getting the government off people's backs — which he favored, of course — but also getting rid of what they called the Jews and the Jigs and the Rag-heads. That part made him uneasy to the point that he decided he was going to collect his pay and get out, but it took him too long to decide.

I was in darkness then, Ray said to himself, working on either the sermon or how he was going to explain this to Dinah. *That's what I was then. When I needed money for my pleasures, I took it from wherever. I don't think I would have put a gun to the back of a man's head and fired, but thank you, Jesus, I was never tested. I did take money from people whose lives were about hate, not love.*

He had thought all he needed was money, and here came Poke who knew someone who needed men to drive trucks, just carry a few things here and there. And they were paying $50 a pop, sometimes a hundred, for an hour or two of work.

Raymond never doubted for a minute that they were hauling contraband, because the pay was too good and got better as time went on. Also the loading and driving was usually at night from garages to deserted barns and vice versa. Sometimes he was pretty sure they were stealing, but mostly they just seemed to be relocating material that already belonged to the Colonel, a man named Floyd Looker, a fellow in real estate, and somewhat of a preacher himself.

The Colonel wore fatigues and a beret, and Ray saw him maybe three times but never had a conversation.

The meetings drew in all kinds of people, sometimes big meetings, especially after certain things happened in the news, especially after the federal building in Oklahoma. Up until then, Ray had figured it was all about drugs or the semi-secret marijuana fields all through the West Virginia hollows, but then he realized Floyd Looker and the others had more on their minds. Oklahoma City got them real enthused.

Ray remembered thinking, *But those boys in Oklahoma City killed little children. What the hell good is that?* Ray complained with the best of them about taxes and people sneaking into the country and taking your jobs. All the Savages, his whole family, were independent to their toenails, believed in taking care of their own and devil take the hindmost. But when Bobby Mack started going on about how there was something to it, you had to be ready to blow away the ape-people and fight the government, Ray had said, "Now wait a minute, Bobby Mack, my big brother Duke, he was one of the very last ones to die in Vietnam."

Poke said, "Bobby Mack supports our troops, don't you, Bobby Mack?"

That was when Ray started thinking about getting out of it, but again he was too slow. He never even knew if Bobby's last name was Mack or if that was part of his first name. That was how careless he had been in those days. *Straight to the Devil for fifty bucks.*

Jesus loves the Second Chancers. Praise Jesus.

They got paid a hundred when it was explosives they were hauling, and that was when he was sure they were stealing, although he was also pretty sure that someone had paid off the guard at the quarry to be out in the woods pissing at 2 a.m. It was very precise, that they had to drive in at 2 a.m. and break into a shed where they found about 500 pounds of blasting caps and old fashioned dynamite. So by that night if not before, Ray knew these so-called patriots were planning a big explosion of some kind. He was sick of their meetings and he decided this was it, he was finished. The next time there was a dead-of-the-night job, he opted out, although he still did some daytime hauling for them.

Then the whole thing broke loose: It turned out Colonel Looker and the Mountain Militia Patriots were going to blow up the new FBI fingerprinting facility down in Harrison County before it even opened. This fingerprint center was a gift from West Virginia's Senator Robert C. Byrd, who always took care of his own and got the facility moved from D.C. to West Virginia, so people would have jobs. *Good old Robert C.*

But Colonel Looker got the idea in his head that the fingerprint place was going to be the command center for taking away men's guns and organizing gangs of black men to rape little white children, both sexes. So the idea was to blow it up before it opened.

Most of what Ray knew about it, he got from the newspaper and TV like everybody else. The Colonel talked a fireman into giving him blueprints for the new facility, and he was collecting the explosives to do the job. Then the Colonel had some meetings with an Arab terrorist (What was he doing in West Virginia anyhow? Didn't anyone have the sense to ask?) and the Arab terrorist turned out to be a federal agent, and what's more, there had been other agents following the whole thing all along.

So Floyd Looker was at least as stupid as I was, Raymond thought. More stupid, because Floyd got eighteen years. Some of the inner circle got ten, and the rest of them, the drivers like Ray and Poke and Bobby Mack, got two years that ended up being a year and a half. He had read about the whole thing in the paper and congratulated himself on being out of it, never realized he was about to get arrested till they picked him up one afternoon working under a car at his brother Junior's garage.

Those were the details Dinah didn't know.

She did know about how prison was the beginning of God's part of his story and about the old man who aimed Ray straight at Jesus. *That old man was a gun and I was a bullet, and he shot me into the heart of Jesus, and I have lodged there ever since!* He used that whenever he had an opportunity to preach, which wasn't as often as he'd like. He wanted to check out the opportunity Poke Riley told him about because he wanted more preaching and less shit jobs and maybe someday that Lighthouse of the Cross of Jesus church..

He wasn't quite sure how to present it to Dinah. He knew she was going to say, "That sounds real good, another bright idea from the man who got you sent to prison."

The fact is, Ray thought, *probably nothing is going to come of it. The idea of a rich businessman wanting to start a radio church up on some mountain don't make much sense, anyhow.* He knew it was time to tell the whole story to Dinah, but he thought he would pray on it a while first in the gentle glow of Jesus before he exposed it to Dinah's searchlight.

*From Chapter 4 of a novel-in-progress entitled *Safe Houses.*

Dave
Okey Napier

I knew the moment I walked backstage into the dressing room that I liked him. The him in question was Dave, otherwise known as Miss Dawnita Devereaux, though at that moment he was more Dave than Dawnita.

He sat in a chair, cigarette dangling from his lip, as another queen plastered his foundation on—Stein's Tan B theatrical base for the gurl plagued by that five o'clock shadow.

He stood, smiled, and introduced himself.

"Hi, I'm Dave,"

Without stopping what she was doing, Blaze, the queen doing Dave's makeup, scolded him. "Will you sit still and shut the fuck up," she bellowed. "I cannot do this with your lips flapping!"

He took a sip of his beer then sat back in the chair quiet, for the moment.

The backstage was at one of the two gay bars in town. It was dingy, dusty, at times smelled like piss, and tonight it was packed full of queens. We queens took our places in front of the mirror like royalty, sitting by seniority. The oldest, and I stress the word oldest, most popular queen sat beside the door AND in front of the small air conditioner.

Our thrones were mismatched chairs placed in front of a long table made from a piece of plywood, painted black. I have to tell you—fucking splinters—just saying. Above the "table" was a long set of mirrors of various sizes likely nabbed at the local Goodwill. Above the mirrors, was a row of bulbs that were so bright they would put you blind.

The background noise was heavy thumping from the bass in whatever the DJ was playing—at that point Janet Jackson sang about a *Rhythm Nation*. Of course all of us had cocktails, lots of them. The music was so loud, it jarred the liquor or beer in our glasses that sat on the table in front of us. You could watch the liquid jump around, almost like it was dancing to the beat of the loud music. There was a never-ending smell of pot, and one of the queens periodically pulled out her eyeshadow case and snorted a line of coke from the little mirror in the case.

Percussion in Janet's song added to the pounding beat that enticed people to the dance floor. It also enticed us. Periodically, some queen would jump up from the makeup table and lip sync and dance along with Janet or whoever the DJ happened to be playing. Yells of, "Get it gurl!" or "Work it gurl!" erupted from the rest of us as she danced.

I chose the chair beside Dave, sat down, and unpacked my makeup. He was talking again before my ass could arrange itself on the seat. If he wasn't talking to me, he was talking to someone else. To be honest, I was usually guarded backstage. I usually talked a little to be polite, but was otherwise quiet. I came into the drag scene naïve and trusting. After getting my ass scorched and stabbed in the back a few times, I learned quickly that words could be twisted and confidences were usually not kept. I learned the quick lesson that a gurl couldn't be too careful with some of the evil queens in town. "Honey, some of those bitches would stab you in the back quicker than they'd turn a trick in the alley for a $50." But, Dave's smile was infectious, and before I knew it, we were talking like old friends.

Dave was an older guy. He was forty and at the time, that meant he was an old queen to me. He regaled me with stories of times past, the adventures of his youth: bars that have come and gone, tricks who had come and gone, his virginity that he kept losing, and a little gossip on some of the regulars at the bar — okay, a *lot* of gossip about some of the regulars at the bar. We had a grand time talking as we got ready.

"If you ain't careful, this bar will chew you up and spit you out, gurl," he warned me. "Always someone who wants to lead you down the wrong path or use you or steal from you. Don't forget that, Miss Ilene." That was my name, Miss Ilene Over.

Blaze told Dave that he was done. She tossed Dave's lipstick onto the table in front of him. "You can do that," she said. Dave asked if she'd come back after the first half of the show and retouch his makeup. Blaze half agreed as she all but sprinted out the door.

Dave hopped up, bent over and put on his lipstick, grabbed his now empty glass and headed for the door. "Gurllll, I'm gonna go out and mingle. Dawnita Devereaux has just come to life and she needs a cocktail!"

I finished my makeup, put on my wig, accessories, and sprayed a half can of Aquanet on my wig to hold it all in place, then headed out into the club to refill my cocktail and mingle — remember when you mingle it increases the chances of earning more tips — people who come to a drag show come up and tip you a $1 or $5 or $10 if they like you, how you look, how you dance, etc. If you go out to the audience before the show and mingle around, get to know them, they are way more likely to tip you. And, even better than a tip, if you mingle you might get lucky and find a husband for the night.

"Showtime, ten minutes, SHOWTIME TEN MINUTES," the DJ announced.

The smoke from all the cigarettes and pot backstage was so thick I could barely breathe. The haze hung over the room like fog off the river and clung to the various sequined costumes hanging backstage, giving it an almost surreal feel. It had a very "dream sequence" from a B movie feel to it.

Dawnita came in and was a bit tipsy. Well, perhaps more than a bit tipsy. With a plop, she sat beside me, legs gapped open like a linebacker on a locker room bench.

"This is my first time doing this. I'm as nervous as a whore in church. What if I forget the words to the song?"

I was tempted to name one of the queens in the room and point out that she never remembers the words to a song and still gets tipped — only to comfort Dawnita, of course. I thought better of it. "You'll be fine," I told her. She stood by the door, waiting for her song to start. The queen ahead of her, my drag mother Kandi Barr, finished her number and came through the door. The stage lights went out and Dawnita walked out behind a small curtain that protected the backstage door from the eyes of the "audience."

The DJ's voice boomed, "Please welcome to the stage lights a new vixen here at the club, Miss Dawnita Devereaux!"

The audience responded well, clapping and cheering. The music started and Dawnita made her her way onto stage for the very first time — a grand entrance.

"I know, I'll never, love this way again..."

She picked an old but good song for her first number. From the sound of the crowd, the magic of Ms. Dionne Warwick was with Dawnita. I could see her in my mind's eye, standing on stage wearing that beautiful white gown with it sparkling as the stage lights hit it, her hair piled elegantly up on her head. Dawnita's lip quivered and she moved her arms gracefully, lip-syncing to the song as if Dionne Warwick herself were crooning the ballad. I knew she would walk to each person who tipped her, smile at them, then almost curtsey as she accepted the tip. Dawnita's attention would place a smile on the face of the tipper, a smile that told all it was as if he or she were meeting Dionne Warwick herself.

The song ended, the crowd applauded, and Dawnita came through the door backstage and was ecstatic. She clutched dollar bills in both hands, and I could tell from the look on her face that she'd had a blast.

"Not bad for a gurl's first time on the stage," I told her.

Dawnita dropped into the seat beside me and immediately started talking. She chattered at me until it was my turn to take to the stage. In fact, she was still talking to me as I walked out the door and onto the stage. I wondered if she even noticed if I'd left my chair. I performed my number, the last in the first half of the show, then returned backstage.

"I need another cocktail — I'll be back," Dawnita said. She was out the door with empty glass in hand.

When it was time for the second half of the show, a much drunker Dawnita came in and was, well, how shall one say it—a hot mess. It was July, so the bar was hot as the 7th plane of hell. Her face was melted and mostly gone. The only makeup that remained was her smeared eye-liner, which made her look like a big raccoon. She had no lipstick on, it was all on her beer glass, which she clutched to her big but false bosoms. The only thing missing from this picture was her having one broken heel. I'll give her credit, she managed to get into the seat beside me.

"Gurl, what am I gonna do?! I can't find Blaze. My makeup needs a little touch-up."

I looked at her and all I could do was blink. "Gurl, maybe more than a little touch-up."

She looked at me with those big raccoon eyes and asked if I'd help her. "Oh, I don't have the strength," I thought to myself, but I smiled and said yes. I handed her a box of tissues and told her to sop up all that sweat. "Get cooled down and dry your face—we'll get it fixed."

I'd never done a drag intervention before, but I managed. I helped her get her face back on using my makeup. Though drunk and in a panic, she still had that sweet smile and friendly disposition. She thanked me over and over for helping her. "You don't know how much this means to me," she told me. I told her it was all cool and to get changed for her number. I needed to retouch my own makeup. She wasn't the only one sweating—*Goddamned heat*. I dabbed my face with tissues, re-applied my makeup, then used so much powder it looked like a crop duster had flown through. As a finishing touch, I added more Aquanet on the wig and then a little on my face to help keep the makeup in place—it is harder to sweat off with the Aquanet.

After Dave was out on stage, my drag mother Kandi tapped me on the shoulder and motioned for me to join her. We moved over to the other side of the dressing room away from everyone.

"You shouldn't loan Dave your makeup or brushes because you might catch something."

I cocked my head and looked at her. All I could think of when she said "catch something" was, *OH MY GOD lice or scabies or cooties or something!*

"What do you mean?" I finally managed to get out.

Exasperated, she turned us around so our backs were to everyone and said, "Gurl, he's got AIDS!"

I was speechless.

I stuttered, "B...but you can't get it that way."

"Gurl, be careful," she said and then walked away from me to rejoin the others.

I discovered later that Dave moved away from West Virginia after coming out as a gay man at a young age—sixteen, I believe. His family wanted nothing to do with him when they found out he was queer. They condemned him and kicked him out with nothing. He traveled to Florida where he worked in the service industry. I often teased him and said he worked in the "servicing industry."

In a large city, he was free to be himself, to love and fuck who he wanted. Dave lived in Florida until he got sick. In those days, a diagnosis of AIDS was a death sentence. He was too sick to work and there was no one to help him there. It was cheaper to live in West Virginia, especially on the limited income of social security. So, like many other gay men from this place, he packed his things and moved back. He couldn't stand the thought of having to move back to his hometown with his family. He was from a very small town with a lot of closed minds, so he moved to Huntington, a larger university town. Of course, once back he was soon out in the gay bars. Before long, and with a little encouragement, he decided to give drag a try.

I did several shows with Dave and after a while, he and I started hanging out. One evening we hit Burger King for dinner and I found out that he had to move. It wasn't one of those situations where he could take his time and choose a place. No, gurl had to vacate the premises by order of the County Magistrate. I later found out that it was because he hadn't paid rent for three months.

Dave couldn't work because of his health. He received a minimal amount monthly from social security. He was also one of those generous and carefree spirits. He was one of those types that always wanted to buy you a drink, take you to get something to eat and pay for it, help out someone who was in need. I remember him helping several people pay various utilities. He was a kind and giving soul. Sadly, he gave so much and so often that his social security check quickly vaporized, and he was left with nothing. Aside from being an angel of mercy for other people, Dave was also more likely to spend his money on weed and/or cocktails than for rent, food, and utilities. So, between the two things, he was ever and always broke.

I agreed to help him move and showed up on the appointed day (arriving before the Sheriff did to throw him out). I was there along with some of his other friends. He met us outside and took us into the apartment—the third floor naturally. When I came through the door, my jaw dropped to the floor. He wasn't even packed. He had a few small boxes sitting on the table, which still had dirty dishes on it as well. All of us pitched in and stuffed his belongings into garbage bags and then lugged them down and loaded them to the truck. We managed to get all of it out and give the apartment an adequate cleaning before the deadline to be out.

A person who worked with the local AIDS task force volunteered her garage for Dave to store his belongings. After unloading the truck, Dave and I stood by my car. He had a garbage bag filled with clothing and a big suitcase. Everything else he owned was now stored in the garage. "Can you drop me off at the Mission?" he asked me. The mission was the only shelter for the homeless in the city. I told him to get in my car. I didn't take him to the city Mission. I knew that someone who was gay and had AIDS would not fare well there. He would likely have ended up getting hurt or worse. I drove us to my apartment. I lived in a one room efficiency at the time that had a living room, kitchen, and bedroom all in one room, and bathroom off to the side.

When we arrived at my apartment, I told him he could not stay at the Mission, that he would be staying with me until he could get his own place again. At first, he said no, that he didn't want to impose. I told him, "Listen, Dave, shut the hell up, I'm offering." He brightened up and gave me a hug.

It would be crowded to say the least. I had room for a TV stand, a bed, small loveseat, small apartment sized stove, and a refrigerator — that was it. "We'll have to share the bed and keep your hands to yourself, bitch," I told him. He laughed and poked his head into the refrigerator. "What am I cooking for supper?" he said as he was already pulling out items.

Dave was one of the best roommates I ever had. He bounced around that tiny place cleaning and cooking, making it truly feel like a home. At night, we'd head to one of the bars to do a show and then come stumbling home at all hours of the early morning. His being there chased away some of the loneliness and sadness that haunted me at the time.

Dave moved in not long after I'd been outed to my family. Someone took it upon themselves to call each of my family members and report to them that I was 1) gay and 2) a drag queen. The person told them my drag name, the bars where I performed, and even the color and type of bag I used to carry my drag in. It was a difficult time for me, and so having Dave there with me was a huge help.

We were always broke, but I made sure the rent was paid. Oftentimes that meant Dave didn't have any weed because I made him cough up his part of the rent. Actually, he generally wasn't the one who had much weed — ever. He was always asking people, "Gurl, have ya got any papers?" — his way of asking people if they'd share a little weed with him. Usually, they did.

Dave was always laughing and goofing around. One time he was leaving to go get cigarettes and I dared him to wear a pair of stiletto heels he had. He laughed and put them on. Miss Thing marched three blocks up that street, into the store, then back to our apartment in broad daylight. Doing that took guts. It was a different and more dangerous time for queers. There was no *Will and Grace* or *RuPaul's Drag Race*. People were much more ill-disposed toward us. The country was in a panic about AIDS—the kind of panic that caused people to run a family out of town because a kid, like Ryan White, had AIDS.

That year on my birthday, I didn't receive a card or hear from my parents. We had not talked for several months. After I was outed, they gave me hell—my father told me to choose between "those people" or my family. I told him I'd live by his decision. I had no contact with anyone in my family other than my granny.

I tried to not let it get to me, but of course it did. On my birthday, I was down and not in a celebratory mood. I left for work that morning and when I came home and opened the door, I smelled cake. While I was out of the apartment, Dave baked a birthday cake. We were so poor we couldn't have bought a dust bunny. I have no idea where he got the money for the ingredients. He probably shoplifted them. He also got me a birthday card and wrote the sweetest verse in it. When I got home I was so surprised. As if that wasn't enough, he had made a delicious birthday dinner from the fine fixins of the food pantry. We had BBQ, made from commodity pork, green beans, mashed potatoes, rolls, and, of course, birthday cake. It was one of the most meaningful birthday celebrations I've ever had.

It wasn't long after my birthday that Dave got sick. In those days, there wasn't a drug cocktail and a cadre of physicians you could rely on. The only treatment was a drug called AZT. It was prescribed in such doses that people often wondered if it was worse than the disease itself. The side effects were terrible—teeth crumbled and fell out, constant nausea and diarrhea, to name a few. Dave took it, but he worsened.

Nights became difficult. Each night I was awakened several times by his coughing and choking. He would flail and kick in the bed as he tried to raise himself up so he could get his breath. I started getting up with him—propping him up and talking quietly to him, holding him so he would calm down and breathe a little easier.

I didn't need a doctor to diagnose what was wrong; I knew it was pneumonia—likely pneumocystis pneumonia common for people with AIDS. He told me over and over how sorry he was. I reassured him it was ok, that I was glad to be there to help him. There were usually a lot of tears involved. After he settled down and I could lay him back, I sat there in the dark and silence with my eyes closed, listening to him gurgle and struggle to breathe until he was finally asleep.

About a week later, he told me that though he and his family did not get along, he had called his mother and was going to go home for a little while. He reassured me that it would only be until he was better, and then he'd be back. I asked him several times if he was sure. "Yes," he would say, "I need to get better, then I'll be back."

Early the following Saturday morning, I helped him get dressed. He struggled to breathe and we took several breaks. I made breakfast for us, but he didn't eat much. We mostly sat in silence. I took him by the arm and helped him walk downstairs. We had to stop several times so he could rest and get his breath.

The streets were still empty and the city was silent. The mist from the river covered everything. You couldn't see more than a few feet in front of you. We walked out onto the damp sidewalk. It was just Dave and me.

"You'd better keep that apartment clean, gurl, or I will kick your ass," he joked and laughed a little.

"You're the slob," I told him.

Before long, a large, four door, burgundy car came down the street and pulled into an open parking spot in front of us. The person driving didn't speak or get out. He was in a sports jacket and had short-cropped, graying hair. He sat stiffly and stared straight ahead. He never acknowledged either of us — his hands gripped the steering wheel.

"My father," Dave said weakly. The tone that he used told me everything I needed to know — the sadness, fear, and anguish in the tone told me just how much he dreaded what he was about to do.

I helped Dave into the car and loaded his suitcase into the backseat. I moved to close the passenger side door. Dave looked up at me, a half-smile on his face and said, "See you later."

"See ya later," I replied. I closed the door and they drove away.

That was the last time I saw him. One week later, Dave died in the hospital.

CORAL LIP, SAGE TONGUE
Spaine Stephens

It was a listless dawn that cast first light on Willett Street, where the pocked road bore fresh neon orange loops and lines like some strange abandoned game of hopscotch. The jaunty scribbles no longer marked the spots where shell casings had come to rest, but people still stopped to point and cup their chins in their hands. "What a shame," they said, and shuffled on.

An occasional car would ease down Willett Street, pausing as if to draw a hesitant breath, and roll past the house, its occupants staring at the ribbons of glass that still hung in the front bedroom window's chewed wood frame. Sometimes the people in the cars would murmur to each other, mounting their theories of how the shooting went down and why. Others would stay silent, meeting Jettie's eyes with a mix of sympathy and distaste. They knew there would be no real answers on Willett Street.

Jettie stood in the squat front yard, hating the morning. Her eyes stung with grit and grief, and her exposed arms and legs looked purple in the mean summer sun. Jettie wasn't what they called "high yella" like her mama had been. Her darker brown skin was mottled with plum-colored bruises that puckered and deepened at the centers like angry bites. She rubbed them absently and her hands felt dusty. A fine, dry ash clung to her skin, and she wore it like cloth. Jettie looked as if she'd been beaten up, like someone had held her down in the yard's eastern Carolina sandy silt and viciously twisted her skin in their fingers, causing angry risings to form and swell, the air around them darkening too. But the fingers were her own, and the times when she gathered her clammy skin into sharp peaks and pinched, the flash of hot pain and the itchy prick of tears in her eyes made her almost laugh with relief.

Jettie looked down at her feet. Her toenails were thick and discolored. They looked older than the feet of a seventeen-year-old. She turned her back to the house and blinked.

"Man, *damn,*" she hissed.

Stoke Meyer, her mama's landlord, had left a big blue pail, a mop, and an assortment of bleach and other cleaning supplies sitting on the top step of the little yellow house on the corner of Willett Street. Jettie had until dark to clean what she could and go away for good. The morning after the shooting, Stoke — that hateful old white bastard whose hands were too loose when around Jettie — had come around just as word was getting out about the shooting and bellowed that he had already begun the eviction process on Jettie and her mama. The news vans, cops, and neighbors who had flocked to his property for this latest incident were too much for Stoke; the fewer prying eyes on his slummy properties, the better.

Jettie couldn't even remember how she had gotten outside this morning, how she had come to be standing in the sad, square yard in front of the yellow house. She had slept fitfully last night on the old orange couch in the front room, crawling across the floor to keep her head below the windows when she needed to use the bathroom. She didn't know if the shooters would come back. Just two days ago, Jettie and her mama, Marketta, called "Coral" by both family and acquaintances because of her trademark shade of drugstore lipstick, had walked down the street together as always. Their arms had been linked like sisters as they strolled in tank tops and ripped denim shorts to the corner store up on Highsmith Street, just like any other day. The days had all run together in Jettie's mind, and she wished for a split second that she had been the one that got shot.

It took Jettie two trips to carry all the supplies into the house, which was already sweltering. She wandered into the bathroom, which smelled like stale shit and Lysol. Hair was stuck to an oily sheen in the sink. She threw back the shower curtain and waited as a roach retreated into the drain. She pushed aside an assortment of cheap body wash containers and found the purple travel-size shampoo bottle that Coral had hidden behind them. She grabbed it in shaky hands and unscrewed the lid, her nose burning as she took a desperate lungful of the sharp tang that wafted out. She closed one eye and peered inside it, then brought the bottle to her dry, crusted lips. The liquor snaked through her like runoff rolling over the stagnant Tar River after too many weeks without rain. Relief forced her eyes closed, and she fought the wave of heat that alcohol drew to her blemished cheek.

Jettie heaved, then swallowed back down the bitter remnants. She sprinkled Ajax in the sink and swirled tepid water in it for a few short seconds. She had to hurry. Besides Stoke giving her only hours to clean and leave, her caseworker Betsy Best—a mousy white lady who no better understood Jettie's life than what it was like to live on the moon—would come looking for her soon. She dreaded the whiny, nasal drawl of her preachy voice and the way her cool blue eyes darted past her like all she wanted in the world was to get away and wipe her hands on her skirt.

"There are scholarships for girls like you," Betsy Best had told her last year, when Jettie had been caught skipping school again, back before she dropped out altogether.

"Girls like you," Jettie had spit back stupidly, as Betsy Best cocked her head and wrinkled her creamy brow, her long jangly earrings brushing the shoulders of her Lilly Pulitzer dress.

"Girls like you" had played on repeat in Jettie's head for the rest of that day. What had the lady meant? Poor? Black? Retarded? Ugly? A "self injurer," like the doctor at the clinic had explained to Coral one day when Jettie had pinched herself until she bled? His gaze had skittered over the marks on Jettie's body, which were covered only by a flimsy paper gown. He had not offered any referrals for counseling or care. There would be no scholarships for Jettie.

She moved silently now to the bedroom she had dreaded entering and had avoided since the shooting. It had been "neat," she had overheard the cops say, and she saw now what they meant. The blood had stayed on the bed. The walls were left untouched, dotted only with chipped green paint. There was one inexplicable smear of blood across the floor where Coral's feet first touched in the mornings when she climbed out of bed.

When those boys had driven by and opened fire on the little yellow house on Willett Street just after 3 o'clock those few mornings earlier, Coral had been fast asleep in her lumpy, sour bed. Jettie knew her mama always slept on her right side, and that had provided a perfect path for the bullet to pierce the window and Coral's bare brown back. Coral's new boyfriend, Leonidas, had not been in bed when the shooting went down, but staring at the watery light of the TV in the living room while Jettie had been tossing and turning on the couch. She wished it had been him instead. She knew it had been his sons who had taunted the Willett Street boys and invaded their turf and invited violence to her house.

Go big, girl, Jettie thought suddenly.

It had been the thing Coral had said to Jettie all her life. When Jettie was small, she had laughed and clapped her little hands together when her mother said this, and as she grew, she took it to mean, "Go, big girl!" In later years, it had evolved into an affectionately sarcastic intonation that her mama used when Jettie fucked up bad and when she had quit school. Lately though, her mama's voice had been edged with urgency when she addressed Jettie's future.

"Go big, girl," Coral had said in her coarse rasp, her voice scraping Jettie's ears and causing them to burn. "Make something of this life. You can be better. Listen to your mama's sage tongue, now, Jeannetta."

But Jettie had not listened, and now she longed for Coral to grab her by the shoulders and tell her what to do next. Coral had been smarter than she looked, and the young neighborhood kids who had been observant enough to notice that had often sought her out for advice. She took her role as neighborhood mother seriously, never letting any of the kids see her bottles, pills, or roughhewn, rolled cigarettes lying about. When they would throw open the front door, she sent them on to the kitchen for a snack while she swept the cobwebs

of addiction away with a hand or a foot. Under the couch, under the rug. Then she sat the boy or girl down, angling her head forward until she looked him or her full in the eye.

Once, it had been Dobie Russell, the high-school junior who had been blessed at football, who had burst into the house in a full-on panic. Dobie insisted that God had just called him to the ministry, and he begged Coral to tell him that no, his life was bound for football. She hadn't been able to tell him to choose God or football; she told him to be the best Dobie he could be, whatever it took. She had never been one to follow her own advice, and she surprised herself with the words that spilled out and into the kids' ears. But years later, Dobie came home after a magical football career at Furman University. He had earned a degree in sociology to boot, and now he was the preacher of the big African Methodist Episcopal church out on Highway 64. Coral had always felt shell-shocked when she thought about it, but the neighborhood kids eyed her with respect and got her alone to seek her truths whenever they could.

Jettie smiled tightly at the memory and grabbed two black trash bags from the Glad box in the corner of the room and opened up the two dresser drawers she knew Coral used. With both hands, she crammed her mama's clothes in them and tried not to breathe the familiar scent of her. Jettie went through all Coral's pants and came away with two small white pills that she quickly popped in her mouth and washed down with the last of the liquor. She threw the shampoo bottle into the far corner and dropped its cap where she stood.

Jettie turned and surveyed the bed. Beside it, on the nightstand, Coral's water glass still bore the lacy webbing of the outline of her lip, in her signature shade of lipstick. The glass was half-empty. Jettie unscrewed the tops of the two bottles of bleach she'd found on the stoop, and poured them over the bloodstains on the bed. The brown blood was baked into the bottom sheet, and it stank of rot and death. Where the sheet was peeled back, the mattress was stained with blood as well as years of sweat, grime, and sex acts both consensual and not. The stench was replaced by the bleach's antiseptic tang. *Girls like us get washed away*, Jettie thought. She wanted to rub bleach all over her body and start all over on a different street with a different name, a different face, a different skin. Each splash of bleach, each swipe at the smear on the floor, felt like erasing the memory of her mama.

When the shots had crackled and echoed and the glass in the back window exploded, Jettie had sat up and met Leonidas's glittery, tired eyes. They both elbowed each other as they tripped down the hallway to the bedroom, and stopped short. Jettie flipped the light switch, and the naked bulb in the ceiling flickered to life. Leonidas vomited and backed out of the room. He had stumbled off into the night, and Jettie hadn't seen him since. She had not been able to take her eyes off of Coral, who looked somehow smaller in death in her already-shrunken frame. Jettie had felt stricken, but somewhere inside her she was relieved that something had finally happened to them, something that released the pall of dread that defined the days of their lives.

Jettie shook off the weight of the memory and scraped off the rest of the sheet, stuffing it in its own trash bag and gingerly pushing it through the shards of glass in the window. She found the mattress surprisingly light as she clambered over the bed frame with it and pushed it over the gritty tile floor and out the front door. She paused at the open door and looked back into the recesses of the house where she had lived with her mama. She couldn't think to take anything from the kitchen that she would use. Let Stoke deal with the mess in there.

Jettie pushed the mattress to the curb and let it fall, bloody side down. She went back in for the empty pail and bleach bottles and threw them in a pile beside it. She knew that when the city workmen arrived to pick up the mattress, they would pause, exchange a knowing glance, and snap on extra rubber gloves. *Another day, another one*, they would think, shaking their heads. *Careful not to touch it and catch anything from her blood; who knows what all she had.*

Jettie peered up and down the street, her vision fluid and cloudy. The neighbors stayed close to their curtains, peeking out occasionally, their stares cold and closed. There would be no cakes or casseroles, no ham beans in pots stirred by generations of mama- and granny-cooks. There would be no funeral day, no tears spilled, no preacher in staccato breath bidding the gates of heaven to open and "Lord God, please welcome our Coral."

Jettie felt the drugs she'd found in Coral's pocket finally take hold of her brain and started back up to sit on the stoop, out of the worst of the heat. *The pills*, she thought. Warm piss pooled between the fatty sacs at the tops of her thighs and ran down her legs. She was acutely aware of her jerky movements, like she was trying to walk through a swimming pool with only her head above water. She could even smell the chlorine, or something like it, a pungent odor stinging her nostrils and eyes. The sound of her breath punched out a thunderous rhythm in her head; she clawed at the skin on her forearm and pinched hard but felt nothing. She would never wear coral lipstick, or have a sage tongue that said all the things someone else needed to hear. Jettie watched the world turn upside down as she squinted toward Willett Street. She waited for Stoke, for God or anyone, to come and say to her, "Go big girl, go on now and get on out of here."

PRIDE AND PREJUDICED
Lacey Schmidt

I tried to stifle my tear before it hit my waffle. I stared down at the text from my mother, "Supreme Court recognized same-sex marriages. Heart. Smiley Face."

My wife was alarmed at my sudden change of affect, but I was too choked up to vocalize an explanation so I settled for passing the phone across the table.

Our eyes met.

I'd like to say unfettered joy crossed our faces and that we stood up and did a dance, but our prejudices ruined the moment.

We thought about holding hands but didn't.

We dashed the palms of our hands at the tears in our eyes while cautiously peering around us hoping no one would notice our odd behavior and ask if we were okay. We might be prejudiced and even occasionally hypocritical, but we're also both horrible liars and we know it. Don't ask after our welfare unless you want an honest answer, and on that day we were afraid (because of our prejudices) that an honest answer might get us lynched.

We were having breakfast at a Waffle House in Fayetteville, Arkansas, on our way to a lakeside cabin near Eureka Springs. I knew Eureka Springs was relatively hippie and LGBT tolerant, but we weren't there yet.

My wife bit her lip and gave me a smile.

She handed me back my phone and squeezed my fingers as our hands touched in the passing.

Our smiles trembled. *This was just too big to celebrate silently.*

I come from a long line (156 years back on the newly immigrated side of the family) of Texans. My wife comes from an even longer line of Texans. Parts of both of our families have been in America since 1690. In short, we live in our ancestors' ancestors' homeland; and neither of us was about to abandon our families and careers to move out of state any time soon—even if that was the only way to obtain legal recognition of our relationship our status as a family.

Sudden legal recognition of us as a family was momentous. Not because we or our family needed it to validate our relationship. In our eyes, and the eyes of our friends and family, we had already been married for over three years. We already had the illegal ceremony and marginally legal (if we don't talk about the city ordinances we broke) wedding reception. We had even already obtained a legal marriage certificate from Martin Luther King County in Seattle, Washington, while we were passing through for work (and where more friends than we knew we had in town showed up uninvited to the impromptu ceremony to celebrate it with us).

Legal recognition of our marriage in Texas was momentous for us, because it restored our faith in our homeland.

We were suddenly free to chase our dreams, buy a house, officially take care of each other's aging parents, and pay our taxes...as a couple (which meant paying more taxes by the way) in our ancestral homeland. We could have some of the same freedoms that our great, great, great, great grandparents came to these lands hoping to find and secure for their progeny.

Somehow it made me feel safer at home again.

But it didn't make me feel safer about expressing my love and happiness in a Waffle House in Fayetteville, Arkansas.

Of course, I have an excuse for that. *My prejudice prevented it.*

That morning when we wandered into the Waffle House, we were greeted by a spirited, balding Caucasian septuagenarian named Joe, who proclaimed himself to be a lay minister and witness to Jesus, "Blessing upon us and all strays."

As I said, I'm from Texas, and I'm no stranger to adamant fundamentalist Christians. I wasn't offended by Joe's strong expression of faith. I blessed him back, and we chatted about his life and the shared points of our faith for several minutes after he showed us to our table.

But I didn't give Joe the benefit of the doubt. I let my stereotype of adamant fundamentalist Christians convince me that Joe would be rabidly opposed to same-sex marriage as a sin and that he would want to tell me all about how I was bound for Hell rather than share our joy. And I let this prejudice convince me that everyone in that Waffle House would share this condemning attitude.

Fortunately, my tears did hit my waffle, and Joe did notice.

He bustled his way back to our table, slid into the booth next to me and asked the dreaded question, "Are you okay?" In my hesitation, he continued, "I'll pray right with you, whatever it is."

I thought he would find my answer nutty and offensive, but I had to be true. I told him we were just happy. Happy that our marriage of three years was finally legal everywhere in our great country.

Joe was so happy that he cried too. Then he thanked God for us with enough volume, enthusiasm and specificity for everyone to hear and understand... and people clapped. Then he sang a celebratory hymn and people joined in, including me.

I am ashamed that I did not sing with more courage with Joe in that Waffle House. I should have suspected better of Joe in Fayetteville.

I am sad that I didn't realize until after we left breakfast that the Waffle House was on MLK Street—I should have taken that as a sign from the universe probably. Joe and God wanted us to be proud of our love and to share the joy and light that love brings without fear born of prejudices. I should have already known that.

I believe this is America's greatness: that we can all so easily choose to know and love a great diversity of people.

And one lesson I have learned from my fortunate existence is that most people prize and share two primary objectives: to love and be loved. I strive to let this lesson always be my first prejudice now.

Coconut Heads
Bonnie Schell

Ten minutes into the concert by the New Jubilee Jazz Ensemble, my mother leaned her soft shoulder against mine. "Well, if I closed my eyes and just listened," she said, "I don't believe I could tell those boys were colored."

"They are good, aren't they?" I replied, immediately ashamed that she had trapped me, even in California where she had come from Atlanta for Christmas.

"I wish they'd do some of the old spirituals, and if they're going to travel around the country, they ought to have matching robes." The black choirs of my childhood had fifty members swaying in blue robes and white stoles. These Tennessee University students wore a mix of T-shirts, sports jackets, and light blue denim jeans.

"You mean those choirs that sang the we'll-be-rewarded-in-heaven-for-all-our-suffering-here lyrics?" I whispered to her. I confess that I too sometimes longed to hear the sweet bye-and-byes and River Jordan laments.

Instead, the director adjusted the amplification equipment, and the vocalists drifted into an a cappella piece of textured improvisation making a popping sound inside their cheeks. I looked around startled. It was the sound of something I had forgotten—heads swinging above mine. They hung by their hair from the roofs of lean-to stands up and down the highways of Georgia, Alabama, and Florida. Pop, pop percussion. Heads, coconut heads, clicking, drumming, thumping, together. My family always stopped at those stands to buy pralines and pecan logs as well as another coconut head for my uncle.

It was so like my mother, when we returned from the concert, not to mention my leaving before the reception to wait alone in the car. My mother had again leaned over to whisper after intermission, "That white woman on the end doesn't go with any of those black boys. I saw her showing someone a picture of her child; it's light as milk." She had been immensely pleased by her information.

Waiting for Mama, I rolled down the car window to let a welcome breeze blow across my face. Again, I heard the coconut heads banging. I hoped Mama, without me at her side, wouldn't assure the musicians that they were as good as her Methodist choir back home. Or did I slink out to avoid having my residual southern accent identified with hers?

When we returned to my apartment, Mama and I began making our traditional southern ambrosia for Christmas Day. No matter how far away I moved, she always arrived with her envelope of recipes and a hairy coconut.

"That little one who directed and played the electric piano was so cute!" she bubbled. "He jiggled his leg the whole time." She was happy. I almost smiled. A Ph.D. in ethnic musicology, the man was both the arranger and composer.

Mother segmented the oranges, slicing the pulp off the membranes. I hammered a large nail in the eyes of her small coconut, leaking out the milk. Then I put it in the oven, heating the head until it cracked. I cut out the meat where I could, peeled off the hard shell, and dug out the insides for grating.

"Mama," I asked her, "do you remember those coconut heads hanging by their hair along the highway?"

"No, I don't believe I know what you are talking about."

"Of course you do," I insisted. "When I was little, you said they were what became of bad black children when they grew up."

"I never said any such thing!"

I tried to get her to recall how the face was constructed. Not so round as the one we were using in our recipe. The forehead and eyes were sunken, perhaps chiseled out, so that the mouth and jaw jutted forward. Apelike. "Didn't they have old brown and yellow corn kernels for teeth? Eyes darkened with bootblack?"

"Children, dear, get things so confused."

"I always wanted one, but Daddy said no." My voice modulated to a childish whine. The truth is I did want one of my own to put in my bedroom, to help me conquer my fear of even sitting next to a darker skinned person. I first accomplished that in Arizona. And now I was terrified that somehow my clammy alabaster covering might smell like magnolias or chicken coops and give me away as the historical oppressor I did not want to be.

"Your daddy always stopped at those stands and bought your grandmother some divinity and pralines. In those places, they were the best to be had. Louisiana brown sugar, I'd imagine."

"Who do you think made those heads, Mama?"

I persisted. "There aren't any coconut trees in Georgia, Mama. Maybe Florida? Where did the coconuts come from?"

Finally, she answered with one tainted word—"YANKEES."

"Yankees?" I was incredulous.

"Why, yes. You don't think we made those ugly things, do you? Or those ceramic statues of darkies eating watermelons? Yankees sent that stuff down south for other Yankees on vacation who bought them as novelties, thinking they had a specimen of southern culture."

I had counseled myself that on this particular visit, I would remain calm and not upset my mother. We had always grated on each other's nerves, but she had spent a lot of money to fly to California.

Mama passed a hot cup of coffee across the base of my neck. I moved aside to let her take over the sink duties. Standing behind her I stared at the pink scalp and fine soft grey hair. I loved her. I could picture her head hanging by that sparse hair over a dirt road next to my head and those of all my relatives. Together we made a rhythm section for the Jubilee Jazz Ensemble. Mother and I have a look of surprise, our brown eyes wide on Christmas Eve, our kernel teeth exposed. "Mama," I asked, "do you remember Aunt Euphoria's collection of vines, Wandering Jew, sweet potato and Vinca all over the backside of her breezeway?"

"She had a nervous breakdown, your Aunt Euphoria."

"And Uncle Freeman taunted her by pulling back on one of the coconut heads hanging from the ceiling, then letting it swing against her pots and suspended what-nots, just so Aunt Euphoria would scream."

"Freeman never broke anything." Mama always defended her brother. "It's the Chinese conversion trick. The pots in the middle don't move. It only seemed like the end of the world. Everything was alright."

"I was always afraid everything would come crashing down," I said. Was that why I left home to go as far away as possible?

"Your Uncle Freeman was only playing. Children don't always understand adult diversions," she said.

"So, you remember the coconut heads?" I was chopping pear and pineapple.

"Of course I do."

"Mama," I ventured, "don't you think it would be hard to grow up thinking well of yourself with coconut head caricatures displayed all up and down the highways?"

"Why should it, dear?" Her voice was gentle, then conspiratorial. "They weren't supposed to resemble what you call the African Americans, you know."

"Then who, Mama?"

"Native Americans. They were supposed to be Indian scalps. The reason all those tribes disappeared is mostly because they killed each other off. I thought you knew that."

I took the grated coconut out of the refrigerator.

There was a lot I had forgotten

We mixed the white meat and the fruit. Mama added some chopped dates. We sprinkled on the powdered sugar.

"This is the dessert of the gods, nothing better," Mama said with a wistful voice. "We always had it with pound cake in the old days."

"I wasn't born then, was I? I don't remember Ambrosia being this much trouble to make. It's good of you to come to see me and show me how, Mama."

I might never see her again. I would never make Ambrosia for my friends, but I would forever hear the rhythm of those coconut heads hanging above my small self.

SHE CAME TO STAY
Haley Fedor

This peanut butter was never coming off her feet. There was so much of it. The bathtub's spigot was blasting hot water, and Kira stuck her right foot under until it came out a blistery, lobster red. The biggest chunks of greasy peanut butter had fallen off and were swirling around the drain. Kira wiped at the gunk still stuck to her sole with a washcloth. She'd have to do laundry later, or Pap would notice. At eleven o'clock, she figured he was probably snoozing in his armchair in the den over a *M*A*S*H* rerun, so she had until morning to finish. And wipe up the gooey footprints on the hall carpet. The entire house smelled like peanut butter, she was sure.

Maybe she shouldn't have accepted a gig from a guy with the username *Mr. SmoothB87*, especially since he'd only clocked twenty paid minutes of her time. That meant she'd covered her feet in peanut butter for thirty bucks. Next time she'd make sure he got a thirty-minute slot at the very least; this was too much of a hassle to do again for less than fifty.

Even when the peanut butter was gone from that foot, it was still impossibly oily. Kira's foot gleamed in the yellowed bathroom light. Her left foot was still planted on the bathroom mat, keeping her balanced on the thin porcelain lip. The mat would have to be cleaned, too. Kira rinsed the washcloth in the jet of water, burning her hands in the process. It was too hot, but the water temperature in Pap's house was either boiling hot or freezing. She rubbed soap on her foot, noticing with dismay that the peanut butter was already starting to clog the drain.

The bathroom door swung open, and her grandfather walked in.

"Why in the hell is there peanut butter all over the carpet?" he asked.

For a moment, all Kira could do was stare at her grandfather in horror. She was only wearing a lacy bra and underwear. The ones that were sheer white. The ones that were now wet and see-through.

"You know what? I actually don't want to know. Are you alone? In your room?" Pap looked away from her and around the door, as if there was someone lurking behind his moldy bathrobe on the hook.

"There's no one else here," Kira said quickly, grabbing the towel from the toilet seat to cover herself. "Please get out!"

He obliged, but stayed behind the closed door. "Are you going to clean this up? I'm too old to be on my hands and knees, dammit."

"I will, I promise!"

Kira felt her heart pounding in embarrassment and fear. She could hear him swearing and muttering under his breath as he walked away. Then she heard the creak of her bedroom door opening, as Pap checked in there for any participants in her peanut butter-covered shame.

She *definitely* wouldn't do this again for less than a thirty-minute block. At least Pap was so deaf that he couldn't hear her when she was on the webcam talking to customers. Before Mr. Smooth, she had been paid to berate some guy and talk shit about his one-inch penis. She made fun of it, calling it an over-sized clit and not worth any woman's time. Kira felt nothing when she looked at the tiny, stubby thing, but she didn't feel anything from any other dicks she saw while working. They were all weird and gross, some circumcised and some not.

Kira could talk the way they wanted her to talk, though. She just hoped her girlfriend didn't mind that she did webcam stuff for horny men. She would tell Angie at some point, but it wouldn't be until after she'd saved up enough money. They'd only been dating for a few weeks, and this was definitely too weird to bring up so soon.

Shifting to the back of the tub, Kira grabbed the handicap rail on the wall and hoisted her left foot under the spout. Installed after her grandmother's fall, one of the few reminders that she'd ever lived here. The porcelain dogs—all Dalmatians, for some reason—and decorative dishes filled with toffee from her childhood were gone. The front parlor was dusty, and Pap's den, the heart of the house, was full of old newspapers he said would be important someday. Kira couldn't remember the newspapers or any other junk Pap collected before her grandmother's Alzheimer's.

When she came out of the bathroom, Kira could hear the television on in the den. She ran into her room, dodging the peanut butter footprints in the hallway. There was a text from Angie as her phone beeped, but she ignored it and threw on pajama pants and a shirt. She had to get the hallway carpet cleaned up before Pap went to bed, or else he would yell at her again. He might already be rethinking his offer to let her stay until she took the GED. It was still two months away, so Kira had to be good.

An hour later, Kira slipped out the front door, wincing when the hinges protested loudly. She hated sneaking out to smoke when it was this cold. Back home, her mother hadn't cared about her smoking, or at least didn't say anything about smoking out of her window. Not that it wasn't as cold in Mingo Junction right now. Kira had only flung herself so far as to get out of Ohio. Pap's house was in Benwood, out in the middle of nowhere, West Virginia. There was nothing to do here, not unless you had a car and could drive to the next town over.

Her naked hands trembled to try and light the cigarette. The weather website said it was fourteen degrees tonight. As soon as the cigarette was lit, her free hand jammed the lighter in her coat pocket and stayed there.

It was pretty, though.

From the covered porch, she could see the heavy snowfall without getting wetly assaulted. The snow wasn't quiet. It was building up on tree branches and plopping off in big heaps. When falling in thick drapes like tonight, the snow ticked against the thick maple trees, giving them a blasted look on one side. The slenderest of branches were already groaning under the weight. When the ice formed, the air would be thick with sharp cracks of wood exploding, unable to survive in frigid stillness.

There was too much snow to see the sky, she noticed. It was falling pretty rapidly. They'd likely get more than a few inches by morning. Not bad enough to call a blizzard, this storm was calmer, quieter in its intensity.

Kira pulled the cracked phone out of her jacket pocket. Her thumb kept shaking and couldn't catch on the line to flip it open. There were different types of air in winter, and this kind really stung. At least she was standing out of the wind and most of the snow. The front porch had the best cell reception, and Kira would always be in danger of losing service in her bedroom. Using the landline to call Angie might invite too many questions. Squinting to look at the cracked screen, she read Angie's text.

Are you watching the snow?

It was nice to know they were both looking at the same thing. Angie was probably caught up in how pretty it looked, not thinking about anything else.

Yea. If it snows too much I can't make the show, she texted Angie, laboring over the keypad and pressing numbers several times in rapid motions. Pap was nice enough to let her use his car sometimes. The '98 Buick Regal wouldn't make it down the hill in weather like this, let alone to Wheeling.

Kira finished the text and sent it, snapping the phone shut and shoving it back into her pocket.

This was one of those drug dealer's phones. A drop phone. But it was all she could afford. Kira preferred that Angie message her online, so it would save her minutes, but Ange always forgot when she was excited about something. The last time it was for a laser light show in the city at the last minute, and Angie had included so many exclamation points that it split into two separate texts. Kira could never hold it against Angie, but she was running out of minutes. Her girlfriend sure was easily pleased.

Her girlfriend. That had such an odd ring to it, Kyra was always surprised and delighted by the way it sounded on her tongue.

The snow muffled sounds for miles around, and Kira felt like she was truly alone. There weren't cars squealing by, or dogs barking. It was nice to just listen to the echoes of small sounds enhanced by snow. Pap's property was pretty isolated, too. Benwood's few residents all lived pretty spread out. There was too much farmland out here for her liking. Back home, everything was kind of dirty in a well-worn way. Mingo seemed to be caught in mid-exhale, breathing out the bad air and poised to intake the new. Her mother told her that when the mill was running in the seventies, no one could keep their cars or houses clean from the red ore dust. God help anyone in those row houses who strung laundry out at the wrong time of day.

No one here had to worry about ore dust, just wild animals getting into gardens. Benwood was boring.

The phone buzzed in Kira's pocket.

You have to, it's the only nite they're in town, the text read. Before she could reply, another message appeared.

I can pick you up, I got me some snow tires, Angie wrote.

Kira hesitated. She wasn't sure about that. Pap was letting her stay here, but it had only been three weeks. He knew why her mom kicked her out, but she didn't want to do anything else to make him regret taking her in. Not after this peanut butter incident.

Kira couldn't stay with Angie; her parents didn't know about their daughter's sexuality and it had to stay that way. Kira's aunts and uncles all agreed with her mother's decision and wouldn't take her. This job helped her afford a phone and pay for necessities, but shit all besides that.

Maybe, Kira typed slowly.

She sent it and stubbed the cigarette out on the metal porch siding. It left an angry soot mark. Kira would have to clean that up later, or Pap would have another fit. But it was too cold for her to care right now.

The house phone was ringing when she came back inside.

"Don't answer it!" Pap called from the hall. That was code for: *Your mother is calling*. Grace had been doing this every single day since Kira had showed up at the bus station with a duffel bag and backpack.

The phone rang until the voicemail kicked in.

First there was silence.

"Dad? Are you there?" Grace's voice filled the space of the room, oppressive yet stifled, like she was doing something else at the same time or was holding something back.

"Dad, I know you're there, pick up. You're enabling this sick shit, and someone is going to get hurt, ya hear me?"

Pap glared at the phone.

"Don't listen to her nonsense," he said, talking over the recording.

"If you're going to fight for faggots now, that means you're turnin' away from the cause of God and truth," Grace declared. "And I have tried to warn you, but you're dragging this family down into sin with it. You *and* her."

So Kira was just "her" now.

Pap hurried into the kitchen. Kira stared after him for a moment, until she heard the sound of the blender motor whirring, obscuring her mother's voice completely. When he stopped, the voicemail recording ended and beeped to announce that the machine held a message.

While Kira was shrugging off her coat and putting it on the hook, Pap came back into the room and pressed buttons on the answering machine. An automated voice asked him if he wanted to erase the message, and he jabbed another button in confirmation. When he turned back to Kira as if to ask her something, the phone began ringing again. Grace was a stubborn woman, and she left at least one of those voicemails every night.

"Are these your jeans on top the washer?" Pap yelled over the noise. "They're bedazzled on the ass, so they're not mine!"

"Yeah, they're mine."

He held up the jeans and Kira was filled with an uncontrollable sense of loathing, looking at the ugly mommy jeans with their silver, fluttery stitching on the back pockets.

Kira wished they didn't belong to her. Every now and then she went on clothing websites and looked at the men's section longingly. Cargo shorts, polos, and baggy pants. Kira could only imagine pants that didn't cling to and dimple beneath her ass.

Clothes were expensive.

After a moment of hesitation, Kira took the offending jeans. "Thanks, Pap."

"You cleaned up all o' that peanut butter?" Pap asked. His voice was softer, and it said he knew that she already did.

"Yeah, I got it. You don't need to worry about it." Kira was planning on steam cleaning the carpet in the hallway tomorrow for good measure.

"Do I need to know why you put peanut butter on your feet in your undies?"

"Nope." He really, really didn't.

"Good. Don't make a habit of it," Pap said.

"I won't, I promise," Kira said immediately. Next time she would leave a towel in her room, at the very least.

"All right. I'm going to bed, so I'll see you tomorrow. Not too late, okay?"

"I won't stay up too late," Kira agreed.

He had gotten up to go to the bathroom several nights in a row now, and complained that she left all of the lights on. Kira was just glad he hadn't barged into her room that late, because she was almost always working. He also complained about how late she slept. But sometimes she was up until four in the morning. How could she get up before nine o'clock and be functional?

Her grandfather padded back down the hall, towards the kitchen and pantry where the laundry machines were kept. Kira sprayed air freshener in the hall so there wouldn't be any questions about the lingering smell of cigarettes.

There was a text from Angie when she checked her phone safely in her room. Kira hoped her reply would send in here.

Do you not want me to come pick you up? Is it your grandpa?

Angie knew she was living with her Pap, but that was about it. Kira didn't want to bog Angie down with all of her family problems. They had met online, and Kira worried about appearing needy by sharing too much, too soon.

Let's see what the snow looks like tomorrow. Gotta go back to work, Kira sent back. The text seemed to go through, surprisingly.

Hopefully there wouldn't be too much snow on the ground, and she could ask to borrow Pap's old Buick. It was a maroon boat, but it was comfortable. Kira liked that it had volume controls for the stereo on the wheel. It would take at least half an hour to get to Wheeling, depending on what the roads were like.

Taking off the various layers she'd put on to go outside, Kira crawled onto the bed and opened her laptop. She was glad Pap agreed to upgrade their internet service, on the condition that she pay for part of the bill.

Kira shook her long, dark hair out of its ponytail, trying to look less frozen as she turned on her webcam and logged in. Her profile lit up green showing that she was online. The man with the tiny penis had already left a comment on her profile, telling her how great she was and that he'd be back in the future. That didn't take long.

A member — she restricted her profile to members only — logged into her chat. He had a username she'd never seen, telling her she was pretty. His image was slightly unfocused from some kind of delay, probably from a shitty connection. What was the point if all he could see were pixelated bits? He had short dark hair and was shirtless, that much she could tell.

Why do u do this? Do u need the money? Send me ur email, I can help.
Ah. One of those.

Kira occasionally got what was called a "white knight." Some guys got off on visiting cam sites and offering to take care of the women they found. She was willing to bet this guy had already made the same offer to someone else this week, if not tonight. Kira started typing the standard canned line about the website filtering out anything that looked like an email address, as it was against policy.

Do u do paid video chat?

Her profile clearly stated that she did, but they dickered for a few minutes about the price and time slot. The white knight was deterred pretty easily. He was eager to see the rest of her — unpaid chat was waist up, tits tucked away — but her bra didn't leave much to the imagination. His webcam feed seemed to freeze, and she saw him lean forward as though to fix something.

I want to see u.

For a moment, she froze. The image cleared and the dark-haired man was actually much closer to her in age than she'd previously thought. He also looked eerily like Tommy Bresnik from middle school. The same Tommy who had cut off her ponytail with scissors in sixth grade and called her dumb and other names when she joined the cheerleading team.

The walls behind him were blank, and his expression eager. This man had a hungry look to him. Maybe it wasn't sexual excitement, but recognition.

Panicking, Kira exited the chat and closed her laptop. A million people on the internet, and she gets Tommy Bresnik at her cam job? No way. Getting up, Kira paced around the room and kept looking at the laptop like it would follow her.

Maybe mom told other people, she thought. Maybe everyone back home thought she was a slut. How could she know whether or not her mother said anything?

Kira suddenly needed another cigarette. She contemplated pulling on all of those clothes again so soon, but it was too much trouble. Plus, if Pap heard her going out every half hour he would *definitely* say something.

The following evening, Kira tugged the collar of her button up shirt nervously in front of the mirror. This was only their third official date. Angie grew up closer to the city and was going to Chatham, a fancy, private women's college. Kira was a little intimidated by her, already so sure about who she was and what she wanted.

Angie's parents didn't know, though. Kira was just "a friend, from work." It was stressful, having to remember so many lies. But at least Angie was staying in the dorms, so she didn't have to worry about keeping up appearances when she went to visit.

Kira piled her long, dark hair under the cap. She wanted to shave it, but she didn't want to have to buy a wig for work. There weren't really any butch strippers on the site.

Not that she didn't still think about it.

Kira buckled the large, thick belt, and took a step back. The button-up shirt was purple, but it was the butchest thing she owned.

Her jawline was too severe, her ears stuck out too far. Angie would take one look at her and laugh. In a moment of panic, she thought about putting on one of the old church dresses left in her closet. But this was a concert, not some Bible study ice cream social. She felt like a sack of potatoes in dresses, anyway.

Kira hustled out of her room and slipped into her boots, hoping she didn't look like a fool. The thought of Angie laughing at her made her cheeks hot with embarrassment.

"Are you goin' out?"

"Yeah, I'm going to see a concert with Angie," Kira said, turning to see Pap emerge from the kitchen with a beer. She spoke quickly to try and gloss over Angie's name, almost like it was an afterthought. Kira would have lied about her plans if she'd been at her mom's. She felt the instinct to lie about it here, with Pap, like it was a chalky aftertaste on the breadth of her tongue, the backs of her teeth. Kira didn't want to lie to him, though.

"But you're coming back?"

Kira stopped adjusting her purse. Pap was looking away from her, staring instead at a fixed point on the wood panels in the hall as though it were suddenly fascinating.

"Of course I am." She would've smiled at him if he were looking.

"Y'know, you can invite your friend in for a beer, after," he said.

"She's my age, Pap. We're not twenty-one yet."

"I'm not a narc," Pap said with a shrug, downing a hard swallow of his preferred pilsner.

"Thanks, Pap." It meant a lot to her, but she didn't know what else to say.

Pap just patted her shoulder with his free hand, before returning to the kitchen.

Contemplating a smoke, Kira heard a car horn, followed by the crunch of gravel in the driveway. She zipped up her coat and said goodbye to Pap, before stepping outside and feeling very ungraceful. The snow slowed her movements, and Kira had to feel more than watch for concealed patches of ice along the path.

"Thanks for coming," Kira said, opening the door of the Jeep. "I hope you found the house all right."

"I had to hire a guide," Angie told her, laughing. She leaned over to the passenger side when Kira got in, pressing soft lips to her cheek. Kira looked back up at the house and saw curtains move.

"What time is the show?" she asked.

"Shit. Soon. We'll be late if we don't leave now," Angie told her.

Kira watched her pull away and crane her neck to begin backing out of the long, winding driveway.

"They're a pretty cool band, and I think you'll like them," Angie said over her shoulder.

"What're they called again?" It was a band Angie really liked. Kira didn't really care who they saw, but Angie liked to get caught up in the details.

"Garbled City."

She had no idea who they were. Kira probably wouldn't like their music, but it didn't matter. All she could think about was Angie's small, warm hand sliding up her thigh. It stayed there, content for a minute, before turning on the radio. There were no other cars on the road, but it seemed like most folks would rather stay inside on a night like tonight.

Angie said something and she missed it, caught up in looking at the darkness and the blurred side-mirror.

"You look pretty handsome," Angie told her. "I can't believe you fit all that hair under your hat." She laughed a little too loudly as the radio dropped into static, searching in vain for another station. They were in the no man's land before the suburbs started cropping up. Kira hoped this band was worth the long drive.

"I can't believe how gorgeous you look tonight," Kira said at last, glancing over and looking away quickly. Angie had long honey-brown hair that cascaded over everything in waves.

"Maybe you can persuade me to leave the show early."

Angie took Kira's hand and drew it to her lips, kissing and then sucking on a finger. Her car was the best place they had to be alone together.

The din of a train horn struck a midnight absolute. They must be near the water. Kira felt like a bat at the narrowing end of a tunnel. If the road changed from rubble to the smoothness of glazed tarmac, she didn't notice. They were getting closer but the radio still searched in static futility. It was too cold to think straight. It made Kira feel sluggish, tired of caring about how cold her feet and fingers were. She should've worn gloves.

Angie grabbed her hand again and held it for warmth. Kira's knuckles were lily white. She knew she squeezed too hard, but Angie let her do it.

It would be over if Angie knew about her job or what her family was like, Kira was sure. She held onto the other girl's hand, trying to not let herself get worked up about it.

"I'm glad you're here," Angie said at last.

"Me, too."

By the time they pulled up to Pap's house, it took a few seconds of looking at the vehicle parked behind the Buick for it to register. The big black truck with monstrous tires and a Jesus fish on the rear bumper belonged to her mom.

"Oh, no."

"What's wrong?" Angie asked.

"My mom's here. You better get out of here," Kira said quickly.

The front door slammed open, so loud that it echoed with a crack, like the snapping of frozen tree limbs. Out strode a large, tall woman with a white parka and graying hair. They could hear her yelling indistinctly all the way up the drive. Kira tried to unfasten her seatbelt to get out and intercept her mother.

"What's going on?" Angie asked, her eyes wide.

Kira saw her turn off the car and finger the pepper spray on her keyring. She couldn't say anything; her jaw was clenched so tight that her teeth hurt. She got out of the car and shut the door before Angie could say anything else.

"You're over here, living in sin right under your grandfather's nose?" Kira's mother demanded.

"I—I haven't done anything," Kira said, hating how small her voice sounded.

"I have been calling for *weeks*, and here you are, lying to him and taking advantage of him." Grace bore down on her daughter with an intensity barely muted by the marshmallow puffiness of the parka.

"I am not!" Kira said defensively, feeling numb.

"I said you leave her alone, dammit!" Pap was coming outside next, struggling to put on his long coat.

"She's manipulating you! Making you complicit in her sinful lifestyle."

Grace grabbed Kira by the collar of her jacket, yanking her closer. Kira felt numb and helpless as she was dragged, the wet snow seeping into her socks. On instinct, she flinched. She wanted to melt right into the snow and disappear.

That was when her mother clocked her in the jaw.

Kira was lying on her back in the snow, seeing the dark tops of trees and the cloudy night sky. Her ears were ringing, but when they cleared, Pap and her mom were yelling. When she stood up, she saw Angie was a few feet away, her eyes bright with fear.

"Are you okay?" Angie asked. Kira saw her look back and forth between Pap and her mom, expression worried.

"I'm fine," Kira mumbled.

"She's bleeding," Pap insisted, looking at her. He walked closer to Kira, tilting her jaw back to examine the wetness on her lip.

"She'll get more than that from Satan in the fires of hell," her mother insisted. Grace's fists were red and clenched, and Kira worried that she might hit Angie, too.

"Get the hell away from her!" Angie said, but she didn't move closer to try and intercept them. The heat of Grace's rage was palpable, and for a split second Kira had the urge to grab Angie's hand and run, down the snowy driveway and towards—where? There was nowhere to go.

"Is this another one of your whore friends?" Grace demanded. "Do you know what she does, Dad? Stripping in front of a camera online for money?"

"Stop it!" Kira screamed.

Her voice shook and she took another step back, eyeing those meaty fists. Her eyes clouded with tears, and she couldn't look at Angie.

"I don't give a shit what she does," Pap said angrily. He stepped between them and slapped her mother. "Your mother would be rolling in her fuckin' grave if she saw this, right here on the damn lawn!" His jaw squared in determination, he slapped her mother again.

Kira could only watch, stunned, as Grace took a step back, the color draining from her face. Her mother never stopped for *anyone* before.

"You get outta here, because I have to take on your responsibilities and raise your own damn child. Don't you ever come back here, y'hear?" Pap's jaw worked unconsciously, like he had a wad of chew in and was fixing to spit.

"You move your car so this asshole can get out of my driveway, before I call the police," Pap told Angie. Her girlfriend—was she still her girlfriend?—jumped to do just that. Kira worried that, once in the car, Ange would just keep going and not look back. She'd want away from this mess if their positions were reversed.

Pap placed a protective arm around Kira's shoulders while her mother simply stared at them.

"Are you deaf? Get the fuck off my property," Pap spat. "You have two minutes to get in that flashy hunk of junk and leave, before I call the cops."

Kira watched in stunned amazement as her mother backed away. No one had ever cowed her mother like that before, at least not that *she'd* ever seen.

There was a flurry of motion as Angie backed her Jeep out of the driveway, allowing the outlandish truck—and her mother—to back out and speed away in a puff of exhaust. To Kira's surprise, Angie returned, parking hastily before getting out.

"Are you okay?" Angie asked, coming over and taking Kira's hand in hers.

"Come inside, both of you, so I can check out that cut on your lip," Pap said. "I'm sorry you had to see that. Angie, was it? My daughter's a real cunt."

Angie stopped for a moment, surprised. But then she smiled, and let out a deep, musical laugh.

"It's okay. I have aunts and uncles like that, all hopped up on Jesus," Angie said.

"My condolences," Pap told her. He started to walk back to the front door, waving for the both of them to join him.

Angie laughed again, and pulled Kira by the hand to follow him inside.

It was a beautiful laugh, and Kira loved everything about Angie in that moment, even forgetting the blossoming pain on her cheek and jaw.

PEARL ON SATURDAY NIGHT
Tom Ray

Dwayne was wearing his Mackinaw coat, wool cap, and cotton work gloves against the November cold. As he walked along Broad Street, the main highway through Draketon, Tennessee, he would turn and stick out his thumb when he heard a car approaching. He'd walked a little over a mile when a brand-new Dodge pickup truck stopped.

"Where you goin', buddy?" Music was playing on the truck's radio.

"'Bout ten miles outside of town."

"Sounds like you're goin' to Cotton's for a beer."

"I'm going to Cotton's, but I don't drink. I'm going to pick up a friend in some trouble."

"Get in. Glad to help a guy helpin' a friend."

Dwayne climbed in. The driver, an old man in overalls and with a railroader's cap over his gray hair, had the heater cranked up full blast. It felt good, coming in out of the cold.

The old man said, "Where do you work?"

"I'm a minister. I have a little church up by Owenby, the Owenby Gospel Church. I also broadcast a service every Saturday morning at seven thirty." He gave the radio station call sign.

"A preacher hitchhiking to Cotton's of a Saturday night. All the way from Owenby?"

"I'm also cashier at Bowden's Cafeteria. I just got off work there."

"Bowden's. I've eat there once or twice. Not bad."

After they'd listened to the *Grand Ol' Opry* for a while, the old man said, "You ain't got a car?"

"Fuel pump's shot. I'm waiting to get it fixed."

"So you're gonna drive your friend's car?"

"No, sir, she don't have a car."

"If you ain't got a car, how're you gonna help your friend?"

"The Lord will provide me a way to get her home."

"You got a lot of faith." The old man chuckled.

"He sent me you, didn't He?"

The old man laughed. "You got me there, son. I reckon He did."

When the old man pulled into the bar's parking lot, Dwayne had a faint hope he would offer to wait for him, but the old man just said, "There you are, son. Good luck to you."

"Thank you, sir. If you ever are in need of a church, come out and see us at the Owenby Gospel Church, right on the Nashville Highway in Owenby."

"I sure will."

Dwayne was dreading going into the bar. Whenever he picked Pearl up at Cotton's there was always a fight. People would be mad at her for cursing them, spreading out on the bar to take up too much room, and just being a nuisance. They'd be mad at Dwayne for being her friend. He was a natural target for bullies anyway, being middle-aged, short, and pudgy, with thick glasses.

Walking through the parking lot he caught sight of Pearl, sitting outside on the ground next to the front stoop. She was slumped forward, her legs extended straight out in front of her, one hand in her lap, the other on the ground. She wore white vinyl boots that came up over her calves, a bright blue mini-skirt, a white wool sweater with a scoop neck, and a gray synthetic fur jacket. A white vinyl pocketbook hung from her neck. The holes in her stockings exposed the red, chapped skin of her knees, and her skinny thighs with varicose veins. The low neck of her sweater showed the splotchy skin of her upper chest with its prominent ribs. Her wrinkled face and stringy, white hair didn't match her red lipstick, white boots, and mini-skirt. She was staring at the ground beyond her feet and talking to herself.

"Pearl?"

She didn't answer, but continued mumbling in her deep, raspy voice.

"Come on, Pearl, let's get off this cold ground."

She still ignored him, nodding her head from time to time to emphasize a point to someone who wasn't there.

He took her arm and tried to pull her up, but she jerked it away. "Get your goddamn hands off me."

"Pearl, it's Dwayne," he said. He hoped she was alert now, but she lapsed back into mumbling.

He heard a George Strait song playing on the jukebox as the door of the bar opened. Two men came out talking to each other as they headed to the other side of the parking lot. He looked at them as they walked away, and called out, "Larry!"

One man slowed down, but didn't look back, and resumed his pace.

"Larry, can you help us here?" This time he used his sermon voice, pushing a strong, plaintive, gravelly call out from his belly and into the darkness.

Larry, a kid who attended the state technical university in Draketon, stopped and looked back. He worked at the radio station where Dwayne broadcasted on Saturday mornings. Larry started walking back toward him. The other man, who appeared to be a student like Larry, came with him.

Larry was wearing corduroys, a turtleneck sweater, and a windbreaker. The other kid had on dark trousers, a plaid shirt, brown leather jacket, and a beret. Larry's brown hair was long. The other kid's hair was dark blond, cut short, and he wore a thin mustache.

"What's up, Dwayne?"

He was relieved that Larry remembered him. They only saw each other once a week, at the station. Larry collected the money from the preachers, and made sure they didn't exceed their allotted time in the broadcast booth. He wasn't stuck up as bad as some college kids, although he was distant with the preachers who came to the station.

"My car's busted, Larry. Can you help me get this poor old thing home?"

Larry hesitated for a second. Both he and his friend were carrying grocery bags under their arms. They must have bought beer at Cotton's, where the bartender didn't ask kids for proof of age. Finally Larry said, "All right. Let me bring my car around." He started back across the parking lot. The other kid stayed back with Dwayne and Pearl.

"My name's Jim." He stuck his hand out. Dwayne, squatting on the ground next to Pearl, reached up and shook hands.

"Hi, Jim. My name is Dwayne, and this here woman is Pearl."

"Howdy, Pearl. How you doin' tonight?" Pearl didn't look up or say anything. "Must be cold on the ground there, Pearl." Jim's tone was mocking.

Larry pulled up in an old Ford 4-door sedan. He parked with the back passenger-side door facing Pearl, got out, opened the door, and waited.

"She won't stand up, Larry, and I can't pick her up. Bad back."

"What's the matter, preacher? Won't Jesus help you pick me up? Goddamn cocksuckin' preacher." Her voice was clear and distinct now. Dwayne was ashamed of Pearl's cursing.

Larry pursed his lips like he was irritated, but he walked to Pearl's side. "Give me a hand here," he said to Jim.

When they began raising Pearl, one on each side of her, she gave a loud scream. The boys stopped with Pearl suspended off the ground. Her screech was frightening, but they recovered. Larry said "Come on!" They maneuvered her onto the seat.

"Oh, Lord God, what are you doing to me? You're killing me!" After she was seated with her feet on the ground, Jim stepped back and Larry put both hands under her knees and swiveled her around so her legs were in the car. "Why are you doing this to me, Dwayne? You're killing me. Help! Help! I'm being murdered!"

Two men in work uniforms were coming out of the parking lot and heading for the stoop of Cotton's. Looking at Dwayne and the others, they laughed as they went inside. Dwayne rolled down Pearl's window, and slammed and locked the door quickly.

Larry went around to the driver's side and said over the top of the car, "You want to come, Jim?"

"Yeah, what the hell. If you'll bring me back here to get my car."

Larry said okay and got behind the wheel, while Dwayne got in beside Pearl, and Jim got in the front passenger's seat.

Larry said, "Where're we going?"

"Head into town." It was better to give directions a little bit at a time. If Larry knew how far they had to go, he might balk.

They'd just gotten back on the highway when Pearl made a low retching sound. Dwayne knew that if she vomited in Larry's car he'd throw them out for sure. "Come on, Pearl," he said in a low voice. He'd rolled the window down before they started because he knew there was a good chance she'd be getting sick during the trip. Now he pushed her head toward the window, and she, miraculously, climbed up so her knees were on the seat and her head and shoulders hung out of the window. He held her by the bottom of her jacket to keep her from falling out. Her retching became louder. He couldn't tell if anything was coming up.

"We'd better pull over, Larry, and let her empty out her stomach." He didn't want to suggest that, but he was afraid she might slip from his grip and fall out of the window.

Larry didn't say anything, but pulled over on the shoulder. Dwayne lowered Pearl so her belly rested on the seat and her head hung out the open door. She moaned slightly and began retching again. Some beer came out, then nothing more, but she kept retching.

"Do you have a Coke?"

"Just beer," Larry said.

"She don't need any more of that. Give her a minute."

She finally stopped, and became quiet. He raised her up and closed the door. "All right, Larry. Let's go." He wiped off her mouth with his handkerchief.

The car moved back onto the highway and proceeded on toward town. Pearl was quiet, and the two boys didn't say anything. At the city limits Larry said, "Which way?"

"Just keep going straight."

They passed through downtown and reached the city limit on the other side of town, where Route 70-N stopped being Broad Street and became the Nashville Highway. Larry said, "Where are we going, Dwayne?" He sounded angry.

"Just keep going straight. I'll tell you when to turn." Larry didn't say anything more to Dwayne. He and Jim started talking to each other in low voices, about a party they were going to. As long as they were talking to each other they might not notice how far they were travelling.

Jim raised his voice, "How you doin', Pearl?" He was making fun of her again.

"She's sleeping." He wanted to tell Jim to be quiet, so as not to wake her, but decided it was better not to say anything more.

"She must be tired. I was waiting on the bartender to sell me some beer, and she was in there raising hell. The bartender was always having to tell her to shut up and leave the other customers alone. That's why he finally put her outside." Jim was laughing as he said this.

"She's had a lot of rough times. You can't judge her by the way she is now."

Jim just laughed again. Dwayne wondered what Larry was thinking, sitting behind the wheel, saying nothing.

Jim said, "How do you guys know each other?"

Dwayne couldn't think of how to answer. He didn't want to say anything that would embarrass Larry, who finally said, "Dwayne has a broadcast on the station."

"So you're a preacher, Dwayne?"

"Yes sir, I have that honor."

"On the radio."

"Yes sir."

Jim let that rest a while before saying, "My grandmother watches that bastard Oral Roberts all the time. She can hardly pay her rent, and that son of a bitch tells her to send him money. He's rich as hell, and he's sucking that old lady dry."

Larry and Dwayne didn't say anything.

"You hear what I said?"

"Yeah. I'm sorry Brother Roberts has caused you pain. I'm not of his faith." Dwayne faltered as he spoke. "I don't ask anybody to give me love offerings if they can't afford it." He felt guilty answering Jim that way. He didn't tell donors to give only what they could afford when he asked for money in church or on the radio, but he hoped people understood that's what he meant for them to do. Anyway, he wasn't raking in big money like the preachers on TV.

"I bet. Do you cure people?"

"I don't lay on hands, if that's what you mean. I just try to bring some peace to troubled souls."

"Like old Pearl here."

"Yes, like Sister Pearl."

Larry said, "Leave him alone," speaking low. Maybe Larry didn't want Dwayne to hear him, but he heard.

"You asked me to come along," Jim said, in a loud voice Dwayne was sure to hear.

They went on for another half an hour, nobody saying much, until Dwayne said, "You're going to be turning right at the next road."

Larry said, "Finally." They turned onto the county road, paved but with no stripe down the middle, and continued on for fifteen minutes. The countryside was dark, with a few houses, most of which had no lights on.

Dwayne said, "That gravel road to the right." Larry turned without saying anything.

Jim said, "How the fuck did you get to Cotton's from here, with no car?" Dwayne was embarrassed that Jim used that word in front of Pearl, but then remembered that she'd talked the same way back at Cotton's. Dwayne explained he had been working at Bowden's when his wife, Doris, called to tell him Pearl was in trouble.

"How'd you get to work in the first place?"

"A lady at work lives near here, Jim. She gave me a ride today. She had to get home tonight, so she couldn't give me a ride to Cotton's."

"Christ, I don't blame her."

His house was five minutes from where they'd turned off. "That's it, to the right." He figured college kids like Larry and Jim would think his house was a shack. The siding was better than plain tarpaper, but it was cheap, brown with black lines trying to create the illusion of bricks. At least he had an electric pump to provide running water to the house from the well, but he hoped they wouldn't ask to use his bathroom. They'd laugh at his outdoor toilet.

"Pull on around the back." A member of his church who worked for the county came by periodically and spread gravel on the yard, to keep the mud down. The gravel crunched under the car's tires. The kitchen window provided a modest beacon in the otherwise dark backyard.

Larry parked his car so Pearl's door was facing the kitchen door. As soon as they stopped Dwayne jumped out and ran around the car to open Pearl's door. He opened it slowly, to make sure she didn't fall out. He stepped back and looked at the two boys, who were standing behind him.

Jim and Larry surprised Dwayne with how smoothly they moved to get her out of the car. Larry got in the car from the other side, and pushed Pearl while Jim pulled her by her legs and a wrist. She was quiet until her feet touched the ground, and then she started moaning. They stood her up, and each man had one of her arms around his neck. Once they were in position with Pearl hanging between them, her moans became a scream.

"Oh, goddamn, you're killin' me!" she cried. "Oh, Lord God, what are you doing?"

Larry was taller than Jim, and he had to bend his knees and back to match Jim's height. Both men's faces were strained, with clamped jaws, tight lips, and intense eyes.

Larry said, "Just let me carry her. I can't stay bent over like this." Jim took Pearl's arm from around his neck, and supported her until Larry picked her up in his arms. Dwayne ran ahead to open the kitchen door.

Doris was in the kitchen. She was a big woman, entirely blocking the doorway between the kitchen and the living room. They must have awakened her, judging by her bare feet and sleepy expression, but she had managed to change out of her nightgown and into a dress. The kitchen would look poor to the boys, with its little white table with two mismatched chairs, and the linoleum floor with the simulated green and white tiles wearing away in spots to reveal the outline of the floorboards underneath. Still, it was clean and neat. Larry and Jim wouldn't appreciate it, but Dwayne was proud of how Doris took care of their home.

He was glad the boys had come. Without them, Doris would have been the one to manhandle Pearl into the house. He always felt guilty when she had to do the heavy lifting around their home.

Larry came in with Pearl in his arms. She was skinny, but tall, and her long limbs hung limp. She was dead weight, and Dwayne could tell from Larry's face that he was not used to a lot of lifting. Jim followed, wearing a smirk.

Doris said, "Bring her in here," leading them into the living room. Pearl's screams had given way to moaning, which stopped altogether by the time Larry laid her on the threadbare couch. The boy stood up, not moving for a moment, catching his breath before finally turning to go back to the kitchen. Doris was blocking his path.

"Larry, this is my wife, Doris. Doris, this young man is Larry. He and his friend saw me at Cotton's and offered to give us a ride."

"God bless you, son. You're a real Christian."

"It was nothing, ma'am." He showed a teenager's embarrassment at the compliment.

"It was, too, something. Not everybody is willing to help. Stay here and rest a minute. Would you like some coffee?"

"No, thanks. We need to get on back."

Dwayne took Doris by the arm and started her moving to the kitchen so Larry could go on out of the living room. Once in the kitchen Dwayne said, "Doris, this is Larry's friend."

"Hi, I'm Jim," he said, shaking hands with Doris. He sounded friendly, which surprised Dwayne. He was probably laughing to himself about the house and big, fat Doris, like he'd laughed earlier about Pearl. It was nice that he was polite to Doris to her face, though.

She tried again to get them to stay and have coffee. Dwayne knew they wanted to get on to the party they'd talked about earlier. "We better let these boys go, Doris. We've taken enough of their time."

As Dwayne walked them back to their car, Larry said, "Is that woman a relative of yours?"

"Pearl? No, Pearl is just a member of my congregation. She worked with Doris at the sewing factory. Her husband was killed in a car wreck, and she's had all kinds of trouble after that. She's a good-hearted old thing, except sometimes when she's been drinking. You heard some of that tonight. I apologize for her language. She's just had a rough time. I try to help her. That bartender at Cotton's knows to call me if she gets out of hand. I've asked him before to let me know if she ever showed up there, so I can come and get her before she starts drinking. He always lets her spend all of her money on beer before he calls me to take her off his hands."

Jim said, "That sounds like Cotton, all right, that mercenary bastard."

As the boys got into the car, Larry said, "I'll see you at the station, Dwayne. Take care."

"You boys take care, now. God will bless you for this."

Jim snorted. "Yeah, right."

Back in the house Dwayne took off his Mackinaw and hung it on a hook in the kitchen. In the living room he saw the white boots on the floor at the end of the couch. A pair of tattered panty hose was thrown over the arm of the couch, next to Pearl's feet. Doris had placed a blanket over the old woman.

Pearl was crying as he entered the living room. "Oh, God, Doris, I'm so sorry. I don't want you to see me like this."

"That's all right, honey." She sat on a chair next to the couch, holding Pearl's hand and stroking her forehead. On the floor next to the couch Doris had placed a grocery bag with crumpled up newspaper in the bottom, in case Pearl got sick again. "You just need to rest. It'll be all right." She looked up at Dwayne. "You'd better get to bed, honey. Marvin's going to be here early to take you to church."

"Yeah, he will. Thank you, honey." He went over to Doris and bent to kiss her cheek. "I'm lucky to have you."

"No," she said. "I'm lucky to have you."

THE MAN WHO TAUGHT ME TO LISTEN
Gail Tyson

Deep down, I admitted that good-looking men like Mike Moore unnerved me. His photograph in *The Augusta Chronicle* was rough-hewn handsome: wide forehead, high cheekbones, an intense expression framed by long blond hair. In the foreground his muscled, hairy forearm and large, square-fingered hand held aloft a wooden gun rack. The portrait did not show his missing left arm and shoulder, amputated when a tumor had attached itself to the shoulder blade. Although I was an experienced interviewer, I was awed by this one-armed carpenter who flouted Georgia state law by building customized coffins.

Dense woods bordered Mike's home, in the middle of 22 acres. When I drove up to his front porch on an afternoon in May, 2000, his lean form eased into the doorframe as if he was part of the wood. He loped down the steps to greet me, a laid-back version of the man from the seven-year-old *Chronicle*. At 49 he resembled, ever so slightly, the singer James Taylor.

As he walked me around the house to his woodshop, Mike explained the coffin-making was "a little sideline that developed all on its own. In 1989 I sold my farm to a very wealthy landowner and patriarch in the Augusta area, Old Mr. Pete. When he died a few years later, his whole family showed up at my house about 4 in the morning. I had started my woodworking business, and they asked me to build the old man's coffin."

The Atlanta Journal Constitution, CNN, and the Associated Press gave Mike lots of coverage, some of it humorous. "I was a casket maker all of the sudden. I built them to stand on end to serve as bookcases until their owners died."

In 1993 only licensed funeral directors were permitted to sell coffins in Georgia. Seven years later, the authorities were still ignoring Mike's illegal trade. "Every year I build three to four caskets," he told me. "I get calls from people all over the country, from every imaginable, different kind of folk. Some of the calls are very touching; an AIDS clinic in Baltimore wanted to sell my caskets."

The Chronicle also featured a photograph of Mike kneeling inside one of his coffins, finishing a dovetail joint. "Working with one arm is obviously a little slower," he had told the reporter. "It's hard to handle the top of the coffin, because it's a 7-foot-long piece of wood. But I have two sons, and they help."

His shop was cool and shadowy, the floor covered in sawdust. Inhaling a resinous odor that reminded me of incense, I was glad this city girl had worn her boots and frayed jeans. I asked him about his boys, and his story took a fairy-tale turn.

Mike's parents — his father was a neurosurgeon — raised him in Atlanta, but his soul must have been bred in the country. Three years after graduating from high school in 1969, he was growing peaches and apples near Thomson, Georgia. Less than two hours from Atlanta, this rural area was a world away from the state capital's sprawling freeways and seventh new shopping mall. In his early 20s, Mike met and wooed a ballerina, persuading her to give up her pointe shoes and move to his farm. She bore him two sons, but in 1989 she left the family. Three months later Mike lost his arm. Three months after the amputation, the fruit business he'd nurtured for 17 years folded.

"You don't have time to worry about what ails you when you have 9-year-old and 13-year-old sons," he told me as we walked back to the house. "It gave me great focus. Caring for someone or something other than yourself will help keep your priorities straight, which in turn will help you heal yourself."

For Mike, caring also meant moving away from painful memories and creating a home out of this 1903 farmhouse. Stripping the woodwork, removing plaster walls and replacing them with wallboard, tearing down two fireplaces, and joining two others into a single, massive hearth must have been exhausting for an amputee. The renovation was his way of rehabilitating his body while he rebuilt his life as a single parent. "It was a big job, but I was pretty crazy at the time. I suppose it helped put me in the right frame of mind," he had told the *Chronicle*.

Now he walked me through the high-ceilinged main room, the floor freshly planked with heart pine, back into the kitchen. He poured sweet tea into two glass canning jars, and we carried them out to the porch. Leaning back in satin-smooth rockers — Mike Moore originals — we listened to the sandpaper scratch of cicadas' wings, while the balmy air sweated our cold Ball jars.

Already his mellow tenor voice and deliberate cadence had slowed my racing mind. "Tell me about your business," I said. After his divorce, amputation, and move in 1989, Mike had turned his furniture-making hobby into a backyard venture, specializing in custom, heart-pine creations. The name he chose, Single-Handedly Woodworks, struck me as both mischievous and down-to-earth.

"When you start looking for lumber to work with, you find all the old farms around here that are melting into the ground are made of heart pine," he began. "At the heart of a pine tree is a knot so full of resin that it never rots. All the structures that covered this country from the 1700s and 1800s to the early 1900s were made of heart pine wood; so were the tall masts of sailing ships. The virgin stands of longleaf pine were 70 to 150 years old when they were first cut. Heart pine has always been there for the taking. For 17 years I ran the big farms around here for the owners, and they were glad to let me have the wood."

"How do you know the virgin stands were that old at the first cutting?" I asked.

"An inch of heart pine requires 30 years of growth." His tone was tender, the heartwood a cherished friend. "A first-generation timber has very tight rings — 30 to 35 per inch. The heartwood, from the center of the tree trunk, is much harder than the sapwood that surrounds it. Heart pine is as strong as red oak and has a fine-looking reddish-gold color. I make all my drawer pulls and handles out of the knots."

In the past, my craving for answers had made me a better questioner than listener. Now my hand rested on my notebook. Mike waited, easy with silence. He knew I had been hired by a medical practice to tell the stories of their cancer patients. My goal was to relate the wholeness of his life, but we couldn't ignore the fact that he had survived four rounds of the disease. He told me how the first tumor, on his heart, was discovered during an unrelated surgery when he was eighteen. Fifteen years later, in 1984, he had a three-month course of radiation for Hodgkin's Lymphoma. In 1989 his left arm and shoulder blade were amputated. Then last year, a decade after that surgery, tests for his recurrent back pain revealed lung cancer that had spread to the rib.

"This last time," he added, "the radiation was a short, precise dose but there were about three weeks there I could hardly get up. The chemo, though, has been a breeze."

"Do the doctors know why you've gotten cancer so often?"

Mike shrugged. "One oncologist is convinced I have a split chromosome #17; some diseases, including cancer, have been linked to it." He paused. "As a farmer I've worked around herbicides, including paraquat sprays, although the EPA says they aren't carcinogenic." We sat in silence; then he added, "I just think I have a body that likes to get cancer."

I gaped at him. When I met Mike 45 minutes ago, a line from a James Taylor song had popped into my mind: "I guess my feet know where they want to go walking on a country road." Now he sounded like one of the song's heavenly angels. This man had experienced so many losses: his wife, his farm, his first profession, his arm and shoulder. Yet he didn't seem to wonder, "Why me?" The guy rocking beside me sounded as resilient as his beloved heart pine. How did so many losses add up to this uncanny acceptance?

"Eight to nine weeks ago, my doctor told me, 'I don't know whether this is a miracle or the treatment works this well.' I'm grateful that I can go to my son's graduation from Long Island University in two weeks. He's earned a degree in ecology and outdoor education." He rose to his full six feet. "Come around to the side porch. There's someone I want you to meet."

Mike had built this porch recently, so it still smelled like fresh-cut lumber, the sunbaked railing warm to the touch. In a puddle of light curled a spotted fawn.

"I've raised three or four deer," Mike said softly. "Living way back in the woods here, it's like a game preserve. Veterinarians bring me orphan deer; so do the neighbors. This one is 13 days old. A couple came home and their two German shepherds found the baby at the corner of their property. She was walking down the road, her hooves still soft, probably one day old; her mother was hit by a car and thrown into a ditch."

"What do you feed her?"

"I give her bottles of goat milk, which is richer in fat than cow milk." We both smiled down at the fawn—mostly long legs, with a plush black nose. "All my babies have been gentle and sweet and easy to deal with. When they get older, I let them go free, but they decide I'm their mama, and they often come by to visit."

Mike walked me back to my car. Through a break in the trees, I spied a gentle green slope of pasture. A red-winged blackbird flashed past us, trilling *oak-a-lee, oak-a-lee*. "It's so peaceful here," I remarked.

Mike laughed. "It wasn't last weekend. About 100 people and three bands were here—friends of mine with their kids and pets and friends they brought along." He told me the event was a yearly tradition that began as a housewarming a decade ago. "Hold on a minute," he said, going up to a small chest on the porch between the rockers, and pulling one of the heart-pine handles on the single drawer. He came back with a sheet of paper. "Here's the invitation I sent out."

At the top of the page *Single-Handedly, Inc.* appeared in calligraphy with a small handprint; at the bottom was a drawing of routes from Thomson and Atlanta to his place on Stagecoach Road. Between them were these hand-lettered words:

> I've been trying to figure out how to write this particular invitation for about six months now, as I was again made aware of how precious our time here together really is. How does one invite all of those friends and family that he loves to come again, to the woods (that keep shrinking), to celebrate the arrival, the rebirth, the coming of the first glorious growth of the year 2000, by participating in and being a part of the celebration of the rites of springtime. How to adequately

express in mere words how much it means to gather together the spirit that exists only amongst us as a group and that is experienced whenever we are joined in singing, dancing, yabbering, eating, drinking and carryin' on as we approach the ever so serious level of pitchin' that wang dang doodle that each new spring deserves. This will be the tenth time we've done it and not likely the last.

On Saturday, May 6, Buzz Clifford and the Last of the Bohemians and Carl Brown will open up for Robert Moore and Those Wildcats and together will carry us closer and closer to the doodle. There will be the annual hay ride for all ages of chirren and plenty of other entertainment, so please pack your bags and come be a part of it—come again and share the gift of a grateful heart.

After I got behind the wheel, I rolled down the window. "I love that Willie Dixon song, 'Wang Dang Doodle.' Which cover do you like best?"

Mike shook his head. "I don't have a favorite. I've just always loved the song."

In the rural South, drivers show each other a courtly respect by raising one hand from the steering wheel—*namaste*, country-style. As I backed my car away, I saluted Mike, and he raised one hand in return.

I didn't turn on music during my drive back to Atlanta. Instead, my mind replayed all my favorite versions of "Wang Dang Doodle," a blues classic about an all-night party. You never want the song to end—like the party—and you can't help dancing to it, so I swayed a little in my seat. Written in one chord, it requires highly skilled guitar players, and every musician who recorded it has coaxed a different sound, in a different key. The Grateful Dead mixed the driving chord line with some jazzy piano licks and a keening harmonica. On Howlin' Wolf's London studio tape, his voice sounds seductive and intimate, even though he's backed by Eric Clapton, Stevie Winwood, and a half-dozen other musicians.

I loved Dixon's lyrics, too, especially the way Koko Taylor growled them defiantly, a sax riffing on her words partway through:

Tell Fats and Washboard Sam
That everybody's gonna jam
Tell Shakey and Boxcar
We got sawdust on the floor
Tell Peg and Carol Dime

We gonna have a hell of a time
When the fish scent fills the air
There'll be snuff juice everywhere
We're gonna pitch a wang dang doodle all nite long

Once I got home, I found myself humming the song as I wrote up Mike's story. Over the next few weeks Tonya, the graphic designer, put it in a layout with photographs of Mike in his woodshop and bottle-feeding a wobbly-legged fawn. When the song crept into my thoughts I'd wonder, did the lyrics take on different meanings at the twists and turns of Mike's life? I'd never asked him about the private pain of his runaway wife, but when did the "romp and tromp 'til midnight" turn into "fuss and fight 'til daylight"? When he went a little crazy, tearing down the farmhouse so he could build it up again, did that time make him feel "Tonight we need no rest/We're really gonna throw a mess/ We're gonna break out all the windows/Gonna kick down all the doors"? If it did, his life now—like the end of every verse and his invitation—declared, "We're gonna pitch a wang dang doodle all night long." I wanted some of the resilience Mike had, but did you have to go through such a dark night to get to the all-night party?

About a month after I saw Mike, Tonya called. Our client, bought out by a larger healthcare practice, had killed the project. I felt bereft. This man's story had latched onto my soul, and I wanted more people to hear it.

Tonya called again eight months later. Mike had gone into the hospital for routine tests. He was cancer-free, but in those couple of days he was overwhelmed by a staph infection that resisted antibiotic treatment. Mike was dead.

Filing the work we'd done on his story with other closed projects, I prayed for those fatherless boys, the baby deer, the dead he helped send out of the world. From time to time I would pull out his file and reread his invitation from a grateful heart. Year by year, I got a little better at what he had taught me: to keep quiet and listen to the world.

A decade later, opening the drawer of my memories, I picture Mike in his woodshop, carving drawer pulls one-handed. I dwell, grateful, in the time we spent together, imagine him pitchin' his wang dang doodle all night and all day long. And I understand that love, like heart pine, is all around us, for the taking. We just need to learn how to listen, and where to look.

The Importance of Names
Nancy Gustafson

Loretta Katherine held up the seven-dollar hair frosting kit to make a sales pitch to her sister and mother. She tapped the picture of a Marilyn Monroe look-alike on the box front. "Sue, you are going to love having frosted hair. And just think, you'll save about fifty dollars by letting me do it instead of a beauty operator."

Marie pursed her lips in disgust. "Men! They don't know what looks good and what doesn't. I always liked you in short curly hair, Sue. Let your sister frost it and if it doesn't look good, cut it. You're due for a change, girl."

"It's taken me years to grow this hair, Mom, and I don't want to cut it! I'll let Loretta Katherine frost it, but that's all."

Loretta Katherine stepped aside and let her sister and mother forge a path to the bathroom. Sue lead the way, her mahogany mane swishing side to side, brushing proud shoulders.

Loretta Katherine directed the operation. "Here, Mom, put that toilet seat down and you sit on the throne. Sue, you sit on this little rattan stool in front of the sink. Okay, now we're ready to set up a beauty shop."

Loretta Katherine lay out the kit's contents on the countertop — the bleaching powder and cream toner, plastic gloves, a plastic cap, a timer and a crochet hook. She struggled to get the plastic cap over Sue's abundant hair, tugging the cap over one side, then pulling it over the other side, stretching it as much as she could. Sue covered her eyes with her hands, while her head was jerked first one way, then the other.

Marie took out her cigarettes and lighter from the pocket of her pedal pushers. "Do you have an ashtray in here, Loretta Katherine?"

"No, but just take that white candle off its base and use it."

Marie reached across the countertop, removed the candle and pulled the makeshift ashtray to her. She lit up her cigarette and exhaled a yellow-gray specter that drifted in front of their faces.

Loretta Katherine coughed and waved the smoke away. She held the crochet hook, poised like an Eskimo harpoon, above Sue's head. "This room is so small, Mom. I'm afraid you'll asphyxiate us."

"Oh, I'll just take a couple of quick puffs and put the thing out. You know I don't breathe out much smoke. Daddy always did say I breathe in little panties." Marie's husky chortle ended in a hack. She thumbed the corner of the sink's countertop. "Loretta Katherine, you need to round off this corner. It's too sharp. If you ever fell getting out of the tub, you'd stab yourself to death. It's close quarters in here."

Sue's mouth twisted in a wry smile. "Yes, but there are advantages to such a tiny bathroom. Loretta Katherine could be stuck on the toilet with uncontrollable diarrhea and shave her legs in the tub at the same time."

Loretta Katherine grabbed a thick lock of hair with the crochet hook and pulled it with great effort through the plastic cap. Sue scrunched her eyes and yelped. Loretta Katherine, oblivious to Sue's suffering, continued pulling hunks of hair through the cap.

"I know it's a small room. That's why we made the entire wall above the sink a mirror, to make it seem more spacious. Fred says it's efficient."

Sue aimed her decorator's eye around the room. "I like the wallpaper you put up — beige and white stripes. But you really need a little more color in here. This whole bathroom is beige and white. White tub, white toilet, white sink and a beige countertop. You could spice it up with a basket of silk roses or a rose garland above the door."

"I've got a little dark brown in the linoleum, Sue. I went for that fake brick look. I like things simple. I'm a white-and-beige person. Too much color drives me nuts." Loretta Katherine tapped her sister on the head with the flat of the crochet hook and glared at her in the mirror. "You've got roses everywhere. I don't think you have a single room in your whole house that doesn't have roses in it. You're a pink person, but that doesn't fit me."

Marie flicked ashes into the candle holder. "I should have named her Rosy. In fact, I think I got your names mixed up. You're more of a 'Sue', Loretta Katherine. Plain and simple, just the way I like you. And, Sue, you're more of a Loretta Katherine: vivacious, colorful, just the way I like you."

"You're right, Mom. I always hated my name. A name is very important, and 'Sue' doesn't describe me. Why didn't you name me Suzanne Nicole, or something French?"

Marie blew a stream of smoke toward the ceiling. "Do you want us to start calling you Suzanne Nicole?"

Sue rolled her eyes. "It's too late now, Mother. I'm afraid nobody would ever call me anything but 'Sue,' whether I like it or not. But inside my psyche, I'm a Suzanne. Oh, Loretta Katherine, I have an idea for you. Why don't you get colored towels, maybe with a geometric design, if you prefer that to flowers? Maybe a soft blue and green? You'd spice up your bathroom, spice up your life and grow into your name all at the same time."

"That's an idea," said Loretta Katherine as she pulled an especially tough hunk of hair through the plastic cap.

Sue yelled, "You did that on purpose!

Loretta Katherine ripped off a square of toilet paper and blotted tears off her sister's cheeks. "No, I didn't. This will make your eyes water, but it's a small price to pay for beauty."

Marie rested one elbow on the countertop, her chin on her fist and her eyes focused on her daughters' images in the mirror. "Those alligator tears remind me of when you was itsy-bitsy, Sue. Loretta Katherine would start yelling at the top of her lungs the minute she got a little ouchy, but seldom had a tear in her eye. However, you would just stand there and let tears pour like a faucet. You could cry at the drop of a hat! I should have given you acting lessons. I disagree with Henry. You got talent."

Marie reached across the counter and touched Sue's arm. A tear popped like a pea from its pod, traveled from the corner of Sue's eye to her chin and plopped onto Marie's hand. Marie leaned against the back of the toilet, the arroyo between her brows deepening, and brushed away the tear. "I really didn't mean it when I said that I got your names mixed up. I tried to pick the right name for each of you. I love your names and your different personalities. To me, you girls are perfect just as you are."

Loretta Katherine stretched across the cabinet and kissed her mother on the head. "We know that, Mom. We're just teasing each other. Actually, Sue and I love each other very much."

"That's true, Mom. Loretta Katherine knows I love her," Sue ogled her sister's reflection, "don't you, Sis?"

"Sure, I do." Loretta Katherine pulled on the plastic gloves with a snap against her wrists. "Okay, now we're ready for the bleach."

She mixed the bleaching powder into the cream toner, smeared it into Sue's hair and set the timer for twenty minutes. When the timer jangled, Loretta Katherine pulled a gooey lock straight up. "Ummmm—not cooked yet."

Mom pulled out one more cigarette and breathed in little panties for about five minutes while she looked admiringly in the mirror at her girls. "I have the most beautiful girls in the world. I remember when you was a peewee, Sue, how dainty you was. People used to stop me on the street and comment on your brown eyes and auburn curls. It was quite a shock when Loretta Katherine was born, and there in my arms I held a pale daisy of a girl with blue eyes and corn silk hair. People thought she was adopted."

"Well, I still have that cursed fly-away hair, but I seem to have become more substantial since then, Mom. Wish I could lose some weight."

Sue looked sympathetically at her sister. "You're just right for you, Loretta Katherine. I've always admired your long legs and short nose. I just hate my nose."

"You inherited your nose legit from your Indian great grand-father. I think it fits you. And I'd kill for hair like yours, Sue. Okay, time to check it again. Let's see if it's done its thing or not." Loretta Katherine scooped away the bleach and declared it was time to rinse. She handed Sue a washrag to hold over her face, and then she and Marie guided Sue onto her knees next to the tub and pushed her head under the faucet.

Loretta Katherine rinsed the bleach off Sue's hair and watched it swirl on the bottom of the fiberglass tub and drift down the drain. Then she shampooed Sue's hair and rinsed it again.

"Mom, pull that white towel down from the rack at the back of the tub." Loretta Katherine took the towel from Marie, wrapped it around Sue's head and lead her to the rattan stool. She blotted Sue's hair, took hold of the plastic cap and carefully, as if unearthing a truffle, pulled it off.

"Now is the moment of truth and beauty. Mom, reach in that cabinet next to the toilet and get out the blow dryer, please."

The comforting warmth filled the small room. Sue's hair began to dry once again into soft waves. Loretta Katherine turned off the dryer, and for several minutes the only sounds heard in the bathroom were the sisters breathing and their mother wheezing. Through a smoky veil, three faces, drastically different yet curiously favoring, froze as if etched on a frosted mirror. The picture crumbled. Tears began to leak from Sue's eyes, tumble over her eyelashes and splash down her nose.

Marie's face assumed a calm resignation. She took a drag off her cigarette and studied the situation. "Verdy in-ter-westing."

Loretta Katherine's eyes popped wide. "Well, what I think is... actually, what I really think... I think we may just need a little time to get used to it." A way too cheerful smile accompanied her upbeat voice. "And I think I may just have found a new career as a beautician."

"It's *orange!*" cried Sue, her face a picture of horror. Her mouth quivered. "Henry is going to kill me!" Sue slowly lowered her head into the sink, her hair cascading into it like an orange sunset's final plunge. A choked sob filtered through the mass of hair.

Loretta Katherine stood helpless, a failure above the sorrow of her sister. Still, she never could pass up a wisecrack, and now she felt one tickle. "Better get your head up, Sue. If any of that bleach dropped into the sink, your nose might turn orange."

Marie snickered. "At least she'd be color coordinated." She choked and then alternately coughed and cackled until she could barely breathe. Finally, she got control of herself. Her eyes met Loretta Katherine's, and they quickly wiped guilty smiles off their faces and pulled their brows together in mock concern.

Sue lifted her head out of the sink and raised her imperial nose, her expression haughty before the conspirators. "You know what? I think I like it. Yes, I do like it, Loretta Katherine. I think it fits my personality. It is certainly — what did you call me, Mother — vivacious?"

Loretta Katherine opened the bathroom door and kicked towels out of the way. "The real test is Henry. If he likes it, we know we done good! Let's go show it to him."

Sue shuffled down the hall, her wavy orangutan-colored mane brushing over slightly slumped shoulders. Marie, ready to support Sue should her knees buckle, walked behind. Loretta Katherine brought up the rear. The possibility of having ruined her sister overtook her like pond scum. Little self-conscious titters bubbled to the surface through the guilty muck. All the way down the hall she prayed that Henry would be utterly wild about Sue's hair.

Oh, please God, let Henry be crazy about Sue's hair. I'll try to be a nicer sister. I'll cook more vegetables. I'll volunteer in the church nursery. Oh, I better take that back. Not the nursery. I'll visit the sick. Well, if it's not something contagious. Oh, well, I'll try to find something churchy to do. I'll try not to give in to my nastier nature — no more jokes at my sister's expense. I'll call her more often and tell her how beautiful she is.

As they turned the corner into the living room, Loretta Katherine bit her bottom lip and attempted to squelch a giggle. She prayed. *Oh God, help me keep my sick sense of humor in tow!*

Just as Henry leaped out of the recliner, but before the caterwaul began, Loretta Katherine whispered into her mother's ear: "You should have named her Tangerine."

Sweet Green Icing
L. Mahayla Smith

I didn't look all that great—forty-eight hours of stubble, no shower, wrinkled jeans and a coffee stain of modest dimensions on the state-issued baby-blue work shirt. I'd brushed my teeth and combed my hair. No deodorant in the "exit package" and it didn't seem worth the expenditure with only $150 in my wallet. That's supposed to last till I "get a job." And they complain about recidivism.

On the bright side, stinks and stains beat another day in an orange jumpsuit.

But I resented the cow-like stare of the high school dropout at the bakery. When you've got five piercings in your left eyebrow, three on your lip, green and blue dye in your Rastafarian hair and you can barely talk for the olive-sized happy face stud in your tongue, should you look at other people like they're unusual? Ordinarily, a guy whose only company for six years is men would wonder about other places a girl might have hardware. But my libido couldn't swim against the current of attitude coming across the checkerboard counter. My offense: asking for green frosting on a cupcake.

"It's for my grandmother," I explained. "Sentimental reasons."

"What shade of green?" the icing expert managed to drone after yawning. She looked dumpy in her cargo pants. Large breasts strained against a yellow T-shirt that had a pair of spectacles above the words, "Eyes crazy." Perhaps she did have mental health issues. I shouldn't judge. Right, Genevieve? I glanced down at the girl's feet—bright pink Crocs.

I shrugged. "How about that greenish shade in your hair?"

She reacted as though a request for frosting resembling the color in her dreadlocks was unimaginative. "Luscious lime?"

I nodded.

"Yeah, if that's a color. And if it doesn't take that long to make it."

Genevieve was nowhere nearby, but I could envision her crooning the words about not being able to take it, because some rained-on cake took so long to bake and never having the recipe again. The lyrics to "McArthur Park" never made sense to me, but they spoke to her like "Just as I Am" does to Baptists at a revival.

She used to listen to the oldies station and sing that stupid tune at the top of her lungs, swaying back and forth, clutching her arms to her chest like someone was actually trying to steal something from her. She always had the radio on. And Genevieve—who in any other

~ 160 ~

family would have been known as Grandma—had the voice for it. She sang in off-Broadway shows, coffee houses, and after her youth faded, at officer's clubs on military bases. She met my grandfather, whoever that was, in her New York era.

My mama was a lonely child till Genevieve sent her back to live at her aunt's tobacco farm in Greeneville, Tennessee. Mama said if she met her dad, she didn't remember it. I grew up hearing stories about my grandmother, but Mama never let us talk to her. I found out where Genevieve lived when I turned twelve. One of Genevieve's high school friends delivered a birthday card from her. She handed it to me at choir practice and said, "Best not mention this to your mama, Jackson." The card had a goofy dog on it and a hundred dollar bill inside. She'd written contact information and the words, "You're welcome to visit. Love, Genevieve McMurtry."

Back home they pronounced my grandmother's name in the usual East Tennessee fashion, but my grandmother told me it was pronounced the French way—"Shjohn-uh-vee-eff." It took me ten tries to get it right.

In her "later years"—which was probably age forty—Genevieve developed a penchant for colonels and generals plagued by bad coronaries and a love of whiskey—"as long as they didn't ask too many questions." At least that's what she told me. I didn't know any of the "grandfathers." She'd say, "Call me, Genevieve. I can't bear to be known as Grandmother. I never intend to act like one." I can just see her taking a languorous drag off her Dunhill cigarette. "Besides, Jackson," she'd tease, "you never truly know another person."

I met my grandmother when I was thirteen, and she told me I didn't really know her till the day I checked into the crowbar hotel five years later. Once I asked her why she ended up in Memphis instead of L.A. or Vegas or New York, and she said, "I had a fling with Elvis." Then she winked, tossing her long brown hair behind her.

She might have been in her fifties when we had this conversation, but you couldn't tell it. Of course, Genevieve never told anyone her age. She said good scotch and expensive cigarettes kept her well-preserved. Maybe she was right. A woman like that makes an impression on a teenage boy.

She helped me make memories that carried me through six years for voluntary manslaughter at Brushy Mountain State Pen. And compelled me to ask for the travel voucher to Memphis instead of Oliver Springs where my oldest sister and ailing mother still live. And where that worthless Primitive Baptist preacher brother-in-law of mine still holds the keys to the kingdom.

But he couldn't hold the soul of one Michael Justin Hamby from the Oliver Springs Cemetery.

Or hell either. I made sure of that.

"This do?" The pierced counter clerk returned with a cupcake covered in a mound of neon buttercream. She held it up near her eyes, which I'd previously failed to notice were deep pools of turquoise. I coulda gotten interested in this freaky chick with big boobs, crazy hair, and a rotten attitude—except for those eyes. They looked like my baby sister Christal's eyes. The color of blue that people get lost in. They made Christal look just as innocent and gullible as she really was.

Goddamit, Jackson, I thought to myself. *Why didn't you protect your baby sister?* I'd asked myself that question every day for the last six years. I felt guilty leaving Christal at home with Mama, but she was always tangled up in my mother's skirt tails. I doubt I could have dragged Christal away to be with me and Genevieve.

Or was I just selfish?

Funny thing. I wished over and over I had done different by Christal, and now I don't even know where she lives. She'd be twenty now.

I heard a clicking noise—the frosting stylist snapping her fingers at me. "Hey! Icing? Remember?"

I nodded. "It's fine."

"Shall I write something on this cupcake?"

I contemplated my options. Happy Birthday, Genevieve, or RIP? It was both her birthday and the six-month anniversary of her death. I discovered she passed away from Christal, who sent me a free postcard from a cheap motel in Gatlinburg with two words on it: "Genevieve's dead." That's the first and last thing I've heard from Christal since the day I killed Justin Hamby. Not that I didn't expect the sad news about my grandmother.

Genevieve wrote me a letter every week for the first five years I was in prison. Then letters got scarce. She apologized and said she was having "health problems" and "didn't feel up to the writing." Finally the letters stopped altogether. I hated it.

Not only was I lonely, but it turns out my grandmother was right. I never did know her. But her correspondence gave me a glimpse. Turns out Genevieve moved to Memphis because her late husband, "the Colonel," inherited a house there. "Nothing as beckoning as free rent," she wrote. "But don't think for one second that Elvis and I weren't friendly."

I saved one of the letters under my pillow. It was the first one she sent me when I went to the jailhouse. "Well, Jackson, you've gone and got yourself into one fine mess. And I wish I could be judgmental enough to write you off. But since most people don't approve of how I have conducted my life either, it would be hypocritical. I must admit, I never killed anyone, but in this particular case, I believe you did the world a favor." At the end, she wrote, "When you get out, I want you to come to Memphis. You'll always have a place here."

The bakery wench made a foghorn noise in her throat. I looked at her. "Decoration? Inscription?" She twirled the cupcake in her hand. "Or just plain luscious lime?"

"How about a candle?" I looked at her name tag and added, "Heidi." I figured a candle was right for both a birth and a death.

Heidi peered at me like a cat stares at a clothes dryer. "We supply cake. We do not supply candles." She sounded as pissed as if I'd asked her to write the Declaration of Independence on the cupcake's glistening green surface. I couldn't tell if she was mad about the candle or about me daring to use her name. She placed the cupcake in a box and scooted it near the cash register, dismissing me with, "Thank you. Have a nice day."

She never cracked a smile. I had an impulse to say, "Did you know I once killed a man? No preplanning. No nothing. Just got mad and shot him dead. Did it right at his house." But six years behind razor wire living inside my own head taught me that most sudden urges oughta be squashed.

I held my tongue. Genevieve's voice played in my head: "Jackson Hatfield, don't you judge a girl till you've walked a mile in her high heels."

Who knows what that girl's problem was? PMS? Working in a cupcake bakery instead of being an astronomer at NASA? I just knew my mission: get a cake with sweet green icing and get to the bridge before sunset—my grandmother's very favorite hour.

"Look at the colors, Jackson." We'd stand out on the Memphis and Arkansas Bridge and admire the nameless engineer who'd imagined its trusses. Traffic would whir past us. She pointed at the sunset the first time we ever went there together and said, "What colors do you see?"

I looked out and said, "Red? Orange? Maybe a little pink?"

"Oh no, Jackson. Life isn't meant to be lived amongst such pedestrian hues. The sunset is magenta and gold and mango and dusky rose!" She looked at my startled face. She laughed and grabbed my arms, twirling herself around in a swing dance move. And then she arched her arm and with just a look invited me to take a turn as well.

"If you go back to Oliver Springs, you'll go right back to the six shades in the crayon box. You need to stay right here with Genevieve and see sixty-four colors. Or maybe a hundred and sixty-four."

I've had over half a decade now to mull over that conundrum. What if I had gone back home instead of spending my high school years with my fun, crazy grandma? I thought Mama would watch out for Christal—see who she was hanging out with and supervise her every cotton-pickin' move like she did for me and my older sister. In the end, I guess Mama made the same mistake I did.

Genevieve let me call Christal weekly. When my sister started talking about staying after church, cleaning it and babysitting for Mr. Hamby, I never considered the possibilities. I imagined her as a girl who needed a babysitter herself. Truth was, I hadn't seen her for a while. Christal was a young woman. And my mama never looked past herself to see Christal's trouble.

Genevieve wouldn't openly criticize Mama, who left school and took a factory job. She never blamed her for marrying a drunk or taking off to live with Floyd Mason, who owned an Exxon station. Mama stayed gone for a year. She only came back because Floyd took up with a bank teller.

Genevieve never let me blame my mother for me running away and coming to Memphis. She wasn't the religious type, but if I started in on Mama she'd say, "I see a log in your eye."

You could tell my grandmother was never really happy with a normal life. Though she managed pretty well on her fourth husband's widow's pension, she longed for bright lights and the highway.

"Look across that Mississippi River, Jackson," she demanded. "What's out there?"

I peered up and down the water. I didn't see anything out of the ordinary. "The river bank, a barge. Buildings."

"No!" She tapped my arm in a playful slap. "The Land of Opportunity. The sign at the end of the bridge says so!"

I had read that Welcome to Arkansas billboard many times over.

I smiled. She pulled a Dunhill out of her purse, handed me a Zippo and said, "Help a lady out, will ya?" I fired up her cigarette.

She blew a smoke ring that got disrupted by a passing eighteen wheeler. I yelled at the top of my lungs, "It's just Arkansas!"

She glanced back at sinking rays of daylight. "Oh, no, Jackson. It's the first state on the way out."

"Well then, when I get outta high school, I'm going to Arkansas, Genevieve."

"Maybe you will, Jackson. Maybe not. But remember your problems with your mama and no-good daddy are just like that sun over there. It might go down and you might go all night not even thinking about it." She turned her head toward me and offered a thirteen-year-old a drag off her fancy smoke. I took it and just before I started hacking my head off she whispered, "But that sun is coming back in the morning."

When I stopped coughing, I asked her a question that sounded wiser than I meant it to. "Then why the hell are we standing on this side of the bridge, Genevieve?"

She took my hand. "Because, my dearest young Jackson, for once in my life, I am living up to my responsibilities." I heard both sadness and determination in her voice.

And she did live up to them. I gave her a chance to say she finally got something right. I stayed with her until my senior year in high school. I bet I watched two hundred sunsets from the Memphis and Arkansas Bridge and sang Bob Dylan, Rolling Stones, Beatles songs — anything on the oldies station — till we were both hoarse. We danced wildly and I never once worried I was out of place with my grandmother, who saw nearly everything as though she were peering into a kaleidoscope.

Then came the call from Mama. Things had gone all wrong at home. Christal was pregnant. She was in middle school. I was a senior at Melrose in Memphis. It was a tough school, but I didn't miss Oliver Springs High School one bit, even though I would likely have been a starter on the football team with my height and running speed. I had just turned eighteen. I figured some stupid wannabe jock quarterback got her pregnant. Or some skinny Boy Scout with pimples for a face.

I rode the Greyhound through the night to Knoxville and hitchhiked the rest of the way home. I didn't even tell Genevieve I'd left.

When I got home, Christal told me the baby's daddy was Justin Hamby. I knew him. He was a married man, a newly appointed deacon at my brother-in-law's Primitive Baptist Church. He had to be at least twenty years older than my baby sister.

"Who let you date that asshole?" I asked Christal.

"Nobody. We didn't date. I stayed after church to clean up. He always gave me a ride home."

"Sounds like he gave you a lot more than that."

My baby sister's eyes were red. Knowing my mama, she probably didn't spare Christal any compassion. I guess I wasn't really excelling too much at that myself. She was sitting on the bare floor in her bedroom. I bent toward her.

"Did he hurt you?" I asked.

She didn't answer. I started pacing back and forth over the wood floors of Mama's rent house. "If he forced himself on you, Christal, you just tell me and we'll call the police and get them to throw his butt in jail." I pleaded with her. "You can tell me, Sis. I came all the way from Memphis to Oliver Springs to help you. I wouldn't darken the door for any reason but you."

She looked down at her lap, her head held low like a dog that knows it's done wrong. She rocked back and forth, making low-pitched moans. When she finally looked back up at me, she whispered through a cracked voice, "Justin told me he loved me."

I croaked out a laugh. "Love?" I shook my head and looked straight at her. "He told you he loved you," I mocked.

Her bloodshot eyes never met mine. She curled up on the ground and whimpered.

Something inside my heart snapped like a tree branch in an April wind storm. I felt like I couldn't breathe. I went to the cookie jar in the kitchen where Mama kept a .38 revolver in case wild boar got onto the property or intruders got in the house. We lived a mile from our nearest neighbor. Mama was at work, so I had to walk the three miles to Justin Hamby's house. With each step, I planned what I would say and do. I would ask him who he thought he was and why he preyed on my sister? I would tell him he was a mockery of a Christian. I would hold the gun to his chest and tell him to get down on his knees and beg the forgiveness of God and Jesus and my family and me and especially my sister. I would make him go to the phone and call the preacher and all thirty-four members in the directory of the Oliver Springs Primitive Baptist Church and ask their forgiveness and tell them what he'd done. And then I would make him call the police and turn himself in for rape. And while the sirens were blasting in the background, I would make him go out in his yard and scream over them, "I love Christal Hatfield. I love Christal Hatfield," so his wife and all his neighbors would hear.

After that, I'd go home to Christal, call Genevieve, and tell her we needed money for an abortion. Genevieve would see this for the sense it made. No thirteen-year-old girl needed to walk around carrying some pervert's baby inside her.

Mama would tell Christal it was sinful and make her give birth.

On my walk to Justin's, I played out the drama like a movie in my head. I would be the director and Justin Hamby would do everything I told him.

It was getting dark when I got to Justin Hamby's split-level. The company truck was parked in the driveway. There was light in the kitchen. I could see him at a table eating dinner with his wife. Spaghetti. I saw him sucking the sloppy noodles into his mouth. Then they both laughed. He reached his hand out and touch his wife's face. I wondered if he treated Christal with such tenderness.

At the front door, I knocked. I hadn't been around Justin since I was thirteen and moved to Memphis. He didn't seem to recognize me. But I knew his plump face, the doughy protrusion of his belly against his shirttails. He opened the door. "May I help you?"

I couldn't get any words out. He eyed me closer and asked, "Jackson?"

I hadn't expected him to remember me. I was a prepubescent runt the last time I saw him at church. I thought I'd have to reintroduce myself. The first words in my script were, "I'm Jackson Hatfield, Christal's brother."

Instead I stood silent. I don't remember thinking about what I would do next. I pulled the .38 out of my jacket pocket and without hesitation shot Justin Hamby in the head. It wasn't in my screenplay.

He expressed no repentance. Couldn't turn himself in to the county sheriff. I doubt he saw the gun. The expression on Justin's face never changed. There was a loud noise, and then I threw the .38 into the hedge. He fell onto his back. I saw the splatter — blood and white matter against the screen and the door jamb. When I checked, he was raggedy breathing. I felt some wet stuff on my face and saw pink stains on my shirt. I moved across the yard, sat down on the curb and waited. Justin Hamby made it to Methodist Medical Center alive, but that was temporary. The only thing I regretted at the time was his wife's moaning and asking me what happened. I knew there'd be more tears when she found out about Christal. I wanted to explain, but words wouldn't come.

I made my only phone call to my grandmother. "I messed up, Genevieve."

"I know, Jackson. Your mama's already called." She sighed. "I'll get you the best legal representation available in that hellhole you live in."

I broke down and cried until my three minutes were up. I heard Genevieve sniffling. I knew then she understood, even before I got that first letter.

That's why I had to come back to Memphis. I stopped at Kroger and picked up candles. There was a new sign saying NO PEDESTRIANS on the Memphis and Arkansas Bridge. I walked past it. Cars honked. Drivers pointed toward the warning. If cops showed, I'd tell them I couldn't read. I cupped my hand around the candle atop the cupcake with its green icing and lit it. "What do you reckon this color is, Genevieve?" I said into the sunset. "How about iridescent moss? You'd like that."

I drew a pack of Dunhills that I'd bought yesterday out of my pocket. I couldn't afford more than an airline-sized bottle of cheap scotch, but I got that out, took a sip and added it to the shrine I created on the bridge. Shielding the candle's flame with my legs, I watched the sun go down. I sang every word of McArthur Park from memory. Tears came and went and so did the daylight. As the sun sank into the Mississippi, I toasted Genevieve's memory and spoke to the last flashing rays, "You'll be back tomorrow, right?"

I could still make out that the sign was at the west end of the bridge — the sign that long ago proffered welcome to the state of Arkansas. I whispered, "The land of opportunity." Into the air, I asked, "What d'ya think, Genevieve?"

Maybe it was the wind or my overactive imagination. Or maybe it was something else. I smelled faint but familiar aroma of Johnny Walker Black. I swear I heard, "It's the first state on the way out."

The moon rose. I looked at the little cupcake at my feet. The candle had flickered out. I looked in all directions along the bridge.

No one here but me. The old billboard still stood at the state line. But it had been redone with a picture taken somewhere near a lake that I believe was in the Ozarks. And the words had changed.

I knew I'd be breaking parole. What the hell? I had ninety-five dollars left, no job, nowhere to run and no one to run to.

Somewhere near Oliver Springs, Tennessee, my mother's in hospice, my older sister and preacher brother-in-law are living in eternal forgiveness of Justin Hamby. And Christal and my five-year-old bastard nephew? God knows where the winds have taken them.

I read the words to the new sign: "Arkansas. It's a Natural."

I started walking west.

You Never Told Me
Melanie Haws

The summer that I was twelve, Mamma helped me pack the red Amelia Earhart suitcase for my annual week at my grandparents' farm. Kids at school went to summer camps where they learned archery and slept in bunk beds, and they brought back their stories. My sister Tanya, away at college, went to faraway places and sent postcards home. Yet I never envied any of them for that, for I spent part of every summer at the farm, endless summers. I had always been glad to go.

"Your bra, Melissa," Mamma said. It hung on the bedroom's back doorknob, where I hoped she had forgotten about it. To be fair, she said that she had put off buying a bra for me too long, too busy to get around to a shopping trip, but then she had made a big occasion of it. A mother-daughter date, she said. My father was always gone, working to provide for me and Tanya the things he never had. Lunch at Swenson's, a movie, and picking out a bra from Miller's. The brassieres, of many different colors and sizes, dangled sweetly from the plastic hangers. Some of them lacy; I loved lace and flounces and fuss. I put the chosen bra on, liking not the confinement of it but the daintiness, and showed it to Mamma and the gossipy saleslady.

"Fits nice," Mamma said. She reached into her purse for her checkbook.

The saleslady nodded, then nudged Mamma and whispered, "I can see what the school meant when they called you the other day. Somebody here really needed a bra!" She reached over and tightened the left shoulder strap. "Melissa, you are going to be blessed. Very lucky." She waved her hands to mimic the curve of a full bosom, then laughed. Mamma grinned.

Mamma had never told me about the call from the school. "I want to take it off now," I said. The bra no longer felt pretty to me.

"Oh, you can't, honey. I'll take the price tag off—don't you worry." The saleslady said. Mamma pressed her lips together.

"I don't want to wear it." But Mamma insisted, and when I began to cry, she raised her voice—something she almost never did— and told me that all women had to wear a bra, like it or not. I cried so hard that she refused to take me to on to the movies, as she had promised, to see *Arthur*.

Months had passed, but still I hated the bra, only a trainer, but it chafed my skin and left a rash and bound me. Every time my mother's back was turned, I took it off and hid it. I had never worn one on the farm before. "Must I take it?" I asked, in my best British inflection. That summer Lady Diana Spencer would marry Prince Charles, and I was madly in love with her. Not the prince, or the promise of a fairy tale, but Diana herself, a bit awkward, eager as a colt, her blondness, her downcast eyes, even the detail that she chewed her nails. I chewed my own, down to the quick, and I dreamed of what it would feel like to have all the world with their eyes on me, approving, loving even my faults. Mamma had long despaired that I would ever have properly pretty nails.

"Yes, you must," Mamma said, emphasizing the last word. My face burned. I felt she was teasing me. "Put it on now, please."

I took the bra from the door knob and turned my back to my mother, ducked into my closet to put it on.

"Why do you hide?" Mamma asked. "It's nothing to be ashamed of."

This had been pointed out to me numerous times by numerous females—Mamma, my older sister Tanya, even Mrs. Kent, the teacher who assembled all the girls in a classroom and talked in whispered tones about changing bodies. Still, I didn't want to be looked at.

"You'll get used to it," Mamma said, after we were in the car. "The bra, I mean."

"No, I won't," I said, in my most mournful tone. "I'll never get used to it."

Mamma didn't respond, and I turned my head away from her, looking out the window of our Ford Granada. I had always liked the ride to the farm, watching the houses change from closely gathered to spread apart, barns sprinkled about, and cattle lazing in the fields, all the while listening to the car's radio. Mamma usually let me pick the radio station. She turned up Kenny Rogers when he came on. Journey was my favorite; Steve Perry's pained voice made me cry, as it did when it came on today. I reached over and snapped the radio off.

"You're so quiet," Mamma noted. "Are you ok?"

"Yeah," I said. "Just a bellyache." I was needling her now, for Mamma hated that word. She didn't take the bait this time. "You don't say? Why, you hardly ate breakfast." She paused. "Maybe it's your period coming."

"No, it's *not!*" I hated being asked about my period, and the intrusion of it, for having to endure it for years on end. I had been the first in my class to get hers, and the girls secretively buzzed around me when they found out, even the popular ones. For a short time I was the only one, but they were envious of me only briefly. In time, their cycles started, too, and my short eclipse faded.

I folded my arms over my chest and fought an urge to press my nose against the car window and breathe on the glass. A childish thing to do, and I was no longer to be considered a child. I said to Mamma, "I heard you talking to Daddy last night."

"What did you hear, honey?"

"You told Daddy that you didn't know what to do with me, so you're sending me to the farm. That I'm too moody."

"I thought the time away might be good for you. Wouldn't you like to help your grandparents get ready for the big reunion?"

I knew Mamma wasn't in favor of the family reunion. For months she and her siblings had tried to talk my grandmother out of it. "You don't need to do all that work," Uncle Bud, Mamma's eldest surviving brother, told her. "You don't even like company," Aunt Peggy pointed out. But my grandmother said that she had already set the date for the second Sunday in July — it was written in green ink on her kitchen wall calendar — and had mailed out the invitations.

The farm held my first, fondest memories. There was such wonderment there: the orchard trees drooping with fruit, catfish circling in the pond over the hill, the heavy smells of hay and good, rich dirt. I had always liked my grandparents' house, a six-room farmhouse, white with red shutters, more than my own, for it was full of old things and old secrets and hiding places. My grandparents weren't sitting out on the front porch when we drove up, as was their wont, but in the living room, the TV news blaring loudly and the window air conditioner on high. "Too hot to sit outside," my grandfather said, in greeting. "I'm seventy-five years old, and I can't recall a summer as hot as this one." He peered at me and grinned. "Who's that you got with you?"

"This is Melissa," Mamma said, and I joined in, "You know me, Grandaddy." We always played this game with him, with us being the city-living, long lost relatives, and it gave everyone pleasure.

"Sit, sit now, both of you." He loudly thumped on the divan beside him, then went on with the weather. "The other day I heard tell it was snowing in Wyoming. Snow there, and it's hotter than blazes here."

My grandmother was sitting in her rocker, crocheting something rainbow-hued, her head cocked. She didn't talk much. Her words were spare and meaningful. I felt a distance from her, always had, without knowing why.

On the TV the announcer mentioned Moscow. "Where's the farthest you've been, Granddaddy?" I knew the answer, but I still asked the question, and liked hearing the same answer.

"Went to visit my sister Gladys in Michigan. All them tall buildings. Turned around and come right back. It weren't for me."

"Don't you ever want to go places? Like Florida?" I thought Florida was the most glamorous place in the world. I often doodled palm trees and Mickey Mouse and men in Ponce de Leon hats in school when I should have been paying attention.

My grandfather dismissed my question with a wave of his hand. He looked at me closer. "You've grown, Melissa. Why, you're almost a lady."

"She starts junior high after Labor Day," Mamma said. I had almost forgotten that she was there. "A big old seventh grader."

I scooted uneasily on the divan. I looked out the window, wishing I could take off running. When I was a little girl and believed almost anything, my daddy told me one time there was Spanish gold buried in the backyard at the farm. I decided that I'd be the one to find it, and I dug about here and there in the unyielding soil. My grandmother came often to the kitchen window, the one where she kept geraniums in bloom year-round, to watch me. Sometimes she'd step out on the porch, always under the guise of work. Finally, I sat back and cried, exhausted and disappointed and covered in dirt.

"There isn't anything out here, is there?" I asked.

"No," she answered. Her "no" was heavy, and as she walked away, I noticed for the first time how bowed, ever-so-slightly bowed, my grandmother's back was. It was if she once carried something so heavy, and now the heaviness pervaded her whole being. Her voice was sad and so were her slate-colored eyes. My grandmother understood well the word "no" in all its forms. Her eyes told me so.

I thought this week's stay would be like all the rest, long and golden. But that summer was a hot one, just as my grandfather said. The corn and tobacco shriveled in the fields, and there was little hay for the cattle. No cool breeze rustled the curtains of the white farmhouse. Daily, we began breakfast with a prayer that now included a plea for rain.

My grandfather looked old to me for the first time that summer. He was slightly stooped and occasionally forgetful, and when he looked at me, his mouth slid into a wry, regretful smile. Once I had filled the silences in that house with my knock-knock jokes, my shrieks, but that summer the house was hot and still, almost, as if it were waiting. That summer, for the first time, my grandfather and I had almost nothing to say to each other.

He had long been my hero, my friend, even my confidante. He once seemed to me as tall and sturdy as a poplar tree, but I was now as tall as he. He taught me how to bait a hook, to follow the lead of a dancing partner, to spot fall coming by the spider's web, to pray on my knees at night before bed. "Always humble yourself before God," he said. He led the way and I followed as we walked countless times among the apple trees that grew behind the house, the branches gnarling over me. They frightened me, even in the daylight, and I ran to take his hand. It was rough and chapped, but how safe I felt when I held it.

During past summers we had sat on the porch at night, Grandfather holding me on his lap, listening to the quiet, to the chirp of the crickets, the occasional tinkle of a cow bell, carried on the wind. I asked him once if this time could go on and on, happy and safe, just as it was.

"Oh yes," he answered, his eyes looking off. "Always."

"And the house will always be here?"

"Built like the Rock of Gibraltar."

"And you and Grandmother will never die?" That fear was my biggest. "And I'll never move away?"

"Always," he replied, his voice sure and strong. "Always." It was a voice I trusted, a voice that guided nine children, my mother among them. I believed it.

But that summer, there was almost no sitting on the porch. My grandfather and I often looked at each other as if we were meeting for the first time. I was too big to sit on his lap now, he told me. And that summer, he never said, "Always."

I wasn't close to my grandmother up until then. She had always been there, with her faint scent of White Shoulders, but she was always in the background. As little as she talked, she laughed even less. She acted wary. A smile from her was almost as rare, and when she did smile, it was when she thought she was alone, working in her garden or working on her crocheting.

"I brought my Lady Diana scrapbook for you to look at, Granny," I said. I cut up our *People* magazines every week, gathered every picture of Diana, and then reverently pasted them in a book. Mamma wanted me to leave it at home, but I couldn't spend two weeks without seeing Diana's face. I brought it out so that we could look at it, together.

"Oh, the Queen," Granny said, thoughtfully.

"She isn't the Queen. Not yet, anyway." I considered myself an authority .

"She is lovely, isn't she?" Granny said, and she pointed to a picture of Diana that was my particular favorite. I couldn't resist taking her hand and giving it a squeeze, and she folded her other hand over mine. "Reckon she knows that we are way over here in Tennessee looking at her picture?" Granny said. I laughed, because I wondered the very same thing, and Granny smiled.

She spent much of that summer visit teaching me to crochet, her bony, slender fingers wrapped around mine as she guided the needle and yarn. She regarded me with a sad shadow in her eyes.

I asked her about her younger days, but she said she didn't want to talk much about the past.

"There isn't much to talk about," she said, when I pressed her.

"But wasn't everything better back then?" I asked. Surely it must have been, from the talk of people who were older. People who remembered the sky being bluer, people kinder. Everything seemed surer to me.

"Well, it was my experience that the old days weren't always so good," my grandmother said. "At least not for some." I wanted to ask what she meant by that. With finality in her voice, she added," I don't look back much." It was true. She spoke only vaguely about her young married years or how she'd had her babies or even how she'd decided to marry my grandfather.

She remained a mystery to me, this woman who had given me my round face and my upturned nose. I thought that maybe I could find out who my grandmother had been by looking in some old family albums. I found a stack of them, seemingly untouched, dusty and smelling like no one had thumbed them in years. I turned page after page of stern-faced, determined ancestors, until I found my grandmother as a young woman, tall, pretty, satin-skinned, with a mouth like a kewpie doll, her auburn hair bobbed and marcelled. She had a distinct twinkle in her eye. Turning the pages, I noticed with each one, that twinkle receded. She was now old and worn and sad, and her mouth was a gash cut into her face.

Nothing remained of that tart kewpie doll mouth. I loved the shape of it—I hungered to have one just like it; of everything else, why couldn't she give it to me? And now she didn't even have that little mouth anymore. I wondered where it had gone.

The Reunion Day came—the second Sunday in July—and my grandmother thanked God that rain held off, as much as it was needed. But it was an unbearably humid day, the stickiness of which only a Southerner knows. My grandmother had cooked for four days, letting me help with some dishes. Only she could make the desserts—her famous stack cake, four types of pie, and a Jell-O mold. My grandfather and I sat up the chairs and the folding tables we'd borrowed from the church.

My mother called me that morning. "Now, Melissa, your father and I will be driving over later. I'm bringing fried chicken and potato salad. You need to wear something proper, because we want to make a good impression. No jeans and definitely no shorts." She paused. "And don't forget your bra."

I had already chosen to wear a terry cloth short set, modest enough, I thought, but I put it back into the suitcase. Instead, I took out a Sunday dress and the bra, which I hadn't worn all week. I put it on, fastened it reluctantly.

My parents arrived, and then suddenly the big front yard of my grandparents' house was teeming with relatives. People came from Michigan and Ohio, Florida and Texas. People I didn't know, people who had last seen me as a baby, who were not expecting me to be so tall and already twelve years old. Old ladies pinched my cheeks. "Are you Brenda's girl?" they asked. "Are you J.A. and Lottie's granddaughter? Are you the attorney's little girl?"

"Give me some sugar," they demanded, and I looked to my mother, who nodded. Be a good girl, her eyes seemed to say to me, so I brushed my lips against one or two wrinkled cheeks, refusing a full kiss, or even enthusiasm. "The youth of today lack for manners," said one.

My mother piled my plate high with fried chicken, a slice of ham, green beans, and her own potato salad. Usually her potato salad was my favorite dish on earth, but today it had sat out too long in the heat and was too heavy on the onion. I took a few half-hearted bites and then slid the rest into the garbage.

My mother tried to coax me toward some of the young people there. I was too young for the big kids who sought each other out. They spent the reunion sitting in adjoining parked cars, sneaking cigarettes from their parents' packs, and saying "Fuck you" back and forth. One of them, a freckled boy wearing a Dallas Cowboys jersey, kept making fun of all the old people. "Man, I hope I die before I get that old," he said. The younger kids were playing kickball, and they eyed me as an enemy approaching. One of the littlest girls eyed the swollen bumps on my chest. "Hey." She pointed. "You've got titties."

I went in search of a cool place, to be alone. Above all, I wanted to unhook that bra, if only for a few minutes. I crawled under the front porch, always one of my favorite hiding places. It was thankfully dark and quiet and cool under there. Best of all, no one even knew I was there. I curled up in a little ball, almost half-asleep, but then the porch above me began to creak. And then the talk began.

"It's just too hot today. I'm just as wet as if I'd had a bath," said Aunt Tiny, my grandmother's baby sister. She was named Martha Delphine but everyone always called her Tiny, and nothing else. She was short but never petite. In fact, she was a fat, mean little woman with a razor for a tongue. I dreaded the sight and the sound of her.

"Yes, it is." The other woman said. Her voice was flat and thin, and I knew she was a Northerner. "It never gets this hot in Michigan."

"Do you like it up there?" Aunt Tiny considered Michigan as alien as another planet and Northerners as interlopers, even if they were family.

"Oh, it's fine, after you get used to it, of course. But the niggers are just taking us over. The minute some of them move in—"

I winced at hearing that word. I wasn't allowed to say it, but I heard it plenty.

"I know, I know," replied Aunt Tiny. "You can thank the school desegregation for that."

"Or rock music," the woman pointed out.

"Hmm-mmm, pure evil," Aunt Tiny said. "All of them."

On they went with the talk of old ladies—who was getting married or divorced, who was living in sin, who couldn't hold a job, whose baby was the cutest, whose was the ugliest. Then they moved onto the headlines. "Now you knew Reagan would get those hostages freed," said Aunt Tiny. "And if he didn't, he would have made Iran a parking lot first."

"But I don't care much for Nancy," the woman from Michigan said.

"No, and she wasn't even much of an actress either." Aunt Tiny replied.

They went quiet for a minute, then Tiny said, "Look at that Sue Anne. Her on her second divorce and those skirts too short..."

"Wasn't she Miss Knoxville?"

"Third runner up. Did you know she bought a store cake and is trying to pass it off as homemade?"

"Sue Anne did? She probably doesn't do much cooking though, right?" The two of them laughed.

"We always made our own cakes," said the other woman. "And held onto our men any way we could."

"Hmm-mm, yes, we did. Put up with a lot, but that's what you did."

I was still under the porch. No one had missed me yet. The conversation above me was dull, so I closed my eyes. Then the other woman said, almost in a whisper, "Charlotte looks good today."

"All things considered," Tiny said. The ever-present edge in her voice had returned.

"That was so long ago," the woman said, almost as if she were defending something. "I think we forgot about that."

I opened my eyes. Charlotte was my grandmother.

"Maybe, maybe not. Does a tiger change its stripes? Ask yourself that," Aunt Tiny said. Her voice began to rise, and it was like a force unleashed. "Remember, I was only a little girl when they got married, but that time after Mamma died and I went to live with them, I heard them at night. Her saying, 'James Albert, please...no...' and him right behind her like the devil."

I swallowed. James Albert was my grandfather.

"They was just newlyweds then," the other woman said.

"Oh no, Elizabeth, this went on for years. It was worse, of course, when he drank. I dreaded the sound of his boots on the porch."

"But James Albert did stop drinking," said the woman.

"Oh, yes," hissed Aunt Tiny. The woman from up north fell silent. Somewhere I heard my mother calling my name, her voice urgent. In the dark underneath the porch I balled up the training bra in my fist. I could not stop shaking. I saw my grandfather's blue eyes and my grandmother's sad mouth. I wanted to shout to Aunt Tiny and everyone else, "He's my grandfather, and I love him!" but I kept quiet. I crawled out from under the porch and followed the sound of my mother's voice.

My mother was inside the house, working in the kitchen. Her brow creased when she saw me. "Melissa," she cried. "What happened to you?" She took me by my shoulders. "You look like someone roughed you up!"

I looked down at myself. My dress was dirty from being under the porch, and my hair was dampened from sweat, hot against my neck. Mamma reached out and took the bra out of my hand.

I pulled away from her. "You never told me."

"About what?"

"About Granddaddy. About him beating Granny. And his drinking. You never told me."

My mother turned, without a word, and went to the sink. She ran the cold water and then dabbed a washrag on my face.

"I want to go home," I said. "I want to go home now." I spoke in a demanding tone, then began to cry.

My mother said nothing. She asked me nothing. She took me in her arms, and I pressed my face into her pillowy breasts, my cheek against her heart, like I had always done. Her flesh, my flesh. The flesh of my grandfather, too. I realized this with a gush of clarity and then I sobbed.

TWO FOUNTAINS
Anna Cabe

"There is this shot in the opening scene of the movie, *Mississippi Burning*, where you see two water fountains. One is broken, and chipped, and water is dripping from it. The other is modern, and shining. A white guy goes up to the nice one, and the black kid goes up to the old one. I remember saying to myself, 'If I was in the scene, where would I drink?'" — Sam Sue, "Growing Up in Mississippi," *Asian American Experiences in the United States*

*   *   *

The Manila Men and I came to the Southeastern United States in different centuries for different reasons, sharing only a heritage of dark coloring and wet heat. Those eighteenth-century Filipino sailors on the ships of their Spanish conquerors probably saw the distant coast of Louisiana and saw freedom. They hightailed it through the bayous and founded the village of Saint Malo. They were masters of their own fates.

I — six years old, scrawny, female — was held captive to the whims of the twentieth-century job market. After my father's stroke cracked his confidence in his ability to perform anesthesiology and brought him to the less-lucrative field of internal medicine, he and my mother, a general practitioner, struck out for brand-new shores: the Mississippi Delta.

We had no thought of fountains. Having emigrated from the Philippines to New Jersey, then Los Angeles then Chicago, what was one more move in America?

*   *   *

Welcome to the Greenwood, Mississippi, Cotton Capital of the World. Demographics: white, 33.1 %, black, 65.3%, Asian, .3%. According to Google Maps, Greenwood is 21 minutes away from Money, Mississippi, site of the famous Tallahatchie Bridge in Bobbie Gentry's 1967 hit song, "Ode to Billie Joe." Money is the site of Emmett Till's 1955 lynching. The 14-year old allegedly made passes at a white woman.

*   *   *

My parents, deeply suspicious of the quality of public schools, particularly those in this isolated place, enroll me in the one decent private school in town, Pillow Academy. My entire first grade class consists of fewer than one hundred people. I am the only Asian, East or Southeast. There are also a number of, to my first-grader's eyes, racially indeterminate people whose backgrounds I later discover range from Lebanese to Syrian to Native American. After a couple of generations in Greenwood, though, they all have the same cast of Deep-South, accents, hunting, vicious loyalty to this or that Mississippi football team, and all.

When I am six and new in town, I learn quickly that I'm different from my classmates. I wear dresses; they wear soccer shorts. I top my rice with various soups and stews; they top theirs with gravy. I don't hunt; one girl explaining the appeal of it to a squeamish teacher acknowledges that it's "sad," but that she finds it "fun." I, like my teacher, think of Bambi.

Yet, despite the surface differences in skin tone and behavior, I'm allowed to attend the school, unlike, say, the 65 percent of the town who are black. I don't notice until after I left, years later, the date of Pillow Academy's founding: 1966. Prime time for white flight from the public schools, the tip of the iceberg when it comes to race relations in town.

My dad confides to me later that he heard of a fairly prominent black family who attempted to enroll their child in Pillow Academy, only to be rebuffed because their child would be *alone* there and would have a *difficult time*. I imagine this being said in a peculiarly polite way, inflected with the voice of an old plantation-owner shaking his head at an uppity and recently released slave. Black people are rarely if ever spoken of when I am at Pillow, and I still wonder that any black person would ever want to come to this school, this last hold-out of segregation. Why walk into a passively hostile environment like this?

This vague belief will turn out to be wrong. I randomly reconnect with an old friend (part-Latina) on Facebook when I'm already attending a Memphis high school:

> Her: Do you remember how segregated it was in Greenwood and at Pillow?
> . . .
> Me: Yes, I do. What kind of segregation in particular?
> Her: . . .Well the blacks vs. Pillow. It is a lot worse now. But there are some very brave students at PA. We have 3 families of blacks and I love them!!
> I actually have gotten to spend time with one of the boys and he is so awesome....unfortunately the kids in our grades like to start rumors...you know that.
> Me: Yeah, I remember.
> Her: So I've heard. I was floored to see an African-American girl in the pictures at Pillow. Hey, integration has arrived!

. . .

Her: Yeah, its about time don't you think? One of my best friends, – – – – –, is one of the new African-Americans and we get messed with a lot.

This, I must point out, happened over Facebook. This is not *Gone with the Wind*, Scarlett O'Hara, with Mammy and Prissy relegated to the kitchen. This is not the childhood of Maya Angelou, in which the separation from the "whitefolks" is so total that she remarks, "I remember never believing that whites were really real." This happened over Facebook.

Greenwood no longer had "White" and "Colored" fountains when I was there, but then, everyone, it seemed, kept to their place.

I cannot tell you what my place precisely was.

*   *   *

"Chinese really didn't have a place in society. Economically, they were better than the blacks, but on a social scale, they didn't amount to much. I think blacks saw us as Jews. We all sort of played marginal economic roles. There were quite a few Jews in town. They weren't accepted by blacks or whites either. I don't think whites knew what to make of us... I left Mississippi in 1973. There was no future for me there. I was so alienated that even if I thought there was something concrete to be done there, I have such bad feelings for the place I wouldn't go back. Being Chinese in Mississippi was definitely a handicap." — Sam Sue

*   *   *

Our Filipino community is drawn tight, tight, tight, as a knot in a string. None of us, I think, would have chosen to be there, except for jobs (with the local hospital and the Mississippi State Penitentiary in Parchman) and in some cases, love. One of my most beloved *titas* (aunts) married a white Southern man back in the day, and stays, even after her husband died, even though the dirt road to her small country home is crumbling, and she can't drive, needing to depend on the kindness of friends and relatives (of which she has many) to take her to places. No one understands it.

Eventually, the community dwindles, bolting for the brighter lights of Memphis, Florida, California, spurred explicitly by Mississippi's tendency towards health-care-related messiness and implicitly by the isolation and limitations of a town of 15,205 mostly white and black people in the middle of the cotton fields. When they leave, I feel lost. I have never learned Tagalog, but the sound of two dozen chattering, Filipino-accented voices acted as a wall against this alien culture. Now, I was naked to its assault, from my fourth-grade teacher admitting she was "partial to the South" during Civil War history to Confederate flags springing everywhere, thick as grass.

They're not knowingly cruel people, though, these Green-woodians. At a grade-school trip to the Mississippi Museum of Natural Science, a black boy looks at me and asks, "Are you Chinese?"

One white classmate looks at him askance and says, "She's *Filipino.*"

But there's a gulf.

A game I learn from my classmates:

"Me Chinese, Me play jokes, Me put pee-pee in your Coke."

Another one with hand-motions:

"Chinese" Pull at the sides of the eyelids.

"Japanese" Pull down the eyelids.

"Dirty knees." Point at the knees.

"Look at these." Point at the underwear.

I participate, of course, and feel no offense. I am neither Chinese nor Japanese after all.

*   *   *

"Strips of bacon spelling 'PIG' and 'CHUMP' were found in front of a South Carolina mosque Sunday. In post-9/11 America, pork—which is unclean in Islam—is a primary form of anti-Muslim protest." —*The Christian Science Monitor,* 2010

*   *   *

A South Asian boy joins my class when I am around ten years old. I am fascinated by him, as someone who is not as touched by the deep-fried Southernness of the rest of the class, not that we ever speak much. But he is there, and he is both a comforting and unsettling presence, to know that someone as brown-skinned as me exists here at Pillow Academy. That I am not a lone speck of dirt in the snow, blown away from some other place.

After 9/11, while no one in my class openly taunts him or a Christian Syrian, one of those whose family stretches back and is more or less a Rebel born, there are reports of at least a couple people yelling at them for being "Muslim," an act which all of us in our grade condemn, since they are two of "us." There are even *more* people of Middle Eastern descent in the school, including a girl with a hijab who is a speaker at an assembly one day. I look at her scarf wide-eyed, even though my nanny has a Muslim friend who wears one also, because she's not a grown-up but a high school girl. A *teenager.*

It was the adults whom I really remember after 9/11:

My Catholic fourth-grade teacher who is also my Sunday School teacher during 9/11. I make the point that many Muslims and even many Christians and Jews say that Allah and God are the same. She

~ 181 ~

looks at me in a certain *oh-you-innocent-little-child* way and asks, "Oh dear, what if they're not the same god?"

So does my sixth-grade Catholic English teacher, who makes *comments* about Muslims, pointing out they only want to, in so many words, "kill us or convert us."

I must have been accepted in some way or they, those good white Christian folks (and truly, they were kind to shy me, showering me with books and buffering me from petty childhood hostility), would not have spoken of such things to me like that. Later, later, though, I begin to be aware of the fact I am not "them" either. There are, certainly, members of my family who have espoused such views both privately and *with* them about Muslims and blacks. I'm *like* them being Catholic, Christian, but I am not "them."

I am not part of their "us." I cannot, do not, drink at their fountain.

*   *   *

Memphis: famous for Graceland, Beale Street the Mississippi River, and the assassination of Martin Luther King, Jr., by James Earl Ray on April 4, 1968, at the Lorraine Motel. As of 2000, 0.79 percent of the city is Asian.

*   *   *

In eighth grade, I move to Memphis and later attend St. Benedict at Auburndale High School, a Catholic institution, crammed with Poles, Hungarians, Irish, Italians. Again, I count and realize I am one of 7 Asian students out of around 230 in my graduating class. There are approximately the same number each of Latino and black students.

My school, though, does its best to wring out every drop of diversity when they can. I was once pulled out of a chapel service to pose for an advertisement. In it was one white boy, a biracial girl, a Mexican boy, and me. I see the advertisement in a newspaper and have to laugh at their subterfuge, pretending they're not mostly white deep inside their red-brick walls.

Still, Memphis is light-years away from Greenwood, being a veritable metropolis with a sizable number of non-hunting non-WASPS. This is reinforced when my white AP Government teacher, former nun and former staffer to Al Gore's dad, regales us about a time when she was a little girl during Jim Crow and decided to drink at the "Colored" fountain because she thought that it meant the water itself was colored.

"This woman came rushing at me, to stop me," she said. "I kicked her."

I can breathe more freely here.

But it remains: After five years here, when I am a senior, when I have, tentatively, begun to think of myself as one of "them," I get into Brown University while the white valedictorian is waitlisted. Some white girl I consider a friend casually says, "Hate to say it, but I wonder if you being Asian helped."

To be fair, affirmative action is a nationwide debate and not exclusive to the South. Asians also are actually overrepresented on college campuses and therefore don't benefit much from affirmative action policies. Indeed, the myth of Asians as a Model Minority obscures the vast gulfs between more established Asian ethnic groups like the Chinese and newer arrivals like the Hmong, who struggle with lower educational rates and higher rates of poverty.

It still stings, though, to discover that I haven't outrun scenes like that and probably never will, no matter where I go. My father, after all, barely escaped the Los Angeles Riots in 1992, when he was working at a hospital in the middle of all the action, when the tensions among whites and blacks and Latinos and Asians blew into a wildfire, and a couple of black coworkers had to escort him to the highway so he wouldn't be mistaken for Korean and be dragged out of his car.

The South may have a well-earned reputation for racism, but it's by no means the only place where people look at me and ask "Where are *you* from?" which translates to "You're not one of *us*."

*   *   *

"What do Sweet Potato Queens, Steel Magnolias, Ya-Ya Sisters, and Southern Belles have in common? They're Grits®—Girls Raised In The South!
Now you, too, can benefit from the unspoken rules, rich traditions, and distinctive style of the Southern woman. . . Inside these pages you'll find advice, tradition, recipes, humor, quotable wisdom, and vital lessons such as:
- How to eat watermelon in a sundress
- How to drink like a Southern lady (sip...a lot)
- How to say darlin' like you mean it
From tending your heirloom iron skillet to avoiding a Southern girl's deadly sins (bad hair, bad manners, and bad blind dates), this handbook is a bible of Southern style for the Grits® girl in all of us." — *gritsinc.com*

*   *   *

My parents try their best. They pack me and my siblings off to the North to relatives every summer, in Illinois, Michigan, and Indiana, so we wouldn't get Southern accents and start saying, "y'all." As educated, well-traveled foreigners, they can't help but look down on our neighbors in Greenwood (or bluntly, many Americans as these nephews and nieces of Uncle Sam had trouble identifying most other countries on a map in a study and alarmingly, even some American states). Some of them, after all, have barely left the South or even, when living in Mississippi, the state.

But the mark is already there. Reminiscing about hushpuppies to an Indiana family friend, I am chastened to discover a blank face. Those delicious little fried balls of cornmeal exist primarily south of the Mason-Dixon Line (Possible origins: Slaves were told to whistle to prove they weren't sampling food in the kitchen. To keep barking dogs from drowning their whistling, they threw them proto-hushpuppies).

Also, my delight when I discover my sophomore English teacher has family and connections with Greenwood (she's an Ole Miss Rebel, by the way). I start yelling names of the leading Greenwood families across the room. She knows most of them, and my classmates look on in astonishment as we casually toss out tidbits about this family or that family and whose son or daughter I went to school with.

I feel, oddly, happy, that someone else knows Greenwood is *real*, not a living history museum of Ye Olde Southern Segregation. Not that she, my teacher, a true GRIT, thinks of it that way.

GRITS, Girls Raised in the South, is a merchandising brand founded by Deborah Ford. I see memorabilia everywhere I go when I am in Mississippi, even tucked into my family's favorite fish-fry place, Larry's. Since the models are always blonde or brunette, white-skinned, I never think to myself that *I* am a GRIT.

One week during high school, I go up to Massachusetts to visit colleges and am startled when a professor, who has some roots in Virginia, casually points out that he hears "the Southern in [my] voice."

I have been in the Deep South since I was six. *Of course*, I'm a GRIT, although I'm not sure I, mango-eating, green-tea-sipping, am what Deborah Ford envisions as the prototypical Southern girl.

*   *   *

"In the first comprehensive accounting of multiracial Americans since statistics were first collected about them in 2000, reporting from the 2010 census, made public in recent days, shows the nation's mixed-race population is growing far more quickly than many demographers had estimated, particularly in the South and parts of the Midwest . . . In Georgia, it expanded by more than 80 percent, and by nearly as much in Kentucky and Tennessee. — *The New York Times*, 2011

*   *   *

I spent over a decade of my life refusing to say, "y'all." I counted the days until I could waltz on out of there.

Why the hell, then, did I stay for my undergraduate degree, even going deeper South towards Atlanta? Why the hell do I now, attending graduate school in the Midwest after two years wandering around Southeast Asia, feel such bittersweet nostalgia for the place? Why the hell do I long for mild winters, biscuits and gravy, strange old women who smile at me in the street and call me "honey?"

Some cosmopolitan Chicagoan relatives of mine like to mock Southerners alongside a billion anonymous Internet commentators and Northern and West-Coast media personalities as racists, rednecks, hicks, trailer trash, white trash, crackers (note the conspicuous absence of black people from the equation; they apparently don't count as native Southerners). Before, I used to join them.

But when I unexpectedly found myself in Atlanta, attending Agnes Scott College, it was different: a city reborn as international after the 1996 Olympics and a haven into which fleeing global refugees pour year after year. It's no Chicago, but it's no Greenwood either.

Maybe it's just because I was in Decatur, a particularly blue and intellectual dot in the city, but it was hard to sneer at the Southern-accented "y'all" when you realize that the person you're talking to was either a) working at the Carter Center, b) about to protest Georgia's draconian anti-immigration policies at the Capitol, or c) the recipient of a Fulbright, Truman, or other fancy scholarship.

Or maybe it's because when I eat barbecue in the North, I just have to say the magic words—"I'm from Memphis"—and restaur-ateurs shower me with free brisket and sauce, even if I sneer at one restaurant's attempt at Southernness: Checkered shirts? White picket-fence? A wall that consists of a solemn print of a nondescript country road? A server who says, "y'all," even though I'm not entirely convinced he's been further South than southern Indiana? I like the restaurant's tender Kobe brisket but deride the sauces. Come on down to Corky's, folks, and you'll get sauce good enough to spread on rolls.

Or maybe it's because I have gradually realized, frankly, that not every white Southerner is George Wallace reincarnated and that I gain nothing by stereotyping others as I have been stereotyped.

I can't say I'm comfortable using "y'all" or that I am recognizably Southern when I venture outside of the Southeast. I'm too "Asian": I'm not a sorority girl or a hunter in camouflage or a Southern belle debutante (at least, I refused to do cotillion when I was invited; I did do a Filipino debut when I was eighteen). Yet, I'm not sure if *all* of the Souths I grew up with would be recognizably Southern if I presented them to an outsider.

Slowly, painfully, I'm coming to terms with my sixteen years of history in the South, my supposedly incompatible mix of Filipina and Midwestern and Californian and Northeastern and yes, Southern. I lived there far longer than those other places, after all.

But the South and the rest of the country, then, will have to admit *I'm* Southern, too, that I'm a part of them. That we—the Latino immigrants agitating for their rights at the Capitol, the Koreans clustered in Duluth, those Manila Men who landed in Louisiana all those years ago, the African-Americans who marched with Martin Luther King, Jr., or not—are *them*.

That we are an *us*.

We are the history, the present, and the future of the South. Not white, not white-and-black, or even white-and-brown-and-black, but some chaotic mess of elbows and marriage and friendship and bitter enmity and "bless her hearts" and those damn antlers hung up over every mantel and colors mixed so hard and fast that you don't know what to call anyone anymore because you're plain exhausted of trying to nail blood down. The stuff *flows* after all.

It's too strong to say I'm proud of being Southern. But, if you ask me where I sip my water, I have to say I prefer sweet tea, thank you very much.

Contributor Biographies

The Authors:

Laura Argiri is the author of *The God in Flight* (Random House 1995, Penguin 1996, Lethe Press 2016) and *Guilty Parties: Leighlah and Others*, which includes "Cottage Industry." Lethe Press will publish *Guilty Parties* in spring of 2017. The collection is about the fine gradations of bad behavior and its impact on both targets and perpetrators. Laura is a bicultural Southerner/New Englander who plans to become an expatriate soon.

Anna Cabe now calls Memphis, Tennessee, home, though currently an MFA candidate in fiction at Indiana University and the web editor of *Indiana Review*. Her work has appeared or is forthcoming in *The Toast*, *SmokeLong Quarterly*, *Necessary Fiction*, *Split Lip Magazine*, and *Cleaver*. She was a 2015 Kore Press Short Fiction Award semifinalist, a finalist for *Midwestern Gothic*'s Summer 2016 Flash Fiction Series, and a finalist for the 2015 *Boulevard* Short Fiction Contest for Emerging Writers.

James E Cherry is the author of three volumes of poetry, a collection of short stories and two novels. His latest novel, *Edge of the Wind*, was published in 2016 by Stephen F Austin University Press. Cherry has an MFA in creative writing from the University of Texas at El Paso. He resides in Tennessee with his wife, Tammy. Visit him on the web at jamesEcherry.com.

Haley Fedor is "a queer author" originally from Southwestern Pennsylvania, but has recently lived in parts of West Virginia and Louisiana. Her work has appeared or is forthcoming in *Crab Fat Magazine*, *The Fem*, *Guide to Kulchur Magazine*, *Literary Orphans*, and the anthology *Dispatches from Lesbian America*. A Fulbright Scholarship recipient, she is also a 2014 and 2016 Pushcart Prize nominee, and is currently a PhD candidate at the University of Louisiana at Lafayette.

Nancy Gustafson moved with her family from Missouri to Texas when she was young—therefore, she is a Texan. She and her husband, Jan, live on a farm in Huntsville, Texas, where they raised their four children. They have eleven grandchildren, a growing passel of great grandchildren, and way too many rescue dogs. Nancy has published poetry, short stories and memoirs in anthologies and journals, including *Stories of Music*, *Time of Singing*, and *Don't Write Your Memoir Without ME*.

Melanie Haws is a lifelong Knoxvillian. She has worked in her family's rental property business since graduating from the University of Tennessee in 1986. As a fiftieth birthday gift to herself, she enrolled in Spalding University's Low-Residency MFA to pursue her lifelong desire to study writing fiction. She is married, the mother of two daughters and companion to Opal, her spaniel-mix muse. "You Never Told Me" is her first published piece.

Randall Horton is the author of three collections of poetry and most recently, *Hook: A Memoir* (Augury Books 2015). He is a member of the experimental performance group: Heroes Are Gang Leaders and is Associate Professor of English at the University of New Haven.

David Hunter was born in 1947 and grew up in Knoxville, Tennessee. He is a Vietnam-era veteran who enlisted in the U.S. Army at the age of 18. He served as a police officer for 15 years until he was disabled. He was an editorial page columnist for the *Knoxville News Sentinel* for 27 years and first published in his teens for *Mad, American Legion* and *Reader's Digest* magazines. The author of eighteen books, fiction and nonfiction, he now resides in Powell, near Knoxville with his wife Cheryl, his son, a German shepherd named Lady and three cockatiels.

Robin Lippincott was born and raised in a small, rural town in Central Florida, pre-Disney World. His latest books include *Blue Territory: A Meditation on the Life and Art of Joan Mitchell*, *Rufus + Syd*, a novel for young adults co-written with Julia Watts, and the novel *In the Meantime*. His fiction/nonfiction have appeared in *The Paris Review, Fence, American Short Fiction* and many other journals. He lives in the Boston area and teaches in Spalding's low-residency MFA Writing Program.

Jeff Mann grew up in Hinton, West Virginia, and attended West Virginia University. He has published five books of poetry: *Bones Washed with Wine, On the Tongue, Ash, A Romantic Mann,* and *Rebels*; two collections of essays, *Edge* and *Binding the God*; a book of poetry and memoir, *Loving Mountains, Loving Men*; five novels, *Fog, Purgatory, Cub, Salvation,* and *Country*; and three volumes of short fiction, *A History of Barbed Wire, Desire and Devour,* and *Consent*. He teaches creative writing at Virginia Tech.

Okey Napier lives in Huntington, West Virginia, where he teaches sociology at Marshall University, Mountwest Community & Technical College, and Ohio University. He is working on his MFA in creative writing at West Virginia Wesleyan College and also writing a novel, *Make Me Pretty Sissy*. Okey is currently touring as his drag persona, Ilene Over, in his one woman show, *Rainbow in the Mountains: Queer and Fabulous in Appalachia*.

Chris Offutt grew up in Haldeman, Kentucky, population 200, in the eastern hills. He has published 6 books set in Kentucky. He also wrote screenplays for *True Blood, Weeds,* and *Treme*. His work is included in many textbooks and anthologies, including *Best American Short Stories, Best American Essays,* and *The Pushcart Prize, 2017.* His most recent book is *My Father, the Pornographer,* from Simon & Schuster.

Lynn Pruett, a ninth generation Kentuckian who has returned home, has lived in the southern states Alabama, Delaware, Mississippi, and North Carolina. She teaches in the Low-Residency MF program at Murray State University and at the Carnegie Center in Lexington. She raises Katahdin sheep on her farm in Salvisa. She is the author of one novel and numerous stories and essays, the most recently published in the *Michigan Quarterly Review, Arts & Letters,* and forthcoming in *Appalachian Nature.*

Cynthia Rand was born and raised in Asheville, North Carolina. Her recent story "Waiting" appeared in Spring 2016 Issue of *The Louisville Review.* She writes fiction, plays, and poetry and is a graduate of Spalding University's MFA in writing program: May 2014. Her careers have included teaching theatre arts in Charlotte and Newton, North Carolina, and directing plays in community theatres. She returned to Asheville in 2015 and works in retail and writes during her breaks. She enjoys gardening, attending her son's football and baseball games, and loves going on long walks with her husky/lab Luna.

Tom Ray is a native of Knoxville and a graduate of the University of Tennessee. After serving in the U. S. Army, including a tour in Vietnam, he entered government service as a civilian. Following thirty-five years in the Washington area, he retired to Knoxville, where he devotes his time to writing fiction. His most recent stories are "Benjamin Franklin and the Witch of Endor" in *New Pop Lit,* and "Thumbing to Morristown" in *Fiction on the Web.*

Erin Reid was born in Eastern Washington and raised in Southern California. She has lived and worked in Huntsville, Alabama, since 1998, recently moving to the hills of middle Tennessee, where she shares an old wood home with her partner and their menagerie of critters. Her short story, "The Resurrection and the Life," appeared in *The Louisville Review,* and her poem, "Religious Education," in *NO'ALA Magazine.* She is a regular contributor to the Sundial Writers broadcast on Tennessee Valley public radio.

Bonnie Schell was raised in Atlanta, Georgia, where she was inspired to write by reading Flannery O'Connor and Eudora Welty. In California she ran a drop-in center for the neurologically diverse, printing their poetry in *Voices & Visions* chapbooks. She now lives in Asheville, North Carolina, with a large Russian Blue cat. Bonnie's words have recently appeared in *Knuts House Press Insanity Edition, The Monterey Review* online, *Barking Sycamores, WNC Woman, The Well-Versed Reader, Coast Lines: Eight Santa Cruz Poets,* and the anthology *What Does It Mean to Be White in America?.*

Lacey Schmidt, unlike most of her family, was born on an Air Force base in Georgia, but she grew up on the gulf coast of her family's beloved Texas and completed her doctorate in Industrial-Organizational Psychology in the international city of Houston. In addition to a slew of scientific articles and chapters on effective teamwork and leadership, Lacey has published poetry and best-selling lesbian romances as, *Catch to Release.*

L. Mahayla Smith is a denizen of downtown Knoxville, Tennessee, where she lives with her jazz aficionado husband and a yard full of songbirds, a mouse, and an occasional possum. Her prior short fiction has appeared in *Women. Period, This Ain't No Rodeo, A Knoxville Christmas, Jackson and Central and Three Bridges* anthologies. She is a past recipient of the Knoxville Writer's Guild's award for both short fiction and creative nonfiction.

Spaine Stephens grew up in Sylva, North Carolina, in the heart of mountains. She made her way east and now lives in Greenville, North Carolina, where she is senior writer/editor for Creative Services at East Carolina University. This is her first publication, and she is currently at work on a book of short stories in the Southern fiction genre.

Gail Tyson After living in Philadelphia, Berlin, Stanford, and New Orleans, she married a Southerner and sank her roots in the red clay of Georgia and rocky ridges of east Tennessee. She has published poetry, nonfiction, and fiction, with forthcoming work in *Appalachian Heritage, Cloudbank, San Pedro River Review, Presence,* and *Still Point Arts Quarterly*. An alumna of Rivendell Writers Colony, she has also honed her writing at Collegeville Institute and Dylan Thomas Summer School in Wales..

Charles Dodd White is the author of the novels, *A Shelter of Others* and *Lambs of Men*, as well as the story collection, *Sinners of Sanction County*, published by Bottom Dog Press. He's also co-editor of the Appalachian anthologies, *Degrees of Elevation* and *Appalachia Now*, also published by Bottom Dog. He lives in Knoxville, Tennessee, where he teaches at Pellissippi State Community College and directs the annual James Agee Conference.

Anne Whitehouse was born in Birmingham, Alabama, and grew up there during the civil rights era. She is the author of six poetry collections— *The Surveyor's Hand, Blessings and Curses, Bear in Mind, One Sunday Morning,* and *Meteor Shower* — as well as a novel, *Fall Love*. Recent honors include 2016 *Songs of Eretz* poetry prize, 2016 Common Good Books' poems of gratitude award, and 2016 F. Scott and Zelda Fitzgerald Museum poetry prize. www.annewhitehouse.com

Allison Whittenberg is a poet and novelist (*Life is Fine, Sweethang, Hollywood and Maine,* and *Tutored*, all from Random House and *The Sane Asylum* from Beatdom). She lives in Philadelphia with her family and loves life.

Meredith Sue Willis was born and bred in West Virginia where both of her parents were school teachers. Her mother's father was a witness to the Monongah Mine explosion of 1907 in Monongah, West Virginia. Her father's mother was a country store keeper in Wise County, Virginia. Willis has published more than twenty books of fiction and nonfiction and is a veteran writer-in-the schools. She presently teaches novel writing at New York University's School of Professional Studies and volunteers with an anti-racist organization in the inner ring suburb of New Jersey where she lives.

Katie Winkler, born in Alabama, says that just about everyone in her family is a teacher or a Baptist preacher. She upholds the family tradition by teaching English composition and literature at a community college in the mountains of North Carolina. Her fiction has appeared in numerous print and online publications, including *Saturday Evening Post* and *Mulberry Fork Review*. In addition, two of her plays have been produced, an adaptation of *Frankenstein* and a musical called *A Carolina Story*.

THE EDITORS:

Larry Smith, a native of the industrial Ohio River Valley, is a poet, fiction writer, biographer, and editor-director of Bottom Dog Press where he has edited over 60 books and published 200. He is a professor emeritus of Bowling Green State University's Firelands College in Ohio. His most recent books are *Lake Winds: Poems* and *The Thick of Thin: Memoirs of a Working-Class Writer*. With Charles Dodd White he edited *Appalachia Now: Stories of Contemporary Appalachia*.

Julia Watts was born in Southeastern Kentucky. She is a quare-identified (that's Appalachian for "queer") novelist who has lived in Appalachia all her life. She is the author of fourteen novels for adults and young adults, most of which focus on the lives of LGBT people in the South. Her 2001 novel *Finding H.F.* won the Lambda Literary Award in the Children's/ Young Adult category, and her 2013 novel *Secret City* was a Lambda Literary Award finalist and a Golden Crown Literary Award winner. Her recent titles include *Gifted and Talented* (Bottom Dog Press) and *Rufus + Syd*, co-written with *Unbroken Circle* contributor Robin Lippincott. Julia holds an MFA in Writing from Spalding University. She lives in Knoxville, Tennessee, and teaches at South College and in Murray State University's Low-Residency MFA program.

BOOKS BY BOTTOM DOG PRESS

BOOKS BY BOTTOM DOG PRESS

APPALACHIAN WRITING SERIES

Brown Bottle: A Novel by Sheldon Lee Compton, 162 pgs. $18
A Small Room with Trouble on My Mind
by Michael Henson, 164 pgs. $18
Drone String: Poems by Sherry Cook Stanforth, 92 pgs. $16
Voices from the Appalachian Coalfields by Mike Yarrow and Ruth Yarrow,
Photos by Douglas Yarrow, 152 pgs. $17
Wanted: Good Family by Joseph G. Anthony, 212 pgs. $18
Sky Under the Roof: Poems by Hilda Downer, 126 pgs. $16
Green-Silver and Silent: Poems by Marc Harshman, 90 pgs. $16
The Homegoing: A Novel by Michael Olin-Hitt, 180 pgs. $18
*She Who Is Like a Mare: Poems of Mary Breckinridge and
the Frontier Nursing Service* by Karen Kotrba, 96 pgs. $16
Smoke: Poems by Jeanne Bryner, 96 pgs. $16
Broken Collar: A Novel by Ron Mitchell, 234 pgs. $18
The Pattern Maker's Daughter: Poems
by Sandee Gertz Umbach, 90 pages $16
The Free Farm: A Novel by Larry Smith, 306 pgs. $18
Sinners of Sanction County: Stories by Charles Dodd White, 160 pgs. $17
Learning How: Stories, Yarns & Tales by Richard Hague, 216 pgs. $18
The Long River Home: A Novel
by Larry Smith, 230 pgs. cloth $22; paper $16
Eclipse: Stories by Jeanne Bryner, 150 pgs. $16

APPALACHIAN ANTHOLOGIES

Unbroken Circle: Stories of Cultural Diversity in the South
Eds. Julia Watts & Larry Smith, 200 pgs. $18
Appalachia Now: Short Stories of Contemporary Appalachia
Eds. Charles Dodd White and Larry Smith, 160 pgs. $18
Degrees of Elevation: Short Stories of Contemporary Appalachia
Eds. Charles Dodd White and Page Seay, 186 pgs. $18

Bottom Dog Press, Inc.
P.O. Box 425 / Huron, Ohio 44839
http://smithdocs.net